# Rick
# Gangraw

# Escape from His Past

Published by White Feather Press, LLC

ISBN  978-1-61808-125-4

Printed in the United States of America

White Feather Press

Reaffirming Faith in God, Family, and Country!

## Acknowledgments

Thanks to my wife and kids for giving me the time to write this story, and for providing feedback along the way.

*A prayer for the one*
*the true, the near and the dear;*
*the closer and better half of me;*
*A prayer for the one whoever she may be.*
*My feet have travelled far*
*To all the lands around under sun and star;*
*My eyes have seen countless faces,*
*but not she, who with me, makes "us".*
*I long for the days and storied nights*
*for a woman to make me breathe;*
*for a friend that makes me whole;*
*for an angel to bless my soul.*
*Here it is simple and true;*
*A prayer for the one-*
*A prayer for you.*

*– Paige Cutshaw –*

# Chapter One

**K**IM **D**EMUND STOOD IN FRONT OF her class, studying the expressions on the faces of her six-year olds as they anticipated the arrival of their guest speaker that morning. She deliberately didn't give the students many details about this person but was certain they would enjoy his presentation. Their guest speaker was her older brother, a man who had a way with kids and was good at keeping their interest, although he claimed to only like them from a distance. Her class was polite now. Hopefully, the kids would keep it up while he discussed different countries and animals of the world.

Her big brother, Will Sayre, had such a fascinating life that most people would find it interesting. His travels were entertaining to hear about once someone pulled a story out of him. If only he would talk more about the various trips around the world and across the United States but for some reason he honestly didn't think people would want to hear about those experiences. When she was finally able to encourage Will to tell about some of the foods he had eaten over the years, she was mesmerized by the vast assortment of unusual things he had tried, as well as the circumstances he found himself in for many of them. Asking him to speak to her class was one of many tactics she had used to coax him into discussing his travels and she looked forward to hearing what he had to say.

A movement to her left caught her attention and she glanced over to see Will's smiling face in the window beside her door. She walked toward it to let him in.

"Okay, class. It looks like our special guest is here now, so let's be very quiet as he comes in and I introduce him." She opened the door and Will walked in carrying a small box under his arm. He waved to the class and kissed his sister on the cheek, which immediately got the kids' attention. Kim's face instantly warmed up. Her cheeks had probably turned bright red. Putting her finger to her lips, she attempted to hush the gasps and laughter that erupted from her group of six year-olds.

"Eww, he kissed her," exclaimed one little boy in the back of the class.

Will responded with a surprised expression on his face. "Wait a minute. Don't you all kiss your baby sister?"

The class stayed silent as they appeared to digest their guest's statement, and they looked back and forth between Will and their first grade teacher. Will then turned to Kim.

"Didn't you tell them I was your brother or are you ashamed of me?"

"No, I wanted to surprise my students, but I'll make sure they understand it now. Yes class, this is my big brother, Mr. Will Sayre, and he's going to talk to you about some of the different countries of the world. Since we're learning about geography and different cultures, I asked him to tell you about his experiences traveling to Europe, Asia, Africa, Australia, North America, and South America. Would you welcome Mr. Sayre to our class today?"

"Good morning, Mr. Sayre," said the entire class in unison.

"Wow. Good morning. I'm really glad to be here with you today," replied Will.

"Hey, let me out of this box," said a muffled voice with

a British accent that appeared to come from inside the box Will brought into the class. The eyes of every student opened wide. The room quieted as Kim smirked while she walked unnoticed toward the back of the room.

"What's in your box, Uncle Will?"

Will turned and looked at the little girl with long, straight brown hair who asked the question and recognized his sister's daughter.

"Well, hello Nicole. I'm glad you asked."

"It's dark in here and I need to go potty," said the British voice.

The class erupted with laughter as Will tried to calm them down.

"There's nobody inside the box. I just have some things I've brought back from around the world."

"Can we see inside?" asked another curious little girl.

"Well, let me just make sure it's okay to take off the lid," said Will while he acted out the mystery as if something would jump out as soon as he opened it. He glanced nervously at Kim, who enjoyed this as much as her students and he gave her a crooked smile while reaching inside.

"Nope, there's nothing in here, so let's begin."

"Wait, let me out. I want to see the kids," said the silly voice while Will pretended to struggle with something inside.

The students laughed and squealed again, bringing the Kindergarten teacher from across the hall to the door.

Kim whispered, "This is my brother and he's helping with our geography lesson. Bring your class over."

The other teacher then disappeared, only to return seconds later with her entire class of five-year olds. They filed in to the back of the classroom with wide eyes. It was amusing to watch them all trying to figure out what that man was doing with the box and probably wondering why the first grade students were laughing so much.

Suddenly, a funny looking frog puppet with big eyes stuck its head out a hole in the side of the box and glanced around at all of the students, causing even more laughter. The Kindergarten teacher smiled as Kim just shook her head and commented to her colleague, "That's my brother."

"He's dreamy. Is he still a bachelor?"

"Yes, he's still single, unfortunately."

"Hmm. It may be fortunate for me," the other teacher replied.

Will acted exasperated. "I don't know how Mr. Slimy got in this box. He was supposed to be at home asleep. I'm so sorry for the interruption."

Will lifted out the puppet so each student could see it and then made the frog move its mouth in different ways which caused the kids to laugh even more. It gave the appearance that the frog was really alive with its own personality and not just an extension of Will Sayre.

"Mr. Slimy is a Brazilian tree frog and he sometimes sneaks into my suitcases and bags to go for a ride. He's getting sleepy now and needs to take a nap."

"But I'm not tired," said the silly frog with his accent.

"Yes, you are. Please show the children how well you can obey. You wouldn't want to set a bad example for them, would you?"

The frog looked in Will's eyes, then out at the class, then back at Will.

"Alright, I'll take a nap now."

"Boys and girls, would you say, 'Have a good nap' to Mr. Slimy?"

"Have a good nap, Mr. Slimy," said the entire class as Will gently put the frog back in the box.

"Whew. Sorry about that class. Now where was I? Oh yes, I'm Will Sayre and your teacher is my little sister. Don't we look alike?"

"No, she's pretty and you're not," said one little boy.

Will turned to the two teachers at his left, who both laughed.

"Well. This is going to be a tough crowd."

Will proceeded to talk about different countries, along with animals from each region, and he showed the kids some of the souvenirs he had picked up over the years. When he talked about India, he showed them wooden elephants. When he talked about France, he revealed a miniature Eiffel Tower. His collection of trinkets included pyramids of Egypt and Mexico, the Tower Bridge from London, the Great Wall of China, kangaroo charms from Australia, and more. As he discussed each country, he showed pictures from his laptop onto a screen at the front of the class and displayed a map that showed where each country was in the world. They seemed to enjoy the pictures of Will with various animals the most, especially Malaysian orangutans messing up his hair, the expression on his face when the pigeons swarmed him at Trafalgar Square in London. They also laughed at a photo of Will when he made a face after tasting coconut milk in the Philippines.

It was good her brother agreed to talk to her class today since it turned out better than she could have ever expected. He related well with kids, even though he didn't have any of his own and he targeted the stories perfectly for this age group. Too bad her brother hadn't found the right girl yet because he would certainly make a great father to some lucky kids. In all appearances, he seemed happy with his life but there was something missing.

"Well, that's about all I can tell you today, so thanks for listening," said Will.

"Students, did you enjoy hearing about faraway places in the world?" asked Kim.

"Yes," the thirty-plus students from both classes shouted.

"Let's give a polite thank you to Mr. Sayre." She led the

class in applause as Will bowed.

"I do have a few souvenirs for each of the kids here but they'll need to come up one at a time. Kim, can you help with that?"

As each child lined up single-file to Will's box, he asked them a question, then let them select something from his presentation as a gift they could keep. Some of them were so shy he had to encourage them to pick an object but others were a challenge to keep them from grabbing more than one.

There was a little girl with long blonde hair who came up to Will and he asked, "What's your name?"

"I'm Rebecca and I've always wanted a baby elephant. Do you have one I can keep?"

The expression on Will's face dropped. He must have already handed out the last of his wooden elephants. Kim almost stepped in but her brother recovered admirably.

Will said, "I'm all out of elephants here but I do have one at home I think you would really like. Can I bring it to your teacher and she could give it to you next week?"

The little girl smiled and gave him a hug, which surprised Kim. Will looked up at his sister with a confused expression and she laughed at the scene. Putting her brother in situations with little kids to watch him squirm was entertaining. Children always liked him but he was hesitant to get too close to them, as if they had some kind of dreaded disease or were breakable objects he didn't want to touch. He appeared to like them from a distance and would make them laugh, but nothing more.

Finally, as each of the kids made their way back to their seats, one of the boys asked, "Have you ever been eaten by a tiger?"

Will raised his eyebrows at his sister, who shook her head as if she wasn't surprised by anything anymore. He then cleared his throat and gave a serious expression while looking down at the floor and walking across the room.

"As a matter of fact, yes I was once eaten by a tiger in Southern India."

The class gasped and another little boy asked, "Did it hurt?"

"Well, it was difficult to get past all of those teeth and claws but that wasn't the worst part."

"What's worse than getting bitten by a tiger?" asked Nicole.

"The worst part was coming out the other end of the tiger when he was done with me."

The class sat silent for a second then everyone said, "Eww" and started laughing again.

"Of course I've never been eaten by a tiger, you silly kids, but thanks for asking. Have a great day everyone."

Will picked up his box and waved to the class as he stopped next to the two teachers.

Kim commented, "A Brazilian tree frog with a British accent? How will I explain that to the kids?"

"That's your problem," Will responded.

The teachers both laughed, shaking their heads at him, and Kim asked, "So you'll be over for lunch by 12:00 tomorrow?"

"Let's see, that's Saturday, right? Yes, I'll see you then." He kissed his sister on the cheek again, amidst groans from the class, before disappearing through the door.

# Chapter Two

THE NEXT DAY, KIM'S DOORBELL rang and Nicole ran to see who was there. "It's Uncle Will," she said turning back to her mom with a big smile.

"You can let him in," said her mother.

He stepped through the open door, leaned down to pick up his niece, as Kim and Doug walked up to him from the kitchen.

"Thanks for having me over for lunch today. It's always good to eat a home-cooked meal before I travel."

"Where are you going tomorrow?" Doug asked as his wife took their guest's coat and hung it up by the door.

"I have to be in Paris for a few days to meet with some customers there. I'll bring back those dark chocolate truffles you like, okay Kim?"

"Well, no need to twist my arm. You don't have to get me anything but I'll be glad to accept whatever you bring back for us." She led them all into the kitchen since the meal was ready, and she carried the last platter to set it on the table. "Did you bring the little elephant you promised for Rebecca?"

"Of course." He held it up for Kim to see. "Nicole, do you think your friend will like this one?"

"Oh, yes. She loves elephants so much and that one will make her very happy. She actually wants a real baby elephant but for some reason her mom won't let her have one."

"I can't imagine why not," Kim added. "Everybody please take a seat." The group filed around the table to their usual spots.

As Will sat down, he said, "This smells delicious."

Kim asked, "Nicole, would you give thanks for the food?"

They all bowed their heads and Nicole proudly sang the 'Johnny Appleseed' prayer, finishing it with 'Amen' and a big smile at her favorite uncle.

"Wow, that's from the old Disney movie, isn't it?"

Nicole nodded and reached for a biscuit while the rest of them dished out something from the table. Kim always worked hard to make every meal special and this one was no exception. A simple, yet colorful tablecloth provided the perfect background to the dishes and different types of food.

Will commented, "Kim, this is awesome. It's as though we're at a fine restaurant."

She blushed and looked at her husband, who had his mouth full but nodded in agreement. Even though her family might not comment on how nice it appeared, she was proud of her accomplishment and that's all that mattered to her. She could always count on Will to notice.

"So Will, are you dating anyone right now?" asked Doug.

Will laughed and turned to his brother-in-law.

"I guess you could say so but not one girl in particular. I usually date a few at a time."

Doug laughed. "You're kidding, right? I never can tell if you're just putting me on."

Will shook his head with his mouth full of mashed potatoes and reached for his drink.

"No, I'll probably go out with a few stewardesses this week and maybe a couple of French girls I'll meet at the hotel. That's usually how it works out."

"But you're only going to be gone for three or four days.

You take out a different girl every night while you're traveling?"

"If I'm gone over a week-end, I try to take one out in the afternoon and a different one for the evening. It gives me a nice variety to sample."

Kim interrupted, "Will, these are human beings were talking about. They are not inanimate objects for sampling."

"I'm sorry. I didn't mean it disrespectfully. I just meant that I want to meet as many different types of girls as I can. That's all."

"Wow. How many girls do you think you've dated in the past year?"

Will glanced over at Kim, who gave her husband the evil eye for being so interested in her brother's dating life. "Good question. Let's just say dozens of different girls in the past year. I don't really keep track."

Doug spilled his drink when he heard this and Kim scolded him. "Don't get any ideas, Doug. You're a one-woman man, remember?"

"Oh, of course, Honey. It's just an amazing way of life…" He stopped as a scowl appeared on his wife's face. "I'm not saying I would want to go back to that kind of singles' lifestyle but it's so different from what I expected from your brother."

"You never had that kind of single's lifestyle, Doug," Kim replied dryly with a grin and her husband wisely stuffed another bite of potatoes into his mouth.

"It's all just a simple date, with dinner, the theater, a river cruise, carriage ride around the city, or something similar and then most often I don't ever see the girl again. Never anything long term."

"Still, it would be interesting to see your little black book," added Doug.

Kim laughed slightly as she wiped her mouth on a clean red cloth napkin and added, "Well, it sounds like someone is working on being in the doghouse tonight, eh Doug?"

Doug glanced over at his wife and replied, "No, I mean it would be an interesting study of the dating lifestyle, don't you think?"

"I think my brother should focus on the one girl who'll be the right person for him to settle down with for the rest of his life," and she peered over her glass at Will.

"Kim, believe me, I've been searching but just haven't found her yet. She may be out there. I figure the more girls I meet and get to know, the more likely I'll find the future Mrs. Sayre."

"I think your standards are impossibly high and the girl you're searching for doesn't exist."

Will paused as he chewed his last bite and stared at his plate for a moment. Should she have made that last comment? Without looking up, Will replied quietly, "She does exist. I'm sure of it."

There was a sadness in his expression and Kim wished she hadn't said this girl didn't exist. Will had been stuck in the past for years, lamenting the loss of his 'happily ever after' when the girl of his dreams walked out of his life. He had been trying to escape all of the 'what ifs' ever since, but despite his positive appearance, he was haunted constantly when he was alone. Realizing she was staring at her brother, Kim quickly moved her eyes to the table. At least he was still trying to find someone to replace her memories, but none of those girls had a chance against the one from his past. He seemed to idolize her beyond compare. He would never find someone unless he gave in a bit.

"Does anyone want the last biscuit?" Nicole asked excitedly.

Will tuned to his niece. "No, I'm getting full Nicole. I think you should have it."

She glanced at her mom, who smiled and nodded, then

grabbed the biscuit as her prize. Everyone finished eating and Kim brought out a crème brulee dessert for each of them.

"Very impressive. Did you make this yourself, with the blow torch and everything?"

"Yes, I did. Nothing too good for my big brother, right?"

Doug added, "I'm glad you came over, Will. We don't eat like this unless we have special visitors like you."

Kim laughed and punched Doug's arm. "That's not true. You're special too."

Doug looked at Nicole, raising his eyebrows and she replied, "Sorry Mom. It's always better when Uncle Will comes over."

All of them laughed at that and quickly devoured each dessert, closing their eyes while making 'mmmmm' noises with each bite. It was obviously delicious.

"Will, I know you're leaving for the airport tomorrow but what if we drive over to Rebecca's house now? You could deliver the little elephant to her yourself."

"I don't know about that, sis. It would probably be best if you just bring it to class on Monday and give it to her then."

"Hmm. So you meet a six year-old girl and even dump her after only one hug. That may be fine for your foreign ladies but this just doesn't seem right."

"Wait a minute. It's not like that at all. I figured you're busy after a week at school and wanted to be home with the family. That's it."

"Well, Doug's in the doghouse and Nicole has a bit of homework he's going to help her with. That leaves me some time to visit Rebecca and her mother while you give the little girl her souvenir. Simple as pie. Besides, I've called her and told her we're coming over today so she's expecting us."

Will laughed and said, "Alright, I'll ride over there with you if it'll make you happy."

"It will. Doug and Nicole, we'll be back in a little while.

You can take care of cleaning up the table for me, okay?"

"Mommy, can I go with you? Rebecca's my best friend."

"Not today dear. We're just going to drop off the elephant to her, say 'hi' to her mom, and come right home. You'll see Rebecca at school on Monday."

"Doug, thanks for having me over," said Will, offering his hand.

"Anytime Will. Be careful."

"Bye, Uncle Will. I love you. Have a safe trip over the Atlantic Ocean."

Picking her up and giving his niece a big hug, Will replied, "I sure will, Sweetie. I might even bring you back a surprise if you're good for your mom and dad this week. I love you."

He grabbed his coat as Kim followed Will through the front door.

Will said, "I'm parked behind you. Let's take my car. Just tell me where to turn."

She gazed at his silver convertible and nodded toward it. "I wanted to ride in your little sports car anyway, so that was the plan all along."

"Sneaky," Will replied.

They drove for a few minutes and she had him park on the street across from some apartments that came right up close to the road. Kim watched his expressions as his eyes inspected the front of the building. Just the opposite of the newly reno-vated downtown buildings where Will's office was. The skies even turned ominous momentarily while they stood there, probably to match the gloom of these run-down apartments.

"Doesn't look very safe to leave my car out here unat-tended. Is it?"

"We'll only be a few minutes. Maybe you should close the roof though, just in case."

Will did that and they walked across the street. Not much traffic here.

"Rebecca's mom is a single-mom, struggling to make ends meet, and she's hoping to find a nicer area to live in soon."

Will didn't say anything as they came up to the front door. It was a first floor apartment, with patches of dingy paint on the old bricks and dirty, broken shutters. However, there was a nice flower arrangement outside the window and a colorful welcome mat, which did brighten things up for at least this one apartment.

As Kim reached to knock on the door, there was a scream and a crash while Will turned quickly, looking into her eyes. He immediately rapped his knuckles on the door several times and she listened for a response. Heavy footsteps grew louder, as the sound of someone unchaining a lock jingled in front of them. The door then opened slightly.

A large man, taller than Will, put his face in the crack of the door and demanded, "What do you want?"

Suddenly, a little girl's voice screamed, "Mrs. Kim," and through the crack, Kim saw Rebecca run toward the door.

"Get back to the table," the man yelled as he turned his head and knocked the little girl back with a violent wave of his hand.

Without hesitation, Will kicked the door hard, smacking it against the man's head. He pushed his way through the entrance, while Kim rushed in behind him and ran to Rebecca. Her brother punched the man in the face again and again. Everything happened so quickly but it seemed like slow motion with complete silence. She picked up Rebecca, who had tears streaming down her face, and she examined the room only to see a mess. Her brother repeatedly pounded the man's face and stomach as the big man swung aimlessly, reminding her of a bear trying to swat a swarm of bees. She turned her head to find Rebecca's mother. The whole scene was surreal. Was this really happening? A woman lay on her back in the middle of a broken table that had collapsed on the floor.

Newspapers and magazines were strewn about and Kim recognized her, although wet hair covered most of the woman's cheek.

Will rammed the man's face into the front door, slamming it closed, and then did it again, although this time the door didn't budge. He forcefully twisted the giant's body to his left and caused him to go headfirst onto the tile floor, immediately stopping the man's struggles.

The sounds of her brother's heavy breathing came to life along with the crying of the little girl, and when he looked at Kim, she pointed to Rebecca's mother on the floor. Will got up and ran over to see how she was, while his sister called 911. He wiped the tears from the woman's face with his hand and gently brushed the hair from her eyes. Kim watched Will's expression as he saw the beautiful face behind the hair, tears, and smeared mascara. There was a concerned expression in her brother's eyes.

"Are you okay?" he asked the woman.

She tried to stop crying and forced out a weak response. "Yes, just embarrassed you two had to get involved."

"Can you get up and walk or do you need to go to the ER?"

"I'm fine," she said as she stood up slowly. "He hit me in the face and I fell against the table, breaking its legs. My pride is hurt more than my face. I'll be fine."

Kim quickly introduced these two. "Will, this is Renee Woodson, Rebecca's mother."

"Hi, Renee. I'm Will Sayre, Kim's brother. It's good to meet you, although I wish it was under better circumstances."

Kim set Rebecca down and she ran to her mother to give her a hug. Within minutes, a knock on the door announced the arrival of the police while Will let them in and handled as much of it as he could. They asked Renee a few questions too, so Will and Kim kept Rebecca occupied as they watched the big man from across the room. One of the policemen handcuffed the bully and got him to stand up. He questioned the abusive man, who made slurred, threatening comments to Will and even to Renee, and the policeman eventually walked him out the door. Paramedics arrived to check out Renee, who seemed happy to not have to go to the emergency room, and they left soon after. The other two policemen finished their questioning, took everyone's statement, and eventually left as well, which presented the room with an awkward silence for a few moments.

"Rebecca, I almost forgot the reason we came over today. Do you like this elephant?" Will knelt down, reaching out the little wooden animal to Rebecca.

Her eyes lit up as she came over to see her gift and she beamed as she looked up at Will, then to her mother. "It's perfect. Thank you so much."

The little girl hugged Will, while Kim and Renee raised their eyebrows at each other.

Renee said, "I appreciate you giving this to Rebecca. She loves elephants so much."

"My pleasure. It was good to meet you and I hope you have a much better day now."

Will watched while his sister hugged Renee and Rebecca and then the siblings headed toward his car. He opened the roof of his Mazda Miata and they both climbed in.

This was certainly an unexpected turn of events with today's visit but as they drove home in silence, she was glad her brother was able to meet her friend, Renee. The way things turned out, Will had come across as heroic and Kim smiled as they continued under the warm sun.

# Chapter Three

SEVERAL DAYS LATER, WILL HAD returned from his business trip and played an exhausting yet challenging game of racquetball with his friend, Patrick Wilson, his first day back. As they finished up the game, Patrick served a good hit to the lower left wall, which Will returned with some effort. Patrick responded along with another hard hit, but Will crushed it up the middle. Patrick then smashed the ball into the lower right corner of the court, as Will returned the ball with ease. Patrick hit the ball hard in an attempt to get it past Will, but his opponent placed it perfectly to Patrick's weak spot. Patrick missed the ball and ended up on the floor staring up at Will, breathing heavily.

"Wow, excellent placement, my friend," said Patrick. "You might actually be considered an adequate racquetball partner someday if you keep playing like that."

Will helped him up as they caught their breath, while Patrick went on to get the winning point after the next serve and another good volley. The two of them slowly gathered their things from the back of the court and continued without speaking as they headed toward the men's locker room, accompanied only by their footsteps and labored breathing. Both men showered and met in the hallway before continuing their walk through the health club.

"I thought you might have jet lag your first day back to the

US," said Patrick.

"No, I like to get back on the local time as quickly as possible," responded Will. "I flew in last night, so I wanted to do something active this morning."

"Thanks for calling me. It's always a pleasure beating you in a game of racquetball."

"Yeah, you got a good workout from me today, eh?" said Will.

"Maybe. So did you meet anyone new in Paris?" Patrick asked as he glanced over at his friend.

"I guess you could say that," Will responded. "I took Jeannette to the opera, Valerie on a dinner cruise on the Seine, Hannah on a walking tour of the city, and spent a few hours with Annika during my layover at the airport in Frankfurt."

"Four different girls in four days?" asked Patrick in disbelief.

"Yep," he responded without looking up. "But none of them was the one for me."

Patrick shook his head as they walked in silence for a few seconds.

Will continued, "It sure feels good to have a great workout. Hey, did I tell you I got in a fight the night before I left for Paris?"

"No, what happened? It's not like you to pick a fight."

"I didn't start it, but I sure had to finish it. I went with Kim to the apartment of one of her students after lunch last Saturday and it turned out the mother's boyfriend was physically abusive. I saw him hit Kim's student and I had to take the man down. The police came soon after and took him away." Will paused and stared into Patrick's eyes. "I don't think I've ever felt such anger toward anyone when I saw him hit a six-year old girl."

"Well, that doesn't happen every day. Probably just a 90 pound weakling feeling tough, right?"

Will laughed and replied, "Yeah, something like that."

Their conversation continued while they headed toward the health club's deli.

"Will, have you ever thought of settling down with one girl rather than seeing a different one every other day? There's a lot to be said about marriage and spending your life with that special someone."

"It's crossed my mind a few million times but I just haven't found the right girl. You sound like you're trying to be my mother. Wait a minute. Have you been talking to my sister?"

"No. It's just that you've met more girls than I realized were on this planet and not one of them is good enough for you? How can that be?"

"It'll happen someday." Will looked away and paused for a few seconds then continued, "I really appreciate you meeting me here on such short notice." Will changed the subject to get the conversation away from him being over twenty-five years old and the only single man in his group of friends. Would he ever meet 'Mrs. Right'? Despite his outwards appearances to everyone, he was the loneliest man on Earth.

"I have to admit you actually played a decent game," said Patrick.

"Thanks. You make it sound as if you're surprised. I always play a decent game."

"You'll never beat me but at least you put up a good fight today."

"Ha. Just wait Racquet Man. My time's coming."

Will picked up a Styrofoam container and headed for the salad bar while Patrick reviewed the menu. His friend always ended up ordering a turkey sandwich from the grill, but he must enjoy going through every item on the list each visit. Patrick probably knew the menu by heart, since he came here regularly to exercise, but he contemplated the choices as though it was his first time here. Will took his time picking through the many different salad options and finally finished his masterpiece as Patrick's sandwich was completed. As usual, he ordered a turkey sandwich even after all of that consideration.

Will carried his tray toward his friend and they both stood in line to pay. He was surprised by a feminine voice.

"It's good to see manly men eating healthy at a salad bar."

Will glanced up to a well-toned young lady in line in front of him. She had captivating eyes and wore short shorts with a tight shirt. Patrick noticeably stifled a laugh at her comment as he was inconspicuously elbowed by his friend.

Will responded, "Well it's always nice to see the ladies eating healthy too. Personally, I prefer a salad after a good workout."

The lady's eyes met Will's and they both smiled as if they were the only people in the deli this afternoon. Her long brown hair was pulled up into a ponytail. He had to admit she was indeed a looker. It's funny how they seem to be magnetically attracted to him. Patrick would probably tease Will today and maybe the rest of the week about this one.

"Hey, Will. You should show her what kind of salad you picked out today."

Will turned his back on Patrick, ignoring him, and stood between his old friend and his new friend. His conversation continued with the dark-eyed lady, "Do you play racquetball?"

"I've never tried but I would love to learn how to play. It must be an invigorating workout."

"Oh, it is. I'm certainly no expert, but I could give you some pointers."

Patrick coughed again, as Will glanced back at him briefly with a scowl.

"That would be great. I'm here Monday, Wednesday, and Friday mornings, so look for me next week."

"I'll do that. See you then."

She paid for her salad and bottled water while Will watched

her walk away to join her friends at a table outside.

"Hey, Will. It's great to see you eating healthy today," Patrick added and started laughing hysterically.

Will finally acknowledged his friend but his smile disappeared as Patrick reached over to open the Styrofoam lid on Will's salad.

"What are you doing?"

"Did you include any lettuce in your salad this time? It looks like it's about two cups of blue cheese dressing smothering several slices of pepperoni, a ton of shredded cheese, some grilled chicken, and oh yes, I do see a couple of small pieces of lettuce sticking out at the bottom."

"Give me a break, man. I'm eating a salad, aren't I? I put a few small pieces of broccoli in it too. You just can't see them because they're covered in dressing."

"You deliberately led that poor woman into thinking you eat healthy, while your arteries cringe in fear from what you're about to put through them. And now you have a date with this unsuspecting young girl? Shame on you."

"You're just jealous the ladies always come on to me and not you."

"I'm a married man, my friend, and I'm surprised you weren't honest with this one. Plus, you should start eating healthy for a change before it catches up with you. You need to take better care of yourself. My dad just had a heart attack this year, and the doctor said it could have been prevented by cutting out this kind of stuff when he was your age."

"So I have a little meat and cheese with my lettuce. Big deal. You act like you're my mother."

"I've never seen so much blue cheese dressing outside of a bottle. You should have let her peek at your salad under this lid and then see what her reaction to you would have been. She might not have been so quick to be impressed by your healthy eating habits. You're lucky she didn't catch you on a day when you have your double bacon cheeseburger with tater tots."

"Listen, she would have gravitated toward me whether it was a salad or a cheeseburger…"

"Double bacon cheeseburger with deep fried tater tots."

"Whatever. She just used the salad as an excuse to talk with me. If it was one of my cheeseburger days, she would have found something else as a start to her conversation."

"You may be right. I'm just surprised you led her on and made her think you're a healthy eater."

"I am a healthy eater. A salad is very healthy."

Patrick stared into Will's eyes and burst out laughing.

Will's face registered with bewilderment. "What?"

"Just pay for our lunches, health food man."

Will turned and reached for his large cup to fill it up with Mountain Dew and Patrick grabbed his arm, his eyes searching around the room.

"Look at this. Where's that girl when she needs to see what you're drinking with your blue cheese, bacon, and pepperoni lunch."

"Patrick, it's just a little drink after a good workout. I'll exercise it all off this afternoon."

"This is about the deadliest lunch anyone is having in the deli today and that poor girl thinks you're such a healthy eater."

"Your point is well taken. I'll let her know that sometimes I don't eat as healthy as she thinks I do when I meet her next week. Would that make you happy?"

"Well, it's a start. You still need to change what you eat now or you'll regret it later."

"I will, but not today. Right now, I want a large cup of Mountain Dew with my blue cheese, bacon, and pepperoni."

# Chapter Four

**W**ILL PARKED ACROSS THE street and walked toward Renee's apartment, looking forward to seeing her again, especially since she wasn't at her best when he last saw her a week ago. She appeared to be so vulnerable then and something made him want to protect her and her daughter, to be with them to make sure they would never be hurt again. Something inside of him insisted he check on Renee, but he couldn't explain it. He wasn't sure why this woman seemed so different from others he had dated, but when her eyes connected with his at the apartment, he was hooked. He just had to see her again.

The sun was out with only a few clouds and the warmth felt good after such a cold winter. Colorful flowers popped up everywhere now and he appreciated the various arrangements the city started growing along the roads, around the trees, and in the parks. He drove his SUV today, since he couldn't take two passengers in his little silver convertible. With any luck, Renee didn't have any plans this morning.

He knocked on the door and stared at the ground, considering what to say when she answered. Finally after a little bit of waiting, there was some noise on the inside and the door opened just a bit. As his eyes slowly worked their way up from the welcome mat, a few things registered in his mind:

red toenail polish, bare legs, an oversized sweatshirt, sleepy eyes, and messy blonde hair. He must have stopped by too early. His heart pounded.

"Oh, I'm sorry. Did I wake you?"

Renee stared at him for a few seconds, and then replied, "Hi, Kim's brother. What brings you here so early on a Saturday morning?"

"Sorry, my name's Will. I just got back in town last night and wondered if you and Rebecca would like to go to the zoo today."

The little girl gazed up at her mother with wide, pleading eyes. "Mommy, I want to go to the zoo. Can we?"

Will tried unsuccessfully to keep from staring at Renee's legs but noticed them again when he glanced down to see an excited Rebecca in pajamas, peering out from behind her mother.

"I appreciate the offer, but I already have plans today."

His enthusiasm collapsed as he quickly looked up at her face and said, "I completely understand. I should have called first. My apologies."

He heard the little girl's voice begging in the background as Renee turned to peer inside. Will's eyes uncontrollably glanced down at her legs and he quickly turned away, scolding himself for eyeing them again.

"We can plan it out some other time if you're interested. It doesn't have to be today."

Her eyes, more awake now than when she first opened the door, seemed to sparkle as she pressed her lips together with the hint of a smile. His heart melted. She was more beautiful than he had realized. She was sensational without makeup and her hair all wild. What was it about this woman?

"Well, if you could give me time to get ready, I think Rebecca and I would love to go to the zoo today."

"Great. How about if I come back in thirty minutes or an

hour?"

"An hour would be better."

"Sounds good. I'll be back at 10:00. The breeze is cool in the shade but it's warm in the sun, so just dress casual."

"How else would I dress to go to the zoo?" she asked.

"Just in case you might have thought it was still cold out."

"Alright. Thanks, Will. See you soon."

She closed the door as the little girl squealed with delight inside the apartment while he turned to walk toward his car. Will couldn't help but laugh. He had put Renee on the spot by mentioning the zoo in front of her daughter. He would be more careful about things like that in the future. It was interesting Renee said she would be ready in an hour. He had been out with some girls that took much longer to get ready. This was a good sign.

He drove a few minutes out to the lake and parked, watching the ducks splash in the shallow water. They weren't the only ones who appeared to be enjoying the spring weather. Joggers ran along the path as birds fluttered in the budding trees all around him. This was a great day to be outside and it was even better since Renee had agreed to spend it with him. He got out and walked along the path by the lake and listened to the songs of the happy little flyers. Some of the birds may have been returning here after going south for the winter. The colors and markings of so many different species were impressive. Rebecca might be interested in birds today.

He couldn't wait to go back and pick them both up. The time dragged as he sat on a bench, periodically checking his watch while he stared out across the rippling water. He closed his eyes, listening to the sounds of nature while the cool breeze pushed his hair into his eyes and the sun warmed his face. Maybe Renee and Rebecca would like to come here sometime. There's a playground too. With no kids of his own, he never had a reason to go there, but it seemed as though his sister mentioned bringing Nicole here to play in the past week or so.

Finally, it was time to go see if the girls were ready for him. Will got in the SUV, sped to her apartment, and parked across the street again. He walked up to the door and stood there for a few seconds before knocking. He really wanted to see what she looked like now. Renee opened the door and smiled when she saw him.

"Wow, you look great. Not that you didn't an hour ago, but …"

"Yeah, right. My hair was an absolute mess."

"Not at all. I like that natural wildness, and you were just fine even with no makeup."

She laughed, stepping out onto the welcome mat in shorts, sandals, and a loose short-sleeved shirt, as her daughter walked quietly through the door with a big grin and similar attire.

"No, I mean it. I'll never forget your hair and your face when you looked at me through the open door this morning. You were breathtaking." His heart felt as though it would pound right out of his chest. Had he just come on too strong? He wanted to tell her his feelings, but he didn't want to scare her away.

She blushed and turned away while Will gazed down at her beaming daughter standing behind her.

"You're gorgeous, Rebecca. Are you ready to see some animals today?"

She just nodded shyly behind her mother's legs, but her grin never went away as she just kept staring up at Will. She almost didn't seem like the outgoing little girl he met in her classroom recently. Her experience with an abusive man might have something to do with that. Anger built up inside over what that man had done to them both, so Will had to put it aside for now.

"I'm parked over there so let's get going."

They followed him to his Ford Escape and headed toward the zoo, only a few minutes away. Will had been there with Kim's family and he knew from experience that Rebecca's age group loved the zoo. He easily found a spot to park and he paid for their admission. Once inside, Rebecca's eyes were on overload as though she had never seen anything like it. She ran from one side of the path to the other, with wide eyes and an open mouth. She raced up to the exhibit of little monkeys, the colorful birds, and a bobcat all in the first few minutes of entering the park.

"Have you ever been here before?" he asked Renee.

"No, I can't afford the ticket prices. But look at Rebecca. She really loves it here. I can't thank you enough for inviting us and paying for us to get in."

"It's my pleasure. I really wanted to see how you were doing after last week and when I saw the weather outside this morning, for some reason I thought of taking you both here. I'm sorry I didn't check with you in advance but I'm a spur-of-the-moment kind of guy."

"Well, I'm glad you did. I have to admit my plans were pretty lame for today. I was going to do laundry and clean the bathrooms. Not very exciting."

Will stopped walking and staggered, hand over his heart. "Wow, so I almost fell victim to the old 'sorry, but I have to stay home to clean my toilet' story? I'm hurt."

She closed her eyes and laughed out loud as she gently punched him in the arm. He was thrilled to be punched by her. It must have meant that she liked him, right?

They walked on for a little while when he stopped her, and she turned to gaze into his eyes. "I shouldn't have mentioned the zoo in front of Rebecca, since I'm sure that put you on the spot. I really am sorry. I didn't know she was right behind you when I asked."

"No, I don't mind. I would much rather be here and let

her see these fascinating creatures. She'll be talking about this for the rest of the year."

Will took a pack of mints out of his pocket and offered one to Renee. She popped it in her mouth, and within a minute, she sneezed.

"Bless you. I know Rebecca likes elephants and if we follow that trail to the right, it takes us to some real big ones. I've heard there's a baby one here now, too."

"Oh, she'll love it. You're such a thoughtful person," said Renee glancing back at him. Their eyes connected for a few seconds again, then she turned to find Rebecca and started walking again.

It was a pleasant surprise to hear her sincere appreciation and Will continued walking along the trail with her. He couldn't wait to stare into her deep blue eyes again.

"Don't be surprised if she asks if we can take one home, Will. I've tried to explain that a small apartment is not the best home for an elephant, even a baby one. And she thinks we could do it with a big litter box."

They both laughed and he stole another candid glance at his date when she wasn't looking. Her wavy blonde hair gently lifted here and there by the breeze, only to fall once in a while on the middle of her back.

"Mommy. There are three elephants up here and one of them is a baby!"

Her squeal was startling at first because it almost sounded like a cry for help from Rebecca, but when he realized it was out of excitement, Will gave Renee a look of relief. Renee's expression changed from concern to joy in a split second and she turned to him again with her incomparable smile. This day kept getting better and better.

"I thought she was scared or hurt at first. This must be like a dream come true for her."

"Just wait until she gets to feed a giraffe in a few minutes."

"What? Are you serious?"

"Yeah, we can climb up on a platform which puts us at their head level, and then offer the giraffes some kind of treat the zoo allows them to have. She'll love it."

Will took photos of Rebecca with the elephants in the background and made sure he included Renee in several of them. He was right about the giraffes because it was obvious in the photos he took of the ladies feeding these giants that they were the highlight of the day. Both of the girls' expressions were of pure happiness, so the zoo turned out to be a great idea.

Will took out another mint for himself, and offered one to Renee. She took one and sneezed again almost immediately. She must have some kind of allergy to mints. This could be fun. He would have to experiment and see if she did that every time he gave her a mint, but it couldn't be too obvious. Although she did have a cute way of sneezing.

Renee used Will's phone and took several photos of him with Rebecca, and he let the little girl take some of the two of them together. He had been with a lot of girls over the years, but he never kept pictures of any of them. Photos of these two ladies, however, would be worth keeping.

They all laughed while scrolling through the photos when they stopped for lunch and ice cream after their visit to the zoo. His favorites were the mother-daughter ones. These two girls were a special pair. Should he ask about Rebecca's father or would it spoil the moment? Maybe he would find out from his sister what their situation was. It seemed as though he had known Renee for years, since she was so easy to talk to, and they had clicked right away. Overall, it was a wonderful day with two new acquaintances. He couldn't ask for anything better than that.

# Chapter Five

**R**ENEE MET WITH HER FRIENDS AT work on Monday and by now rumors about the breakup with her boyfriend the previous week were going around. Could she avoid telling them anything during work hours and justify it by emphasizing they were on the clock and needed to focus on their jobs? She didn't want to talk about it at all, but she couldn't hide it any longer. They all hounded her to tell what really happened, so they convinced her to join them for lunch to discuss the details.

Their work in the distribution center was spent inside a large building with no windows. The employees had to stand for long hours, so an opportunity to take thirty minutes outside in the fresh air, sitting down for a quick sandwich was difficult to pass up. Renee's closest friends led her across the street to a local deli. They laughed as the three of them practically dragged her down the sidewalk. She had to admit the sunshine did feel good after being in a cold warehouse all morning, and the four ladies strode arm-in-arm like schoolgirls. She really did appreciate their company.

The ladies giggled as they walked into the deli, attracting attention as they made their way to the counter. They quieted to figure out what they each wanted to eat, and then one by one placed their orders and walked to a round table by the window. Renee selected the table so they could see outside and be reminded of the sunny day. She couldn't help but focus on her time with Will at the zoo. Maybe she wouldn't mention that part of the story to her friends yet.

"So what really happened with Derek?" Lisa asked impatiently.

"I don't know where you heard the kind of stories you've mentioned this morning, but none of them are true," Renee responded.

"We made them up over the past few days because you wouldn't tell us anything," Retta said dryly. "If you don't tell us, just wait until you hear the new rumors we're going to start about you and Derek this week."

"So fill us in and then we'll have the facts," MaryAnn added, pushing her sandy blonde hair out of her eyes.

"As you know, Derek could be a little bossy..." Renee started, but the girls busted out laughing.

"A little bossy?" interrupted Retta. "He was a control freak who wouldn't let you do anything without telling him where you're going after work, who you talked to, or what the guy at the cash register said to you."

Renee nodded and continued, "So he got mad at me one day last week after he called me and I didn't answer, then he came by my apartment in a bad mood."

"Did he have any moods other than bad?" MaryAnn asked.

Rolling her eyes at MaryAnn's comment, Renee continued. "Anyway, I was a little too assertive and mentioned I didn't have to tell him every little place I went, and he slapped me on the face so hard I fell and broke one of the legs of my coffee table."

The faces of her three friends registered horror at that comment, and Lisa put her hand over her mouth. Their eyes opened wide, eventually getting angry eyebrows as all of them seemed upset she was actually hit by this man. She would have to tell them about Will at this point, although it was a little embarrassing since she hadn't had the best choice of male friends over the past few years.

"Where was your little girl? She didn't see him hit you, did she?" asked Retta.

Renee turned away briefly, but responded, "Yes, she was right there in the living room. I know she was terrified."

"I sure hope you called the police. You can't let him get away with that," Lisa warned sternly.

"Well, after I fell on the table, there was a knock on the door and Derek angrily went to answer it. I heard Rebecca squeal when she saw someone she recognized at the door, and then Derek slapped her to the ground. The next thing I knew, someone kicked in the door and started punching the daylights out of Derek's face."

The jaws of all three girls dropped open, and there was a few seconds of silence as though they were frozen in shock by those words.

"Is Rebecca all right?" asked Retta.

"Yes, it scared her but she's not hurt."

"Who was the mystery man at the door?" demanded Lisa.

"Derek is no little wimp," MaryAnn added. "Isn't he like six foot six and 280 pounds? What kind of man could just come up to Derek and start beating him up?"

"You won't believe this, but it was some man I had never met. He only stopped by with Rebecca's teacher to give my daughter a little wooden elephant."

"What?" they all said together.

"Yes, this guy is the brother of my daughter's teacher and he had come to their class to talk about different countries of the world and their cultures, animals, and stuff like that."

"Was he handsome?" asked Retta.

"Like a movie star. He's a businessman, but with longer

32

hair than most men who dress professionally. Not too long. Just over his collar, his eye brows, and most of his ears. That's not even the best thing."

"We're waiting," said MaryAnn impatiently.

"Well, he promised Rebecca a little elephant in class but he didn't have one, so he brought it to our house that Saturday afternoon. He walked in on Derek, said he saw him hit Rebecca, and took matters into his own hands. He absolutely trashed Derek's face and knocked him out in my apartment. I had to clean up Derek's blood from my cabinets, walls, floor, and front door."

"Eww," exclaimed MaryAnn.

"Awesome," whispered Lisa.

"Where can I get me one of these guys?" asked Retta.

"The police came and took Derek away, and I'm pressing charges."

"Good for you," said MaryAnn.

"Every man should feel compelled to beat a child abuser to a pulp," added Lisa as the others agreed.

"This guy came up to me after pounding Derek and was so gentle and caring. I was too ashamed for him to see me like that and didn't know what to say to him."

"Are you sure it wasn't just a dream, and you'll get a call from Derek tonight asking who you went to lunch with today?" asked Lisa while the others laughed.

"It wasn't a dream, although I seriously considered that possibility. I couldn't sleep at all that night and I let Rebecca sleep in my bed with me. We talked for a long time. And then a few days ago, I heard a knock on my front door early in the morning, and you'll never guess who stood there outside."

"Your hero," said MaryAnn.

"Yes, and he wanted to take Rebecca and I to the zoo. He asked how I was, paid for our tickets, and even bought us lunch and ice cream. Derek never bought anything for me, let alone offered to do anything for Rebecca. This man even liked me with messy hair and without makeup."

"He saw you without makeup?" asked Retta.

"Yeah, he woke me up and I answered the door in nothing but my nightshirt. I looked like a mess, but he still complimented me. He actually said I looked breathtaking. I can't remember the last guy that said anything nice about my appearance."

"What kind of guy says something like that on a first date?" MaryAnn asked.

"He says what's on his mind without thinking much about it, I guess," replied Renee. "It made me feel so special I was speechless. I think he might have been a little embarrassed after he said it, but I'm glad he did."

"Wow. You can't let this one get away," said Lisa.

"This guy is different though," said Renee. "He dressed classy and was more of a gentleman than anyone I've ever met. I just wonder if he's out of my league."

"No, wait a minute. You can't think like that. You deserve a good man," said Retta.

Renee nodded. "He's more than a good man. He's like a dream come true. I only get the cheap losers who care more about themselves and cheat on me because I won't let them spend the night with me. Am I that unattractive?"

"No. You need to snap out of it. Those guys didn't deserve to go that far. However, if Mr. Dream is interested in you and he asks you out again, you had better say 'Yes,'" demanded MaryAnn. "This could be your real chance to find a good man."

"Yeah, don't let him slip away because you don't think you're good enough," added Lisa.

"I know. I've only seen him twice, but everything in me says this guy is Mr. Right. He seems too good to be true. Usually if something is too good to be true…"

"Don't say it," interrupted Retta. "Let it play out and see if he comes back for more."

"That's what I plan to do. I'm just wondering why he's not married or spoken for already, especially if he's at least my age. Rebecca said he was her teacher's older brother, so maybe he's about twenty-six."

"Hmm. I wonder if he's recently divorced. Or maybe he's not interested in someone of the female type, if you know what I mean," joked MaryAnn, amid the laughter of her friends.

"Or maybe he's a serial killer who's trying to get you to trust him and then you'll end up in six pieces inside a dumpster," added Lisa as everyone stared at her with disbelieving eyes. "Um, sorry about that. Not the best thing to say after you just went through a night of domestic violence. My bad."

"Or maybe he's really a nice guy who is shy and just hasn't found 'Mrs. Right' yet," Renee responded as she looked into the friendly eyes of her three nodding companions.

"I sure hope it works out for you. Just don't get your hopes up too high right now and let's see how it goes," advised Retta.

They all quickly finished their sandwiches, and appeared to be satisfied they finally knew the truth about her personal life. Hopefully, she didn't say too much too soon, but it felt good to tell her friends about Will. It felt even better to hear them say she deserved a good man like that. She had a warm feeling inside that lasted the rest of the afternoon.

# Chapter Six

**R**ENEE WAS STILL IN A GREAT mood when she dropped by the school to pick up Rebecca, but was startled when her daughter's teacher came up to her.

"Do you have a few minutes to talk?"

"Is something wrong?" asked Renee.

"Rebecca said she didn't have a lunch packed for her again today, and was a little upset."

Renee gasped. She had forgotten to make anything for her daughter's lunch, and she broke down in tears.

"It's okay. I had plenty extra from my lunch to give her, so she didn't go hungry. She did calm down after a few minutes, but I wanted to let you know so it's not a surprise to you when you talk to her."

"I'm so sorry. I'm just going through a lot right now. I keep trying to do everything and make ends meet, but I still end up forgetting something, or missing a payment, or …"

Kim hugged her as she broke down and couldn't finish her sentence, and they just stood there for a minute as Renee regained her composure.

"I thought my life was actually getting better for me, but I guess some things never change. Why is life so hard? It's always looking for some way to knock me down, and I never seem to win."

"I don't have all the answers, but I know that life isn't trying to knock you down. You're going through some difficult times, but you have friends here who will go out of their way to help you. If you ever need anything, just call me."

"You're a truly wonderful person, and I don't deserve a friend like you."

"Don't say that. You deserve the best for you and your daughter. Listen, how would you like it if I picked up Rebecca sometimes in the mornings and brought her to school with Nicole and me? Would that help you at all?"

Renee looked into Kim's dark brown eyes. Will had dark hair and blue eyes, but she did resemble her brother. For some reason, it made her feel good and she hugged Kim again.

"Did you know your brother stopped by Saturday and took us to the zoo?"

Kim's lips turned into a big smile as she stepped back and held her friend's hands.

"Well, well, well. That's news to me. Did you all have a good time?"

"We had a marvelous time. He is such a gentleman. I need to buy some nice dresses to wear, but I can't afford it. I'm afraid I'll embarrass him with the clothes I have."

"Nonsense. He'd like you with whatever you wear. Although, you're about my size. I'll bring in some of my clothes you can try out and see if you like them."

"You don't have to do that."

"I know, but I don't mind. Plus, I think it might be fun to confuse him with the clothes, and see if he recognizes any of them on you."

"You really think he would remember the clothes you wear?"

""Oh, you'd be surprised at how observant he is."

"You're a lifesaver, Kim."

"Don't worry about it. Plus I know what Will likes, so

you'll have an advantage."

Renee raised her eyebrows. "I'm curious about him though. Why isn't he married already? It seems as though he should have been taken by now."

Kim looked down and shook her head. "I've asked him that same question several times. He says he hasn't found the right girl yet. Maybe when we have more time, I'll tell you some things about Will that might help you understand why he is the way he is."

A serious expression appeared on Renee's face. What could that mean? "Is it something bad? I don't want to pry if there's something he doesn't want me to know."

"No, it's nothing bad. Let me give you the short story for now and we can discuss details later. Years ago, he met a girl who he thought would be his soul mate. She meant everything to him but there was some misunderstanding. She asked him to stop seeing her. He put all his time into his job and started traveling a lot. He didn't date for a while and one day found out this girl had married someone else. Will took a position overseas and spent a couple of years in Europe, while his consulting business took off. He started dating again, but it was obvious to me that he felt he would never find the right girl. His 'soul mate' was now with someone else. He does a lot of incredible things with his travels now and he seems content, but I can tell he's missing something by not being married."

"What's her name," Renee asked.

"Ah, we call her 'she-who-must-not-be-named' since Will still hasn't come to terms with her being married to someone else. He may claim to be over her, but he's not. We don't want to mention her name and risk putting him into a depressed state. She was quite a catch, from what I can tell, and her rejection of him has helped make him such a wonderful person. To this day, he says he doesn't know why she broke up with him, so he's done everything possible to be the most eligible and desirable bachelor in the world. I think he succeeded."

"So is there any way he would ever be interested in me? I'm certainly not looking for marriage right now, but if I found the right guy …"

"Since he took you and Rebecca to the zoo, that's a good sign. He's great with kids, and by him seeing how much fun it is to do things with you and Rebecca, it may open his eyes to what's been lacking in his life all these years. Don't give up."

"I don't want him to go out with me just because of my daughter. I want him to date me because he wants to be with me."

"Oh, I didn't mean he's not interested in you. I just wanted to let you know that he would be great with kids too, hint hint."

Renee smiled at the thought, and she locked eyes with Kim again. "I understand."

"I have to warn you, though. You're competing with a mythical girl from his past who he honestly believes was his one and only. It may not be easy, but I think it would be good for both you and Will to spend time together and see what develops. He really is a wonderful person."

"I know that already."

"After only meeting him twice? No, you don't even realize the tip of the iceberg. He has more in his heart to give than anyone I've ever met, and he's generous of his time and money. I don't think people know just how much of himself he pours out for others every day. I constantly find out from various friends some of the things he does, but he's also private and keeps most of that to himself."

Renee pondered those statements, and looked at Kim. This knight in shining armor had become even more intriguing than she initially realized and she wanted to learn more.

*****

Will stared out the window of his downtown office, watching the squirrels running around one of the large oak trees. They were so playful and seemed to bring out the fun in every activity they did. Was he like them? He turned to Sue, his personal assistant, while she straightened the reception area.

"Sue, I'd like to get something special for that girl I met recently."

"Which one?" she replied back without turning to look at him. "I can't keep up with them all."

"You know, the girl I just took to the zoo. Her name is Renee."

"Right. Do you want me to send her a dozen red roses?"

"Maybe. Is red too serious? I don't want her to think I'm coming on too strong after seeing her only a couple of times. I've done that before and regretted it."

"How about some chocolate covered berries?"

He turned to face her. "Could you do that?"

"I can do anything. You should know that by now." She walked over to his desk with a smirk.

"Sounds perfect. All girls like chocolate, right? And berries are a non-committal kind of gift, aren't they?"

"You're something else. Yes, she'll appreciate it but she won't think you're asking her to marry you."

Sue walked back toward the reception desk and asked, "What do you want the card to say and when do you want it to arrive?"

"You know what I usually put. Just something nice about how much I enjoyed spending time with her. Have it delivered tomorrow. Wait a minute. I don't even know where she works. I guess we could send it to the school and she could get it when she picks up her daughter. Would that be alright?"

"Yes, I can do that and I'll find out where she works too."

"Perfect. Thanks again. I owe you one."

"I think you owe me more than one."

He laughed out loud with his back to her and peeked over his shoulder. Sue wrote something down without returning his gaze, and he stood up from his desk to walk over next to her while she turned to look at his smiling face.

"Sue, I appreciate all of the things you do for me. Without you, I don't think I could even function."

He hugged her while she hugged him back. "You're right about that. You really should do more things for yourself and not have to rely on someone like me to keep things flowing smoothly every day. You don't even know how to use a coffee maker."

"But you're so good at what you do that I can't even picture my life without you taking care of things."

She stood back and stared into his eyes. "Will, I appreciate you hiring me and helping me and my family with expenses. You really don't need a personal assistant but I appreciate the job. You're a lot of fun to work with and I'll be available to you as long as you need me."

"Thanks, Sue, but I really do need an assistant," he responded and walked back to his desk. The squirrels chased each other up and down an oak tree, and he sat down to watch them play before realizing his screensaver had started. A slideshow collection of photos from the day at the zoo popped up for a few seconds before changing to the next picture. Renee's face mesmerized him. What was is about her that made her standout above the others? He didn't believe in love at first sight but he was certainly infatuated with this woman more than anyone since …

He stared at her long eyelashes, her cute little upturned nose, and the way her long hair came down and framed her face. They made a cute couple and with little Rebecca, they actually looked like a family.

# Chapter Seven

**W**ILL DROVE TO RENEE'S house after school and seemed to surprise her with a knock on the door.

"Hi, Will. What brings you around to this part of town?"

"Oh, I just happened to be in the neighborhood, and …"

"Yeah, right. This is well out of your way and you know it."

Will laughed as she beamed at him with raised eyebrows. "So I was looking at the pictures of you and Rebecca at the zoo and I wanted to find out how you both were doing."

"Very nice of you. We're doing great. Oh, by the way, I received a wonderful gift from you at school. Would you like to come in and see it?"

"What? Something from me? I didn't want to intrude if you're in the middle of something, but I'd be glad to."

Renee opened the door for him and he walked inside. His eyes caught hers as he passed by very close to her, and he couldn't help but smile. Her eyes were so captivating he actually craved them. She was playful and it drove him wild. Rebecca ran up to him and he knelt down to give her a hug.

"You sent Mommy some chocolate covered blueberries, cherries, and strawberries."

"Would I do a thing like that?"

"Yes."

She took his hand and led Will into the kitchen, then he looked back at Renee as she followed.

"Listen, Renee, I just wanted to let you know that I appreciate you both spending the day with me at the zoo, and I felt I should apologize for showing up early in the morning that day without calling you first."

"You mean like you just did today?"

Will stopped, embarrassed by her statement. "Uh, yeah I guess so. I'm sorry. I should have called before coming over today, shouldn't I?"

"No. It's fine to show up unannounced anytime. I really don't mind, as long as you don't turn out to be a serial killer."

He gave her a weird expression, but replied, "Sometimes I just don't plan things in advance and end up doing something unexpected."

"Don't worry about it, Will. But the next time it happens, it'll cost you."

He stared at her and they both laughed. Was she serious or joking?

Rebecca took the boxes of berries out of the refrigerator and opened them and Will saw the contents.

"Would you like one?" the little girl asked.

"Who could pass up a chocolate covered blueberry? Thanks."

When he finished the berry, Will took a box of mints from his pocket and popped one in his mouth. Glancing up at Renee, he offered the box to her. She took one out and placed it gently into her mouth, only to sneeze a few seconds later.

"Bless you," replied Will and Rebecca at the same time. That was amazing. She sneezed every time she had a mint. What a fascinating creature. He had to study this more.

"Will, you really didn't have to send me anything. I had such a good time with you."

"No, actually I had to. I changed your plans last weekend

and you should know that I don't want to take you for granted or make you feel like you have to do anything that you didn't want to do."

She took Will's hands and held them while staring into his eyes. She might as well have been looking deep into his heart because he felt her reaching in at that moment.

"Thank you, Will. You made my day when I got to school and Kim gave these to me. Nobody has ever given me anything like this before."

It took a few moments for him to speak, and he actually stuttered at first. "I, um, I just, well I'm glad you like them." He had forgotten little Rebecca was there and soon realized he was being stared at by the miniature Renee, who grinned at both of them.

"Oh, and I wanted to let you know that I'd like to take you out to dinner sometime soon, but I have to go out of town this weekend."

Renee tilted her head and asked, "Where do you have to go?"

Every movement she made captured his heart and he was taken by how attractive she was. "I'll be leaving for Europe tomorrow, then going on to Mumbai, where I'll spend the night. The next morning I'll catch a flight to Bangalore, and meet with some of my colleagues there for the next week."

"India? What do you do that takes you way over there?"

"I can't talk much about it, but I work with companies regarding network security."

"What? You can't tell me who you work for? Don't tell me you work for the CIA or the mafia. That would be my luck."

He laughed and responded, "No, just a normal job with interesting customers all over the world. Most people doze off when I try to explain what I do with computers and networks, so I just leave it at that."

"Hmm. Sounds like there's more to you than you're letting on. Well, have a safe trip and call me when you get back. I'd love to go out to dinner and hear all about India."

"Yeah, it's fascinating. I hope to be back in town next Saturday, not this coming week end but the one after. I'll let you know, and I'll pick you and Rebecca up for dinner that night. Dress nice, because the restaurant is a little fancy."

Renee looked at her daughter, who giggled, and she replied, "What restaurant around here would need us to dress up? I don't even know if I have anything fancy."

"It's a surprise. Don't worry, you'll love it. And Rebecca, wear your prettiest dress."

Will gave the little girl a hug, and she beamed up at her mom. He gazed into Renee's eyes for a moment, then hugged her. It would have been so nice to stay longer and keep holding her, but it wouldn't be good to overstay his welcome, especially since she reminded him he showed up unannounced again today. That wouldn't happen again.

His eyes connected to hers one more time before heading back outside. He was drawn to them over and over again, and she seemed to put him in a trance. She wasn't like other women he had met before, and he enjoyed the way he felt when they were together. There was truly something special about this one.

★★★★★

Will flew overnight to Prague, then spent the next day exploring the Charles Bridge, Prague Castle, and Tyn Church, walking around the Old Town Square with a young lady he met at the hotel. The classic stone streets and old architecture never ceased to amaze him, and it was nice to have company as they strolled through the city. The two ate lunch together and eventually met for dinner, but Will's mind fixated on Renee the entire time he was with this girl. What would it be like to share these experiences with her someday? That thought had never crossed his mind before. He was with a pretty woman in Europe, yet he kept thinking about this young lady back in North Carolina. Something was stirring and gave him feelings he had not experienced for years.

He traveled the next day to India, arriving in Mumbai after midnight to thousands of lights and a crowd of people outside the airport. It seemed odd for so many people to be out and about so late, but this was normal with International flights regularly arriving at this time. His next flight left in about seven hours, but from a different airport, so he took a taxi to a hotel and tried to get a few hours of sleep. The one day stop in Prague helped to break up the trip so he wouldn't be totally exhausted when he reached his final destination, but he was tired enough to fall right to sleep.

As usual, the morning came too quickly but he had a flight to catch and looked forward to his meeting in Bangalore before lunch. A shower was refreshing. It definitely helped him to prepare for a busy day after sitting for so many hours. His car picked him up, and his eyes explored the bustling city on his way to the domestic airport in Mumbai. The sunshine felt good as it warmed him. It had been over a year since his last trip here, but something was different. He wasn't sure if it was with him or with the city. Finally on the small plane, he stared out the window as he always did, and he couldn't get his mind off of Renee. Would she enjoy visiting India someday? Would she like the food as much as he did? Would she be as fun to be around as he suspected she would?

The flight was quick, so he soon arrived in Bangalore and took a taxi to the hotel. This was his favorite place to stay in all of India, even though it wasn't the newest, most glamorous hotel. The one he always selected used to be a British Gentleman's Club over a hundred years ago and had about fifteen acres of gardens surrounded by eight foot stone walls.

He pictured a room full of grey-headed, mustached Brits sitting in a room full of books, smoking and talking about tea. The attendant at the front recognized him and greeted him with a smile.

"Welcome back, Mr. Sayre. It is good to see you again."

"Good morning, Prakash. It's good to be here."

Prakash had a handsome dark green uniform with a turban, and he took Will's luggage inside as Will paid for the taxi. Another doorman held the hotel's front door open for him as someone else greeted him by name. They sure knew how to make their guests feel at home. A familiar face welcomed Will at the front desk as he recognized the girl in a colorful sari that wrapped around her like a spectacular sheet.

"Good morning, Mr. Sayre. It's been a long time since we've seen you here."

"Hi, Vijaya. Yes, it's been a while. I'll only be here for a little over a week this time."

"Well, we'll just have to make the most of it, won't we? Here, let me get you checked in."

She had long black hair pinned up in a bun, big brown eyes, and a red dot on her forehead. Will had some fun times with her after work the last time he was here, even though she wasn't supposed to fraternize with the guests. They would meet outside of the hotel grounds at an outdoor restaurant and roam the city in auto rickshaws, the small motorcycles with a driver and a covered back seat for three. Most of them didn't speak English so he had to rely on Vijaya to communicate with the drivers. Will enjoyed the friendliness of the people in Bangalore and laughed heartily when he rode an elephant with Vijaya though the jungle on the way to an ancient sultan's palace. He had good memories of his last few visits here. Plus the food was always excellent and the city was covered with colorful flowers in the spring.

Maybe he and Vijaya could explore Bangalore together

again during this trip and help the days go by more quickly. He looked forward to getting back home and visiting Renee again, but figured that while he was in India, he would pass the time with some of the local ladies. Or perhaps just this one he knew from the hotel. Compared with Renee, however, even Vijaya meant nothing more than a friendly companion with which to explore the city. Renee was something else, and he missed her more than he expected.

# Chapter Eight

ARELAXED SILENCE SURROUNDED Kim in her nightgown as she poured hot tea and hummed a pretty melody. Stepping carefully on the small rug placed on the dark wood floors, she carried the two cups to her living room and handed one to her husband. He had already sat down on their plush couch by the fireplace and welcomed her with loving eyes and a smile.

"Thanks Honey. You know, the way you've been setting up Rebecca's mom with your brother might not be in either of their best interests."

Kim sat down next to Doug and asked, "What do you mean? It looks like a perfect match."

"Well, you might think so, but what would Will think about it? Would he appreciate you playing around with his personal life like this? Sometimes playing matchmaker turns out disastrous."

Kim sipped her tea and responded, "I've talked with both Rebecca and her mother many times, and they've both been struggling without a man in the house. The men Renee has dated since her husband was killed have all been losers. Rebecca needs a father and Renee needs a good husband. Will would make a great father and husband, and he needs a family. He won't admit it, but I can see something is desperately missing in his life. He wants a wife and a family more than he realizes."

"And you're the expert that knows exactly what he needs, more than he himself knows? Sounds like you could have a show called 'Sister Knows Best'."

"Yes, I'm not a psychiatrist but I don't need to be one in order to see what would make both his and Renee's lives so much better."

"You don't think you're meddling into their personal lives a bit too much?"

Kim set her cup down and repositioned herself to face her husband. "Doug, you've known Will for a long time and you've seen how much fun he has with his life. Yet, even you should be able to see that he is lonely without a steady girlfriend or wife."

"Even me, a not-so-intelligent male, should be able to see that, eh? Well, I notice he has a lot of fun and dates different women all the time. Some people would see that as the ideal life for a man, but you think he's miserable with so many dates and a different type of woman every week?"

"Doug, I didn't mean for you to take it as you being not-so-intelligent. I just mean that as a man, you can see when another man needs a good woman in his life."

"He has a good woman in his life. It's just not the same woman every week. Why don't you think that would make a man happy?"

"So are you saying you would be happier as a single guy, with a different girl every week?"

Doug hesitated in his response and Kim slapped his arm. "I didn't mean that. I'm a different person than your brother and I enjoy being with you every day of my life. The same woman, day after day, makes me happy." He paused, turned away for a second, then stared into Kim's eyes. "What if your brother is destined to be single all his life? He may never be a father and may date a different girl every week for the rest of his life. That might just make him happier than being stuck with, I mean married to, one person for the next fifty years."

Kim stared at him for a second or two, then shook her head. "I just can't see how that would make anyone happy. I know Will better than most people and deep down he wants a great woman to spend the rest of his life with. He actually yearns for it so much it breaks my heart. He once told me he thinks about that day constantly, the day when that girl walked away. I just know his main goal in life is to escape from the painful memories which still plague him from that relationship he believed was his 'happily ever after' woman. He's afraid he'll never find that one woman who can give him what we have." She paused again, "Renee fits him perfectly like a glove, and I believe they could be together forever."

"It's nice to know someone else wants to plan out your brother's life for him, someone who knows what he really wants," Doug replied with a sarcastic tone in his voice.

"I don't want to force anything on him he doesn't want, but I believe if we just lean him in that direction, he'll realize how wonderful it will be to have a family, have that one special someone, and share his life with her. Sometimes men can't see something so obvious, even when it's right in front of them. Plus they don't take hints very well. It often takes a wise woman hitting them upside the head with a two-by-four to get their attention so they can open their eyes and see what every woman around them can already see."

Doug laughed and was about to respond to his wife. Just then, their daughter Nicole walked in the room with a cup of milk, while both Doug and Kim turned to see her.

"Hi, Beautiful," said Kim.

"Hi, Mommy and Daddy."

"So Nicole, how do you like spending time with Rebecca?" asked Kim.

"She's my best friend. You know she's smart and always

nice to everyone in class. We have a fun time when we play together."

"Yes, I agree. What about her mom?"

"I like her a lot. She cries sometimes and she always seems to be late for something, like the rabbit in Alice in Wonderland. She needs to relax more like you, Mommy."

Doug and Kim turned to each other and laughed, while Nicole sipped her milk. "How do you know she needs to relax?"

Nicole looked up at her mother and replied, "You know how you feel after you get a massage or after you spend some time reading a book on the back porch? I don't think Rebecca's mom does that enough, because she doesn't smile as much as you."

"Aww, that's sweet of you, Honey," said Kim as she hugged her little girl.

Doug rubbed Nicole's back and said to Kim, "She's more observant than I realized and she already understands the importance of reducing stress from our lives. You've taught her well."

Nicole gazed up at her mom again and said, "I think you should spend more time with Rebecca's mom and maybe she would learn to relax better."

"Actually, I plan to do that so maybe you and Rebecca can play together more."

"I'd like that, Mommy. Well, I'm going to brush my teeth. I'm getting tired."

"I am too. We'll be up in a few minutes to tuck you in," replied Kim.

Nicole hugged Doug and he said, "I love you, Precious."

"I love you too, Daddy."

They watched as Nicole walked into the kitchen and put her cup onto the counter, then disappeared on the way to her bedroom with the sounds of little footsteps.

"I know you mean well and I know you love your brother very much. I just don't think you should be too pushy. And don't be too disappointed if your 'happily ever after' plans don't turn out to be reality for him."

"But look at how happy we are together. Don't you wish other people could have what we have?"

"Of course, but not everyone has the same goals in life that we do. Not everyone is willing to do what we do to make one another happy. Will has led quite a different life from you and me, and Rebecca's mom has had her share of difficulties in her life. There's no guarantee either of them could change their lifestyles to be compatible."

"I do understand where you're coming from. I also know what I've seen in both Will and Renee over the past couple of years. They are both searching for a soul mate. I believe each of them would do what it takes to find the right person. Plus, I see some of the same characteristics of 'you-know-who' in her, so I'll bet Will has noticed the same things. Will saw a lifetime of happiness with another girl from years ago, but since she left, he has probably had a daily dose of sadness, thinking about what could have been. That's miserable, and I would want to escape from the constant reminder too. It's almost as though that girl from Will's past and Renee are on the same parallel trajectory in Will's life, and he sees this opportunity to change his life for the better by making Renee a part of it. A chance to correct what was once broken."

"Wow. You either have a remarkable intuition or an overactive imagination." Doug sat down his cup and turned to hold his wife's hands. He gazed into her eyes and said, "You are an amazing woman and I am the most fortunate man in the world to have met you. I look forward to spending the rest of my life with you and I'll do everything I can to make sure you're happy."

She smiled with a hint of moisture in her eyes and she

looked down at his hands holding hers.

"You only want what's best for Will, as well as for Renee and Rebecca. You are the most caring person and your plans to match them up are only for their own happiness. I agree it seems like they're a perfect fit, but I just want you to be careful and not try to force it. You can bring them together and encourage a relationship, and I'll do everything I can to support it. However, please realize that only they can make it happen."

"Thanks, Doug. That's all I ask." She gave Doug a kiss and he stood, holding out his hand to help her up.

"Let's go say goodnight to our little angel," said Doug as he led her to Nicole's room. The two of them walked arm in arm across the floor and up the stairs.

# Chapter Nine

**W**ILL AND HIS FRIENDS PLAYED an active game of basketball when he returned from his trip to India. Covered in sweat, they bumped each other out of the way, blocked shots, rushed up to the hoop for a basket, and then Patrick knocked Will to the floor after a good block.

He reached down to offer his hand to Will, who stared up at the ceiling, and commented, "Will, it's good to have you back in town so we can beat you at basketball today. Did you have a successful trip?"

Out of breath, Will responded, "Thanks. Yes, it was a good, productive trip and I think everyone was happy."

The court was indoor and air-conditioned, but the men were still overheated from their hour of intense activity.

"Did you try some interesting food in India?" asked Daniel.

Several men gathered around Will to hear more about his trip.

"Just the usual: chicken cooked in a clay pot, curries, rice on a banana leaf. I did have a fish curry that was probably the hottest thing I've ever eaten. Usually the staff can tell I'm not Indian and they ask me if I want it Indian spicy or American spicy. However, the waiter didn't ask me at this one meal. It was certainly more than American spicy and I had sweat pouring down my face. My tongue and lips were on fire for at least a half an hour, but the flavor was so good I couldn't stop eating. I just wish it hadn't been that hot."

"What do you mean about rice on a banana leaf?" asked Frank.

"I went to one restaurant where they spread out a banana leaf instead of using a plate, and they piled rice and some sauces on the leaf. I waited for a fork, but they didn't bring one, so I looked around to find everyone picking up the rice with their fingers and rubbing it in one of the sauces before eating it. So when in Rome …"

"That's unique," added Patrick.

"The only disturbing thing about it was when I walked by the same restaurant the next day. I saw a stack of banana leaves tied up outside the back door of the place and watched a dog relieve himself on the stack of leaves."

The faces and groans of his friends registered their disapproval.

"There was nothing I could do since I had already eaten off of my leaf the night before, so I just kept walking."

"What was the hotel like?" asked Patrick.

"It was my usual. However, I did have a long-tailed monkey sneak into my room and steal something from a bowl of fruit at my desk. That hasn't happened to me before."

"A monkey?" questioned Daniel. "How did it get in?"

"The hotel sits on a fifteen acre garden, and there are monkeys in the trees. I've seen them around before. I like to walk through the garden path in the mornings when it's cool. My room was on the second floor, and I saw a few of the critters walking along the rail next to me. No big deal. When I opened my door, there was a friendly little thief by the open window, and he grabbed some fruit, escaping through the window. I kept it closed from then on."

"You don't see that at the Hilton by the airport in Raleigh," replied Daniel.

"Did you go out with any of the foreign ladies this trip?" asked Gregory.

"Uh, yes. I did take one young lady out shopping and to eat a couple of times in Bangalore, and I spent some time with another one in Prague." It actually bothered him a little that he had met with two women on this trip even after he had been so enamored by Renee. He wanted to tell his friends about her, but maybe this wasn't the right time.

"Only two? That's unusual for a one week trip," Frank commented.

Everyone laughed and Will responded with his usual charming, "Yeah, I didn't go out of my way to find different women this time. I just explored the cities with the same one a couple of times."

It didn't feel right to discuss these women when he should have been focusing on Renee. She was the one who made him feel so special. Will had watched a movie on the return flight and thought he saw Renee in a background scene. He even played it back again to verify, but didn't notice her the second time. She had already infiltrated his mind and that brought a smile to his face.

Patrick added, "Sounds like you might be settling down a bit. Finally seeing the benefits of having one girl instead of a different one every day?"

Will looked at his friend for second, then glanced at the ground. "Not really. I just knew this girl in India from previous trips and enjoyed her company. That's all."

Maybe it was the last time he would ever go out with someone other than Renee. Something had changed in him and he liked it. She had actually won him over and he no longer felt the need to fill his spare time with someone else.

"Good for you," Frank replied. "It's too bad she doesn't live here. Wait a minute. She isn't married is she?"

"Of course not. I would never date a married woman. You know me better than that."

"I know. I just wanted to see your reaction."

They all picked up their belongings and walked toward the exit door, wiping the sweat from their faces and necks along the way.

Will took a cold Mountain Dew from his cooler and gulped down a fourth of the bottle.

"So you drink one of those this early in the morning?" Frank asked.

Will looked over at him with a confused expression. "What do you mean? This is the breakfast of champions."

They all laughed as he gulped down another mouthful.

Then Will said, "Thanks for meeting me for a game. It was a great workout."

Patrick responded, "Anytime, Will. It's always good to see you again. Take care."

"You too. See you later guys."

Will drove home, thinking of only one woman all the way there. He couldn't wait to see Renee again, so as soon as he showered and dressed, he called her.

"Hi, Will. How was your trip?"

"It went well, but it's nice to be home. Do you have any plans for tonight?"

"You mean you would actually want to spend it with me, your first day back?"

"Well, you're the third girl I've called but none of the others were available."

"You rat. I'd better not be third in line to go out with you."

"No, you're the first girl I've called since I arrived. I haven't even talked to my sister, so you should feel special."

"Hmm, what do you have in mind?"

"Remember I told you and Rebecca to get dressed up before I went out of town? I'd like to take you to a quaint little place I'll bet you've never been. How about 5:30 tonight?"

"5:30? That's a little early, isn't it?"

"No, we want to be seated before 6 PM, so I'll get you at 5:30 to make sure we're in by then."

"Sounds good. We'll be waiting for you."

Will could hardly contain his excitement and kept himself busy to take his mind off of being with Renee soon. There was something about her that made him feel like no other woman had been able to do. Well, maybe one, but not for a long time. He gathered his collection of mail and sat down by the window to go through it all. He looked at the computer and was tempted to power it on just so he could watch the slideshow of photos he took of Renee and Rebecca at the zoo. That would be too much of a distraction while he went through the mail, so he just started working on the first envelope. After getting past some of the mail, he glanced up at the screen and smiled as he pushed the power button. It would be worth the distraction today.

✶✶✶✶✶

Will drove his SUV since he needed room for Rebecca too. He greeted the two ladies at the door with a dozen red roses for each of them. The aroma surrounding Renee pulled him through the entrance and he couldn't take his eyes off of her.

"Wow. You two are the most attractive girls in town. You both look marvelous. Would you spin around so I can see from every angle?"

They did and he whistled at them, respectfully of course. "I am one lucky guy tonight. I think my sister has a dress just like that. Oh, and here are flowers for you both. You'll need to put them in water before we leave."

He didn't know what red roses implied, but without the

help of his trusty personal assistant today, he had to think on his own. That often brought about some unexpected results. His rationale was that since he bought the same kind of rose for Rebecca, then Renee wouldn't look too deeply into the gift for a hidden meaning.

"I happened to see the roses for sale on the way here and couldn't resist a last minute stop. I hope you don't mind."

"Nope. Roses on sale are just as nice as roses at full price. You didn't even have to tell us you bought them on sale. We would have never known. Let me put them into vases and then we'll be ready to go."

Renee gathered the flowers and carried them into the kitchen. Rebecca reached up to hug Will, so he picked her up. The little girl whispered in his ear, "Nobody has ever given me flowers before."

"That's certainly news to me. I thought a pretty little girl like you would have been given flowers by several different boys by now."

She smiled at him and shyly shook her head.

"And you're already in the first grade? Boys today just don't know how to treat a girl, do they?"

"We're all set. Let's eat," interrupted Renee.

Will drove them across town and gave his name to the lady at the desk. Reservations were required, so he was prepared and she led the three of them to their table. Renee's expression was priceless, since the interior was even more impressive than the exterior, and Will was pleased he had chosen the right place.

Exotic plants lined the walkway to their table, while a relaxing bubbling sound softly trickled in the background. After they sat down, Rebecca said, "Hey, there's a little stream behind the plants."

Her mother motioned for her to talk quietly. They all looked at the stream as ducks swam in it, inside the restaurant.

Renee turned her eyes back to Will, who had already been staring at her, and she shook her head. "This place is probably a little more expensive than a fast food place, isn't it?"

He laughed. "You could say that. How do you like it?"

Rebecca burst out first. "I really like this place."

Renee agreed. "It is lovely inside and very tranquil."

Without opening at the menu, Will ordered drinks for all of them and selected an appetizer everyone would enjoy.

At that moment, a commotion started and everyone turned to see what it was. Will, however, knew what it was and kept his eyes on his two favorite ladies to see their reaction. Their eyes grew larger and white teeth sparkled exquisitely when they saw a small army of ducks marching along the path.

Will commented, "At 6:00, they march out to their bedtime quarters so I didn't want to miss that."

"What a cute idea," Renee replied.

Rebecca laughed as the ducks walked by her and she saw they had on tuxedo collars.

The rest of the evening went so perfectly that it was all a blur to Will. He talked about some of the aspects of India he enjoyed the most, described the hotel he stayed at and a palace he visited. He relished how interested the girls were in hearing about Bangalore and his stay in Prague. He wanted to do more of this, specifically with Renee and Rebecca, and he didn't want the evening to end.

After he dropped them off at Renee's apartment, he gave Rebecca a kiss on the cheek and she went inside to start getting ready for bed. Will couldn't resist moving closer to Renee at her front door and automatically pressed his lips to hers without saying a word. It was one of the most magical moments he had ever experienced and when he came up for air, he kept his eyes closed for a couple of seconds, breathing in her perfume. When he opened them, Rebecca quickly closed the curtains and Renee said, "I had a perfect evening.

Thanks so much for taking both of us."

"You are a special woman and I'd really like to see you again soon."

"I'll be looking forward to it.  Good night."

Will watched her shut the door, and he stood there briefly before walking to the big, black SUV which was almost hidden in the darkness.  There was no way he would be able to fall asleep tonight.

# Chapter Ten

RENEE WALKED ON AIR THE NEXT day and doubted she would even be able to work. She moved slowly, almost gracefully, as she dressed and got herself ready for the day. Why couldn't she be getting dressed up to see Will again instead of for her job? She spun and hummed a song, reminding herself of Cinderella dreaming of going to the ball. That made her laugh out loud and seeing her expression in the mirror kept the smile on her face. She hadn't been this happy in so long. She actually did look pretty, and it seemed as though Will thought she was too.

"And what did you think when you saw the ducks wearing collars?" Renee asked her daughter.

"It was funny," Rebecca replied. "They were so handsome and I could tell the owners took good care of them. I want to go back there again."

"It was nice, but we couldn't afford it," laughed Renee. "I'm glad Ms. Kim let me borrow some of her clothes. I didn't have anything classy enough to wear there."

"And I'm glad I could still fit in that dress from the wedding when I was a flower girl a few months ago."

Renee hadn't felt this good about her life in years and she didn't want it to end. They both laughed at everything during breakfast. Rebecca was happier than she had ever been and it was all because of one man. How could this guy have such a positive effect on both of them?

"Mommy, can we go out with Will again? I really like him."

"We'll see. He has to ask us, remember? I think he likes us too, so be patient."

Renee replayed the scene where she was kissed by Prince Charming the night before and couldn't wait to see him again. From the way he looked at her, it was obvious he enjoyed himself as well.

"Oh, we'd better get going to school or you'll be late. Are you almost ready?"

"Let me brush my teeth and I will be."

While Rebecca went to finish at the bathroom sink, Renee cleaned up the kitchen, just in case Will surprised her with another visit. Usually she left her dishes in a pile and only washed them up once in a while, but with the prospect of a special visitor, she was inspired to make her apartment more presentable lately. It was good not having papers stacked up on the counters for the first time in years and she was proud of her new neatness. Even if Will didn't notice the missing clutter, it didn't matter. She wanted to straighten up and it gave her a sense of accomplishment she had long forgotten.

Rebecca came back out and they took their newfound happiness on the road to school. They both chatted and giggled about the silliest things and Renee considered staying home from work and letting her daughter skip school just so they could have a fun day together. Unfortunately, she couldn't miss work, with the bills piling up, and wished it was Saturday instead. They could have a lazy day together then and enjoy each other's company. I guess that would have to wait a few more days, so a mother-daughter day was something to look forward to later in the week.

When they arrived at the school, Rebecca gave her mother

a wonderful hug and a kiss on the cheek, while Renee savored every second of it. If only it could be like this all the time. Rather than rushing off like she did every other day to get to her job on time, she sat and watched her little girl march along the sidewalk to join up with her friends before they all disappeared behind the front doors. Back to reality.

On her way to work now, she sang along to a melodic love song on the radio, surprising herself. She didn't often sing to love songs for some reason. She usually preferred the angry, vindictive songs she heard on the country music stations, where the husband cheated on the wife and she took her revenge on his car, or something like that. Those types of songs had been more fitting for her life until now. It felt good to sing about loving someone for a change, especially after an incredible date with the first really nice guy she had met in over five years, since her husband died. It couldn't be love after only knowing Will for a few weeks, but she could get used to feeling like this.

Renee didn't know much about Will and craved information to satisfy her intense curiosity. He seemed open and honest, so he would probably not hesitate to answer any question she asked him. Yet the last thing she needed was to be too inquisitive and scare him away. Maybe his sister would be willing to give her a few more details on his life. She wanted to know everything about him. His favorite music, if he liked dogs or cats, what his apartment looked like. He was like a good dream and she wanted to think about him all day.

Finally at work. Her friends would ask about Mr. Right, so she tried to figure out something to tell them without letting them know all the details that were really going on in her life. They were her best friends, however, they could be nosy sometimes. She was ready to explode with excitement and tell them everything, but didn't want to take a chance that she might overdo it with them. How could she show an indifferent attitude about Mr. Right and still maintain some sense of dignity around her co-workers? Hopefully the day would go by quickly and she wouldn't have to talk about Will at all. And yet, she wanted to talk about him.

Her friend with the long straight blonde hair greeted her first. "Well, it's about time you graced us with your presence, Renee. Running a bit late today?"

"Hi, MaryAnn. Yes, just a little lazy getting up this morning. I need every second of beauty sleep I can get, you know?"

"Dreaming about your knight in shining armor?" asked Retta with a twinkle in her eyes.

"What knight? Who are you talking about?" Renee responded without looking up.

"You know who we want to hear about. Have you seen him again?" asked Lisa.

"Oh, you mean the guy who rescued me from that cheating Derek?"

"Yes!" they all responded in unison.

"Well, if you must know, he did take Rebecca and I out to dinner last night at a fancy place and had us dress up."

"Oooohh."

"You know the big place downtown with the large fountains out front? I think it's called something like 'Le Chateau'?" So much for controlling her excitement.

MaryAnn whistled. "Wow, I've never been there before. What's it like?"

A smile crept up on her and the story flowed freely. "It was impressive inside, with a stream running through the middle. And at 6:00, a parade of ducks wearing tuxedo collars marched through the restaurant to their houses out back. The food was excellent but the company was even better."

"Must be nice. Did you see what the bill was?" asked Lisa.

"No, I didn't even try to look. I think it was more than

one month's car payment."

"Then he's no cheapskate," added MaryAnn.

"And he took Rebecca out with you two? That's a little odd, isn't it?" asked Retta.

"No, he really likes to do family things, like taking us all to the zoo or getting ice cream for all of us."

"But haven't you two had any one-on-one time together?" Retta probed impatiently.

"Well, no. I guess he wants me to know that he doesn't mind having Rebecca as part of my family and hadn't pushed for alone time yet. No one I've dated has really wanted to include Rebecca in anything. Until Will."

"So has he been married before? Is he married now and hasn't told you? What's wrong with him that he isn't taken already?" asked Lisa.

"Wow, you always think the worst," said MaryAnn.

"Yeah, he's a great guy. I haven't seen anything about him I don't like, and I'm sure he wouldn't have any secrets like that."

Retta and MaryAnn looked at each other with raised eyebrows, shaking their heads.

"Ask him if he's dating anyone else now and see if he squirms," added MaryAnn.

"I'll bet he's a flirt, the kind who never marries," responded Retta.

"Wait a minute," said Renee. "He's a nice guy, very polite, and travels a lot. He probably hasn't had time to settle down and have a family yet."

"Oh, he travels a lot. That means he has a different girl in every city," said MaryAnn with a scowl.

"Well, I'll just have to ask him and see what he says."

The other three girls kept talking among themselves about how many wives this guy probably has around the world. Renee stared off into the distance thinking about the possibilities. Will would never be that kind of person, but she planned to confirm it once and for all.

Lisa blurted out, "Oh, I wanted to tell you I saw Steve last night and he was adorable."

"Not the same Steve you met last week, is it?" asked MaryAnn.

"Yes, that's the one. He's so cute! Plus he's snuggly and adores my hair."

Renee was too pre-occupied to get into the conversation. What was Will really like when he traveled? He was certainly a smooth talker and knew how to act around a woman.

"Where did you meet him last night?" asked MaryAnn.

"At the pet store on Colonial Drive."

"Wait a minute. Steve works at a pet store?" asked Retta.

"No, Steve lives at a pet store. He's a baby hedgehog!" said Lisa.

"What?" they all exclaimed, bringing Renee back to the conversation.

"Yes, he's the cutest little critter and he likes to climb into my pocket and look out at the world. I want to buy him but he costs too much."

Renee turned to Lisa and asked, "So the man of your dreams is a rodent?"

"A hedgehog is not a rodent," exclaimed Lisa dryly.

MaryAnn responded to Renee sarcastically, "Well some you your boyfriends were rats. Why should it matter to you?"

"Touché," replied Renee with no expression.

Retta added, "But this new guy doesn't seem to be a rat. Let us know the next chapter as soon as it happens, okay?"

That brought a smile to Renee's face and she nodded to her friend. It was good to get her mind back on the positive aspects of Will, but she couldn't help but wonder about how he behaved with other women he met on his trips.

# Chapter Eleven

**K**IM PARKED HER LITTLE **SUV** IN front of Will's office and stepped out into an overcast day. The rain hadn't started yet but it was certainly threatening to dump buckets of water on the local residents. The morning sunshine usually lit up the front of Will's office building and gave it a life of its own. Today almost provided the impression that men from the 1890's would be walking in and out of it, with a grey countenance which made the building appear much like it did in black and white pictures from that time period. Will always did like classic antique furniture and old buildings. This one really stood out though.

She moved forward into the year 2015 as she walked into Will's lobby area and was immediately met by Sue's pretty face.

"Good morning, Kim. What brings you here today?"

"Hi, Sue. I need to talk to Will for a few minutes before he gets too busy. Is he in yet?"

Sue gave a sarcastic laugh and pointed up. "He's upstairs. Hasn't come down yet."

Kim shook her head in disbelief. "Why does he sleep here at all? He should just go home after work every day."

"I tell him that all the time. Sometimes he does. It doesn't make sense when he has that nice house to go home to."

It made sense to Kim. He probably didn't like the idea that he would come home to no family there, and figured he'd just stay upstairs in his office to sleep after work. He could avoid the dreaded loneliness he must have with no wife and kids at his house, and just focus on his work. That was his life now, but she wanted to change it all for the better.

Kim walked around the lobby to look closer at the paintings that decorated the room. Will had excellent taste when it came to French impressionistic art and these reproductions gave the room a classy feel with the antique items on display.

"Does Will do the decorating himself?"

"Are you kidding? Does Will do anything himself?" Sue answered from her desk. "I have to give him credit though. He does find some spectacular old furniture sometimes." She stood up and walked to Will's office. "Check out this old Victrola record player he had delivered a couple of weeks ago."

Kim followed her through the open door and looked around. The old desk was a beauty too, but Sue was right about the record player. It did enhance the feel of the room where her brother spent a lot of his time. She appreciated antiques as well, but only from a window shopping point of view. Will acted on his appreciation and bought them when he found old things that jumped out at him. He certainly did seem to live in the past. Yet he was a mystery since he also appeared to be so desperate to escape from his own past.

"Very nice," Kim commented as Sue nodded and walked past her to return to the lobby.

Standing by Will's desk, Kim glanced around his office. There were several souvenirs he had picked up from around the world, including large wooden shoes from The Netherlands, an exquisite dark blue silk jacket from China, a glass miniature Taj Mahal, a shrunken head from Malaysia. What? Hopefully, that wasn't real.

Several classic Beatles albums decorated the walls alongside copies of Renoir, Degas, and Monet paintings. Occasionally, a breathtaking photograph of a sunset or wild animals was interspersed to provide a unique look. She recognized some of the photos he had taken himself. Hmm. He also had photographs of Kim's family and their parents in his office too.

An unusual painting with a melting clock caught her attention and she stopped to stare intently at it. She gave it a weird expression and shook her head. What a strange idea. It really didn't fit with the other classics, but Will was known to have a curious taste in paintings, just like with his music. Actually, everything about Will was fascinating. Not always conventional, but certainly interesting.

Kim walked back out toward the lobby and noticed Will climbing down the stairs into his office. His shirt was unbuttoned and his hair a mess. He had just crawled out of his upstairs bed.

"Will, why don't you go home after work?"

"Good morning to you too," he replied.

"You need to get away from work sometimes. It's not good to be here all the time."

Will paused as he combed his hair in an antique mirror at the bottom of the stairs, then buttoned up his shirt. "It's convenient to just go upstairs and crash rather than drive across town. What's wrong with that?"

"Then why did you buy a house if you're not even going to use it?"

"I do use it, sometimes."

"You need to grow up and stop living like a college student. Find a nice woman and settle down once and for all. You'll never do it living like this."

"My little sister is looking out for me. How sweet."

"No, I'm serious. Before you know it, you'll be thirty

with no family. You need a good woman to help straighten out your life."

"In case you haven't noticed, I've been searching for that special someone for a long time. It's not like I'm avoiding women so I can stay single."

"On the contrary," Kim interrupted. "You overdo it with your dating."

"No, I'm a connoisseur when it comes to everything, including women. My art, my antiques, my music. When I find the right lady, I'll do anything for her."

"What about Renee?"

"What about Renee?" he replied. "I like her a lot. If you must know, I've actually taken her out a couple of times."

"So I've heard. She really likes you, so I hope you're not planning on dumping her like some of your travel girls."

"Travel girls? What do you mean by that?"

"You know what I mean. Women you meet on your trips, who just get a hint of what you're like, then get left in the dust."

"No, it's not like that at all. I just run into someone at a hotel or at the airport or wherever, and find out they just wanted some company for a day while they explore the city. Sometimes it's better than walking around alone on the other side of the world."

"Oh, I'm sure it is. One night stands are probably very convenient."

"Wait a minute. They're one day stands. Never overnight. You know me better than that."

"I know. You do need to be careful of other people's perceptions though. I think some people might believe you're doing a lot more than sightseeing and that can hurt your reputation as a true gentleman."

"Personally, I don't care what other people think. If they know me, then they know my character. If they think I'm a man with no integrity, then it's too bad for them."

"Not the best attitude, if you ask me."

'Sis, you can't please everyone all the time, so I've stopped trying. My intentions are always honorable and my actions are pleasing in the sight of God. My conscience is clear."

"I know that and you know that, but if you stopped going out with every girl you meet, then nobody would have any reason to question your character."

"Who is questioning my character?"

"You're paranoid, Will. Guilty conscience?"

"You said it. What are you trying to do to me?"

"Anyway, I came over her to tell you that Renee has been happier than I've ever seen her, and as surprising as it sounds, I think you have a lot to do with it."

"Well, that's good news, but you shouldn't be surprised. We seemed to click right away and we have a fun time together."

She looked at him for a second and asked, "Do you foresee yourself dating her a month from now?"

"How am I supposed to know that? As of right now, I would certainly ask her out again. Will she feel the same way about me then, I …"

"Yes, she would. I know she will."

"Then yes, I could foresee myself dating her a month from now. Maybe more. I like the way she makes me feel when I'm with her, and I like being with both her and Rebecca. They are quite a pair."

"I think Renee's even better than she-who-must-not-be-named and would make a wonderful wife for you someday."

Will stopped buttoning his shirt and stared ahead. "I have to admit both of those thoughts have crossed my mind as well. It's too early to think marriage yet though. As I know firsthand, something could always surprise me and wreck my life again, so I have to be prepared for that."

"Not every girl you're serious about is going to leave you, Will. You are an ideal man and if any girl wouldn't want to marry you, they would be crazy. There must have been something with that girl from your past …"

"Don't go there."

"Well, I don't think it was your fault she broke up with you."

"Yes, it was something about me that kept her from wanting to continue our relationship."

"You never even asked her why she left, so you really don't know that."

"I didn't need to ask her. It was definitely me."

Kim stood in front of him to force him to look at her. "You don't see yourself as others see you, Will. You're too hard on yourself."

"Since then, I've tried to be the best man I can be, but I don't want to be arrogant and think I really am so perfect. It's just something I'll always strive for, knowing I'll never quite get there."

"That's fine, but I believe she is the one woman who will help you forget about you-know-who. Renee already thinks you're the man of her dreams."

Will turned away again and paused. "How can I live up to that expectation? It sets her up for a world of disappointment."

"You don't have to be perfect. She likes you even with all of the faults I'm aware of."

"What faults? I thought you said I was perfect."

"No, other people think you're perfect, but I know you better than them. Yet I still love you despite your many flaws."

"Now I'm feeling depressed again."

She hit his arm and they both laughed. "Don't worry. You'll get over it. Just meet with her and you'll have your head in the clouds again."

"You know, she does affect me like that. Ever since I locked eyes with Renee the first day at her apartment, when that guy hit her and Rebecca, there was something about her... I can't explain."

"What do you mean?"

"It was as though a feeling inside told me I need to get to know that woman and ever since then, I've been falling for her more and more each time I see her. I can't stop thinking about her. I even had a dream about her last night and I didn't want to wake up. She has affected me in so many ways and I really do like feeling this way."

Kim turned her head to look out into the lobby and smiled. "OK, I just wanted to see how you felt about her. I need to get to work now."

"That's why you stopped by?" Will asked.

"Yes, plus I wanted to see some of your new antiques. I like your Victrola."

"Thank you. You're welcome to stop by anytime."

"But I would rather stop by and see you at your house next time instead of your office."

"I might just surprise you then."

"I'd like that," Kim said as she walked into the lobby. "Bye, Sue. Tell Tom I said 'Hi', and give your little one a kiss for me. We need to get together again soon, okay?"

"Yes, we do. Have a great day."

Kim walked through the door with a glance over her shoulder and a wave back to Will. She had obtained the information about Will that she came for.

# Chapter Twelve

THE PLEASANT SOUNDS OF MUSIC filled the air as Renee and Rebecca laughed together about something funny while changing the sheets on Rebecca's bed. Their relationship had been better than ever the past couple of weeks, with Renee happier than she could remember. It had been miserable hiding feelings of depression for the past year or more, where nothing seemed to go right for her. Yet now, even though things weren't perfect, she could successfully handle problems when they came up rather than crying and lying down in her bed, hoping they would go away.

She opened the windows to get some cool spring air circulating through her small apartment and played one of her favorite CD's while doing the housecleaning. She hadn't listened to this one for a long time. Her daughter's face lit up when she noticed her mom dancing to one of the songs and they both danced silly together in between dusting, laundry, and making the beds.

"Mommy, we should clean the house every day. I never knew it could be so much fun."

Renee laughed. Her little girl really was a smart one. This was typically a mundane chore she dreaded, but by making it like a game, the work went by quickly and gave her time to bond with her daughter. She preferred looking at life differently now and never wanted to go back to her depressed ways again. She surprised herself by having the energy and enthusiasm to clean her apartment after a full day of working, and it gave her a satisfaction she had never known before. She would deal with the challenges life threw at her, and everything would be different from then on.

Renee's phone rang.

"Hello?" she sang with a cheerful voice, even though she figured it would most likely be an annoying salesperson on the other end.

"Hi, Renee. I'm planning out my week and I wondered if you wanted to get together for a little while tonight."

Her heart skipped a beat when she heard his voice. "Hi. I'm surprised you actually called first and just didn't show up at my door this time."

Will paused before responding, then said, "Well, I thought you liked to be surprised by my impromptu visits, but I'll try to call first from now on."

"Oh, I like your impromptu visits. I just want to pick on you about them once in a while."

"Hmm, in that case, peek out your front window."

She walked to her window in the kitchen. There was Will, standing by a little convertible across the street, talking on his cell phone.

"Will, what are you doing out there? Get in here right now," Renee demanded playfully.

She went to the door and opened it, while he leisurely strolled toward her apartment. He looked good in casual dress clothes, but she didn't tell him she thought so. He probably already knew anyway, but she wouldn't feed his ego. After thinking about him all last night and all day today, she was glad to see him again tonight.

"I was just in the neighborhood …"

"You liar."

"I almost came up and knocked on the door, but I remembered to call first, right after I stepped out of my car."

"Hey, that's a different car than the one you took Rebecca and I out to eat in. Did you get a new car or do you have two cars?"

"This old thing? Yeah, I just use it to zip around town when I don't need more space for passengers or whatever. I take the Escape when I have guests with me."

"What do you mean by Escape?" she asked, wondering about something Kim said regarding Will escaping the pain from a past relationship.

"The SUV we went to the zoo in is a Ford Escape. I use it when I need more room."

"Must be nice. I can barely afford my payments on the old beat up car I drive."

"Just pay it off and you won't have any more payments."

She laughed. "Really? It's that easy? You're a genius."

"Don't mention it. Let me know if there's anything else I can help you with."

She playfully pulled him into her apartment and watched him explore the room with wide eyes.

"Very cool. I like what you've done with the place."

Rebecca ran out into the living room and said, "Hi, Will. All we've done is clean it up."

He leaned down and picked her up as she ran toward him and replied, "No, the painting on the back wall is new. So is the decoration on that window. I like them both."

Renee smiled and turned to look. "I've had both of them for months, maybe more, but haven't had the motivation to put them up. Tonight I felt like doing something. I'm surprised you noticed."

"I notice everything." Will stared at Renee, who watched his eyes take in her new appearance: hair pulled back in a ponytail, little tank top barely reaching her belly button, short elastic shorts, and no shoes.  Standing next to her was a miniature of her mother, wearing the same style exactly. A perfect match.  Renee put her hand on her hip and raised her eyebrows, while Rebecca imitated her stance with pursed lips.  Renee just stood there, posing just for him, and his eyes slowly worked their way up to her face.  He went back and forth between the mother and daughter.

"Wow.  You two are really something else, and your cleaning attire is quite impressive."

"Thank you very much," Renee replied without expression.

"Listen, I don't want to mess up any kind of creativity that might be going on here between you two, so I won't stay long.  I brought you each a little surprise from India, and I'd like you to show me how they look.  I forgot to give them to you at the restaurant."

Rebecca's face lit up, and Renee smirked as he handed them each a wrapped package.  They both pulled out colorful, silk cloths, and held them up against their bodies.

"They're incredible."

"Would you try them on for me?"

The girls went into the bedroom and shut the door, leaving Will to listen to their giggling.  It took a little while as the girls tried to figure out how to properly wrap the cloths around them. A few minutes later, they came out walking tall, straight-faced, like a pair or fashion models, and Will whistled at them.

"You look better than I expected," said Will as he held each of their hands and helped them spin around in opposite directions like mirror images.  "And they both fit perfectly."

"How did you know our sizes?" Renee asked.

"Just lucky, I guess.  Here, let me take some pictures of you modeling your new outfits."

The girls hammed it up, with Rebecca emulating her

mother as though she was a shadow. Will laughed and snapped photo after photo of his new models. "Well, thanks for trying them on. I need to get going."

"Thank you for thinking of us while you were overseas. You'll have to tell us more about the trip," said Renee.

Will glanced around the room once again and asked Renee, "Have you ever considered doing some kind of interior designs or decorating? You'd be good at personal or business decorating."

She turned back to him with raised eyebrows and shook her head. "No, I wouldn't have a clue how to get into something like that."

"Think about it. If it's something you're interested in, I could help you get started with business cards, advertising, and so on. I think you'd do a great job. You could even do it on the side for a while to see how you like it and keep you current job."

"Sounds too intimidating for me."

"Nonsense. You'd do just fine and you might even enjoy it. Anyway, I wanted to see if you'd like to have lunch with me this week. I could pick you up."

Renee laughed. "Don't you ever work? I have to work all week and I only get a thirty minute lunch break."

"Thirty minutes? I thought there were laws against that. Then maybe we'll have to go out to dinner instead. Are you available one night this week?"

She looked at Rebecca, who had wide eyes and a toothy grin. "I don't know. I'll probably be washing my hair or doing my nails on whatever night you're available. Sorry."

"Okay. I get the hint."

"Mommy, you can wash your hair after dinner," scolded Rebecca.

"That's right. You should listen to your little girl. She's a genius."

"Oh, alright. I guess I could spare one night for you this week."

"This time you can pick a place you and Rebecca would like to go. Let me know which night and I'll come by to pick you up."

"Will it be in the same car you drove here tonight?" asked Renee.

"Sure, with Rebecca and I in the front seats, there's plenty of room for you in the trunk if you fold yourself up with your knees up by your ears."

Rebecca laughed uncontrollably, while Will gazed into Renee's eyes and softened his voice. "No, I guess I'll have to bring my Escape." He slowly shook his head and said to Renee with a deep Russian accent, "You silly little girl."

She melted as his eyes held hers and she wished he would stay longer.

"Well, that will have to do. Let me talk it over with my princess and I'll let you know. You didn't have to drive all the way here to ask me that. You could have just called."

"I did call but you told me to come inside."

She swatted his arm and he leaned down to set the little girl on the ground. He whispered in Rebecca's ear, "Anyplace but Chuck E. Cheese."

Rebecca shouted, "Yes, let's go to Chuck E. Cheese."

"No, I said anyplace BUT Chuck E. Cheese," replied Will shaking his head.

"We'll talk about it later, okay Sweetie?" said her mom while Will winked at Rebecca.

"I'll wait for your call, Renee. Have a good night," he said as he kissed her cheek.

She waved and watched him go across the street to his little car before shutting the front door.

"Now where were we before he so rudely interrupted us?" asked Renee as she started tickling Rebecca. The little girl giggled and ran into her room while her mother chased her, both still wearing their new silk outfits from India.

"Yay, we're going out with Will again," squealed the little girl.

# Chapter Thirteen

**A** **WAITRESS WALKED AWAY FROM** the table after delivering drinks to the four men. Will looked at his friends sitting with him at the restaurant, raised his glass of iced tea, and said, "Thanks for meeting me for lunch, guys. It's always good to get together with all of you, even Patrick."

They all raised their glasses at the same time and touched the rims together.

"You know we're only your friends when you're paying the bill," replied Patrick. "You are buying today, right?"

"Nope, it's your turn to take me out for a change," said Will.

Daniel asked, "So, are your dates with your lady friends taking a toll on your wallet, Will? You can't afford to treat your friends to a nice lazy lunch on a spectacular afternoon?"

Will laughed and looked around. The breeze on a sunny day made sitting at an outside table a brilliant idea, especially after a long winter. "I've actually cut back on my dating habits lately."

All three of his friends spit out their drinks onto the ground in unison.

"What's so surprising about that?" Will asked.

Gregory felt Will's forehead while Patrick felt for Will's pulse.

"Have you seen a doctor lately?" Patrick asked. "This could be serious."

Will yanked his arm back. "Very funny. It just so happens I met a girl…"

Daniel interrupted, "You always tell us you've met a girl."

"As I was saying, I met a girl that's different than the other girls I've dated, and I enjoy being with her."

His friends glanced at each other and shook their heads.

"It sounds as though your bachelor days are numbered, my friend," said Gregory.

"Hey, it's just a few dates and we're not even exclusively dating."

"Does she know that?" asked Patrick with raised eyebrows. "She may think she's the only one."

"Yeah, you need to be careful so you don't break the poor girl's heart," added Daniel.

Will just shook his head then took a drink.

"Is she local?" asked Gregory.

Will's eyes lit up. "Yes, she's the mother of one of the little girls in my sister's class and she's amazing."

Patrick gave him an odd expression and asked, "She's not the one you visited a few weeks ago who had the boyfriend you didn't get along with, is she?"

The others laughed and looked at Will with curious faces.

"Well, yes she's the same one. I've met her a few times and took her and her daughter out to eat, to the zoo, you know."

"What's the deal with her boyfriend and you not getting along?" asked Gregory. "Are you moving in on someone else's territory?"

"It's not like that at all. My sister and I stopped by her apartment to drop off a gift for the little girl. While we were at the front door, we heard a scream and a crash, he opened the door just a crack, then I saw this big guy hit the little girl. I kicked the door in and performed a citizen's arrest, if you know what I mean."

"Didn't you say it was a ninety pound weakling?" asked Patrick.

"No, that's what you said and I just laughed about it. This guy was a head taller than me and outweighed me by at least eighty pounds of beer fat, maybe more."

"My hero," added Patrick with a girl's voice.

"Never a dull moment with Will Sayre, folks," said Gregory as everyone laughed.

"She's quite a talker too," Will continued.

"Aren't they all," replied Patrick. "I've heard they talk at least ten times more than men."

"I believe it," said Will. "Sometimes I can't keep up with the different topics she goes into, even before finishing the first topic."

"She's probably very excited to be with you," said Daniel, "and talks to relieve her nerves. Just enjoy it."

"I do, but it can be overwhelming trying to follow her train of thought. It's not logical like talking to you guys. Sometimes I end up tuning her out, just watching her beautiful eyes to see if she's asking me a question."

"My wife does the same thing," said Gregory, "but she always comes back to the earlier topics to tie it all together somehow. It's actually impressive the way a woman's mind thinks."

"Impressive or scary?" asked Patrick. "Just remember if she finds out you're not paying attention, you'll regret it. For some reason, women expect you to listen to them, even when they're rambling on. If you get caught, beware of the wrath."

"I've had only a taste of her mood swings, so I don't want to face the wrath too," Will added. "How do you handle when your wives get irrational and moody for no apparent reason?"

"There are college courses on 'Dealing with PMS' you need to take," replied Daniel. "If you can't figure out what to do when she acts up like that, then you're in for it."

"I almost went crazy trying to survive my wife's monthly moods, until I finally was smart enough to ask her what I should do when she acted like she needed to be committed," said Patrick.

"What was her answer?" asked Gregory. "Did she slap you?"

"No, she said when her moods go haywire, just hold her. Don't say a word. Just wrap my arms around her and she'll know I care."

"Wow. I would have never thought of that one," said Will."

"That's years of trial and error wisdom right there," said Gregory. "You'd better write this one down."

"Thanks for the advice."

"Will, you've never talked about one specific girl," said Daniel. "It's always been just generic comments about a collection of girls you've met."

"Yes, this must be serious," added Gregory. "I'm happy for you, man."

Will looked at each of their faces. "I see the happiness in your lives and I crave to be like you someday, with a partner in life. Someone to share my life with and grow old with."

"That's odd. Most men would see your lifestyle and wish they were you," replied Daniel.

"I do have a lot of fun, but it's just not the same as what you guys have," said Will.

Patrick added, "There truly is something awesome about finding the right person to spend your life with. All of us are married," pointing to Daniel, Gregory, and himself, "and we wouldn't trade it for the world."

"Hey, speak for yourself," interrupted Gregory. "No, I'm just kidding. He's right, Will. Men often joke about their wives being the old ball and chain, but marriage was the greatest thing I ever did."

"Wait a minute, guys. I only said I've been dating this girl a few times. Marriage is not even on the radar here. I'm just saying that someday I would like to have a wife, but…"

"We only mean this is a step in the right direction," responded Patrick. "Compared to dating a different girl every week, you going out with the same girl more than once is a major change for the better. You talked about dating that girl from the hotel in India more than once, and now you have someone here in town here you enjoy being with. Good for you, Will. I'd like to meet her."

"I'll bet you would. I just wonder what kinds of stories you'd make up to tell her about me."

"With you the truth is better than fiction," replied Gregory.

"That's what I'm afraid of. Let me get to know her a little better. Then maybe you can all look at her from a distance, but not say anything to her, okay?"

They all laughed as the waitress came back to take their lunch orders.

After they had placed their orders, Gregory asked Will, "So, where's your next travel destination?"

"Actually, I have to leave for London in a few days."

"Is that for work or for play?" asked Patrick.

"A little of both. I have to work, but I'll try to see some parts of London in my spare time on Saturday. I plan to check out more of the Beatles sites, like where their rooftop concert was, where they lived in the early sixties, the recording studios they used. Cool stuff like that."

Daniel responded, "Oh no. Living in the past again. I hate to break it to you but the Beatles broke up a few years ago."

"I know. It's just that London is a great walking town and I usually explore some of the unusual areas not everyone visits. I've already been to Westminster Abbey, Buckingham

Palace, and the British Museum. I may even take a British band walking tour this time or a Jack the Ripper walking tour."

Gregory got Will's attention, looking him in the eye, and said, "That's still way in the past. You need to get up into the twenty-first century."

"Yeah, you'll find some parts of London haven't changed much since Jack the Ripper roamed around the White Chapel area, added Patrick. "I once almost accidentally interrupted a gang fight there, then was propositioned by a working girl one block away, and that was only three years ago. Be cautious around that area."

"I'm always watchful, but thanks for caring." Will hesitated, then continued, "Sometimes I've felt like I've been chasing the past and even ghosts from the past, and it's difficult to break those old habits. Maybe this new girl that has my heart pounding will change everything. Who knows? I kept seeing Renee's face in crowds when I was in Prague the last time, but of course it wasn't her. It seems as though she's already a part of me and I absolutely love it."

Patrick replied, "That's a good thing, Will. I hope she's exactly what you're searching for. If there's anything you need, any questions you want to bounce off of us, we're always here for you, man. Between us three, we have almost fifteen years of marriage experience, so take advantage of it."

"Yeah, don't rush into it. Just take your time and enjoy each day as it comes. If she's the one, then you'll know it, but you have to give it time to blossom," added Daniel.

"Thanks, guys."

Gregory asked, "You've dated a lot of girls over the past five years I've known you. What's so unique about this one?"

Will glanced down at his glass for a moment, then responded without looking up, "Several years ago, I met a girl. I was convinced she was the perfect girl for me, but for some reason I never understood, she didn't feel the same about me."

He paused for a moment, then continued, "Since that time, I've met a lot of great young ladies and many of them were fun to be with, some were interesting to talk to, some were smart, some were very classy. None of them were 'The One' for whatever reason. It's not easy to explain. But this girl I'm seeing now, Renee, she's the closest I've seen to being perfect in every way, not just in her appearance, but what's in her heart and that's what I've been searching for. There's always going to be a pretty face out there, but to find a girl with a heart of gold is better than any treasure you can find."

Patrick immediately raised his glass, saying "Here, here," and they all clinked their glasses together. "You're smarter than you look, my friend. I think you're on to something, and now I really want to meet this girl to see if I can give you my approval."

"Yeah, but you'd need to behave. Maybe when I get back from London I'll bring her to lunch with all of you."

"Hmm. We may have to make an exception and bring our wives along to let them evaluate her and make sure she's just not making a chump of you," said Gregory. "Women always seem to know their own kind better than we do. They can tell what the girl's real intentions are."

"Yep, you can all put her to the test and watch her come through with flying colors," replied Will.

Daniel said, "It's interesting how you're defending her as if she's already your wife. This really must be serious. I can't wait to see the woman that tames Will Sayre into settling down."

Will laughed and responded, "I wouldn't say she's taming me, but the way I feel when I'm with her and I see her reaction when I try to make her feel special, you can call it anything you want. She certainly has something that makes me want to see her more and more, and I like it."

The thought of fitting in with these guys and their wives brought a smile to Will's face as the waitress set out their lunch plates.

# Chapter Fourteen

WILL PARKED HIS SUV AT Renee's apartment and walked across the street to her front door. Wearing his typical casual work clothes so he wouldn't appear overdressed, he was anxious to see what Renee's outfit looked like. He pictured her in his mind and enjoyed the vision as he knocked to get her attention. His heart rate increased as he waited to see her and he was not disappointed.

She opened the door and stood there without letting him in, teasing him, and he grinned silently as he gazed intently into her eyes.

"Hi, Will. I hope you don't mind I'm not wearing jeans tonight."

"Wow. You are absolutely stunning," he said as he examined her hair, colorful short dress, and heels. "I can't wait to be seen in public with you. I just hope I'm not a let-down for you." She laughed, probably embarrassed, so he said, "I'm sorry. I just can't believe you look better and better each time I see you."

"Well, thank you. I'm afraid you planted Chuck E Cheese in Rebecca's mind and she is so excited to go there tonight. Are you sure you can handle dinner at such a high society place?"

"Of course. I'm the one who planted the idea, aren't I?

I've been with my sister and her daughter, so I know what to expect. Plus I brought ear plugs for both of us in case the noise gets overwhelming. We can go now if you and Rebecca are ready."

"Sure. Let me get her. Oh, here she is."

"Hi, Will. How do you like Mommy's hair? I helped her with it," said Rebecca proudly.

"I just told her it's gorgeous. I should have known you had something to do with it. Are you ready to play some games?"

"Yes!" the little girl replied excitedly and stepped outside. Renee locked the door and held her daughter's hand, while Will offered his arm to Renee as they walked to his SUV.

Since it was a week-night, the restaurant wasn't as crowded as it could have been. There weren't as many kids there and the noise level was much lower than normal. It was perfect for Rebecca, who seemed to enjoy trying to play all kinds of games with Will and Renee to keep busy while they all waited for their food to arrive. Rebecca asked to play a game close to their table, so the adults sat down while she played nearby.

Lights flashed across the room, noises filled the air, and the few kids in the place squealed with excitement. "This is a great place to go if you have a migraine," commented Will.

"Yeah, right," laughed Renee. "I really appreciate your willingness to spend time with Rebecca. She adores you."

"Honestly, I've never been much for kids, but I like spending time with her and my niece. They make me realize having kids someday is not such a bad thing."

He took a mint from his pocket and offered them to his date. "You eat these things like candy," said Renee as she took one.

Will didn't respond for few seconds, smiling when she sneezed. "Bless you. I do like to have a mint once in a while, but I especially enjoy giving one to you."

"Why? Because you know I'll sneeze? That's not very nice."

"It fascinates me."

"Well, I'm just allergic to mints, and when I have one it makes me sneeze. Simple as that."

"It's one of the little things about you that drives me wild."

"You're crazy, Will Sayre."

Renee watched her daughter playing a game with another little girl. Will asked, "I don't mean to pry, but what happened to her father?"

She hesitated but eventually turned to Will and replied, "He and I were young and foolish, and we probably married too soon. He joined the military and I became pregnant after one of his leaves before getting deployed to Iraq. I never wanted him to sign up and begged him not to, but he did it anyway and ended up getting killed within a few months. It was only about four weeks before Rebecca was born. His name was Michael."

Will put his hands on her hand resting on the table, and he looked into her eyes to say, "I'm so sorry, Renee. I had no idea. I thought he just left you and moved out of the area, although I can't imagine why any man in his right mind would do such a foolish thing."

"Well, I had to deal with being pregnant by myself, I've raised her all by myself, and I've never forgiven her father for leaving us like that. So yes, he did abandon us when we needed him most."

She glanced away again, this time with tears welling up in her eyes, and Will stood up to come around to her side of the table and put his arm around her.

"Please forgive me for even bringing it up. The last thing I wanted to do was upset you."

"No, it's alright. It happened a long time ago and I've put it behind me."

Will said, "I think you still have a lot of anger toward him, but he couldn't help what happened over there. He's truly a hero and I hope you've let Rebecca know it. She should be proud of him. You should be proud of him."

She looked at him with moist eyes and replied, "No, we don't talk about it and she stopped asking. You may be proud of him, but I see him as a deserter because he left his new wife and baby. He could have stayed home and not become a soldier, then we could have been a family. We should have lived happily ever after. He made his choice, and it wasn't with us."

"Renee, there are times when some things are bigger than the both of us, and defending our country is one of them. He chose that lifestyle to protect you, your child, and thousands of other people, and you need to recognize it."

"Will, you don't..." she started.

Will interrupted, "Don't say anything. Just listen to me for a minute. I've only known you and Rebecca for a few weeks, but I already know that I would give up my life to protect you both if it ever came to it. That's how men are. Your husband was willing to do the same thing, and he actually did just that. You were so important to him he gave the ultimate sacrifice. I guarantee he would have rather spent the next fifty years raising a family with you, but the situation came up that required him to give his life for our country. I'm sure he faced it with courage. You should honor his memory and let Rebecca know about him."

She stared blankly out into the game room at the restaurant. Was she was mad at him for bringing this up and speaking his mind? The electronic sounds of games and kids laughing overwhelmed him during her silence, which seemed like a lifetime.

"Will, I know you're right, but it still doesn't hurt any less. I agree. Rebecca deserves to know about her father, but it's not easy talking about him. I still haven't accepted the idea that something else was more important to him than I was. More important than his first child."

"Fair enough. I never knew him, but already I'm proud of what he did. I'm sad he won't be able to grow old with you and Rebecca, but any man would be honored to step in and fill that role in his place."

She stared at him with a surprised expression. What had he just committed to? He meant to say that he liked spending time with both of them, and hoped she didn't think he had just asked her to marry him. Was silence a good thing right now? If only he could read her thoughts.

"Mommy, look at all of the tickets I won," Rebecca said as she came up and climbed to her seat across from Will and Renee.

"You are so good at these games," said her mother as she touched her daughter's hand. At that moment, a waitress delivered their food to the table and they all started eating.

Renee asked, "So what's it like to travel all over the world? Do you meet a lot of interesting people?"

"Well, except for the hours sitting on a plane, the hours waiting in airports, working past midnight to get a proposal finished, and being alone on the other side of the world, it's not so bad."

Will looked over at Rebecca as she quietly ate while staring at a little girl playing some kind of game with animals. She didn't even seem to be aware of their conversation.

Renee smiled and continued, "How many languages do you speak?"

He laughed and said, "Even though I've probably been to over thirty different countries, I only speak English."

"What? How do you communicate when you're in Korea or Brazil or India?"

"I've been fortunate to have someone from each area I've traveled to that speaks English and can help me out."

"So you never even took Spanish or French in school?"

"No, I was somehow grandfathered out of that requirement and didn't have to take another language. I probably would have done well, and I should have made a point of taking French, since my dad's side of the family is French, but I never did. I can fake the accent, thanks to Pepe Le Pew and Inspector Clouseau, but that's it."

"What's your mom's side?"

"She has a lot of English, Welsh, Scotch, and Irish. It's funny, I love Italian food and figured I must have relatives from Italy, but I don't I have any Italian ancestry in my family."

Rebecca wiped her mouth and interrupted, "This was a great idea."

She had been so quiet that Will had almost forgotten Rebecca was with them.

She continued, "I like playing games for a while, then eating dinner, and playing more games. I'm finished eating. Can I go play some more games?"

"Are you sure you've had enough to eat? There's plenty more," asked Renee.

"Yes, I'm full."

"Okay, but when it's time to go, you're not going to argue, right?"

"I won't," replied the little girl with wide eyes before turning around and going to a game she was interested in.

"This really was a good place to bring her, Will. Thanks again."

"Anytime. I really enjoy spending time with both of you."

They talked for a while before joining Rebecca for a couple of games, and Will just sank deeper and deeper into Renee's alluring eyes. She spoke, but he couldn't pay attention. She had only a hint of eye shadow and it looked perfect on her. She didn't wear much makeup, but she certainly didn't need it. He had seen her without it, and she was a knockout even when she wasn't trying.

It was good to see Renee and her daughter smiling so much and having fun. Rebecca didn't argue when it was time to go home, and they all climbed into Will's Escape for the short drive to the apartment. The moonlight guided Will all the way, although he didn't need its directions. Will opened the door for each of his dates, holding hands with Rebecca and offering his other arm to Renee as they walked across the parking lot.

"Thanks Will," said Rebecca as she disappeared through the front door.

"You're welcome, Beautiful," Will replied, but she had already gone.

"Yes, we had a nice time tonight," Renee added. "Thanks again."

Will leaned in for a quick kiss on her neck, breathing in her perfume as her hair surrounded his face. He moved his head up and their lips touched gently as he wrapped his arms around her. He held her for just a moment before setting her free. For a split second, her eyes remained closed as she took a breath and returned his gaze.

"Good night, Will. Have a safe flight tomorrow."

"Sweet dreams," he replied.

She stepped through the doorway and smiled at him as she closed the door, leaving him alone on her front porch. He would be counting down the days before he'd see her again.

# Chapter Fifteen

THE MOONLIGHT BLANKETED WILL as he walked to his car with a silly grin on his face. The cool air was biting to his skin, so he hid his hands inside pleated pants pockets. As he opened his car door and sat in the driver's seat, his phone went off and he answered it without thinking.

"Hi Ken. What's going on?"

"Will, our bass player canceled on us tonight and I'm hoping you could fill in again."

"Hmm. You need to replace your regular bass player."

"Yeah, we're working on that, but can you help us out tonight?"

"I don't know. I have to catch a flight to London tomorrow and I need a good night's sleep tonight. I was just planning to go home now and get to bed."

"Will, you can always sleep on the plane. This is really important. We're at that restaurant called Captain O'Malley's on Michigan Avenue. Please say you can make it."

"You sound a little panicked tonight. What's the big deal?"

"We're supposed to go on in less than an hour. Come on, Will. We'll make it worth your while."

Silence took over the phone as Will considered being up until after 1:00 AM. "Okay, but you owe me."

"It's a deal. We'll even let you sing some of those weird songs you like to do."

Will laughed and replied, "Hey, they're not weird. They're classics. I'll see you in a few minutes."

"Excellent. Thanks again."

Will started up his car and drove to the restaurant, just a couple of miles away from Renee's place. He didn't mind the thought of losing some sleep tonight. He had a great time with Renee and Rebecca, and it would be fun to play in the band for a few hours. He turned his Escape into a spot that seemed like it could fit a truck twice the size of his convertible. In London, he would never find a parking space this big. Only in America. The brightness of the moon caught his attention again, and he glanced up at it as he stepped out of the SUV. What a great night to stroll around outside.

At least the place appeared to be busy already so it should be a good crowd to start the show with soon. He walked in behind a group of people and looked around the restaurant. Irish sayings decorated the place, with back-to-back booths connecting along every green wall.

"Hey, Will. It's good to see you again," the hostess said to him. "Are you going to be with the band tonight?"

"Hi, Valerie. Yes, I am. I received an SOS call from Ken and I guess they're missing someone."

"Great. Drinks are on the house then for you tonight."

"Alright. Can I get a Mountain Dew?"

"No, we only have Coke products. Sorry."

"Ahhhhh! What am I going to do for the next few hours?" Will paused, shaking his head before adding, "I guess I'll have a sweet tea then."

"I'll bring it back to the stage. The guys are already setting up back there."

"Thanks," replied Will as he made his way across the restaurant.

This was a good place to play, but the stage wasn't raised up. It was better to be on a platform above the floor level. This would have to do. The fun was with the music, the crowd and the other guys in the band, regardless of the stage presentation. The back room of the restaurant, where the stage area was setup, was good for the guests who wanted to see the band and didn't mind the volume. The front of the restaurant was quieter for those who only wanted to hear the music as background ambiance while they ate. There was a nice dance floor in front of the stage which allowed a crowd to stand near the band if they wanted to.

"Hey, Will. Thanks for coming out," said the drummer as he tapped the snare drum a few times.

"Anytime, Glen. I'm looking forward to it."

He shook hands with Greg, the keyboard player, Gary, the lead guitarist, and then with Ken, who turned the knobs on his guitar, while the five of them discussed the songs they planned to play. Will picked up the bass guitar and tested the sound to make sure it was in tune, and they played a few chords to see how it all blended together. Should be a good show with some of the old songs Will enjoyed so much. They relaxed at one of the tables for a little while before the show started, then took the stage and played a great set that went over well with the audience as they ate dinner.

Will always had a group of songs he liked to do, and he sang lead on several of them. They were from the sixties and seventies and some were obscure, but the crowd seemed to like them the most. He was a bit more dressed up than the other guys, since he had been with Renee earlier, and he stood out a bit from the rest of the group. His hair, however, was actually longer than Ken and Greg's so he fit right in with the overall appearance of the band. Just a little overdressed for a night at Captain O' Malley's.

Will said to the crowd, "I just wanted to let you know that

you all have great taste in music, and I really appreciate it. Here's a group of songs you won't hear anywhere else. And don't forget where you heard it played."

The band went into the Beatles' "Sgt Pepper Reprise" and "A Day in the Life" and the crowd went wild. Afterwards, they took a break and several people from the restaurant came to the back of the place to talk to the band. A lot of girls came up to Will, as usual, and he charmed them with his smile and personality. Quite a few of guys lined up to chat as well, telling him they've never heard any band play those songs. The other guys in the band just stared at their substitute player as he basked in the glory of a good show.

A waitress brought another round of drinks for the band, and Will questioned her. "Wait a minute. What did you just bring me?"

"A diet coke. Is that alright?"

"A diet coke? Please, pour this down the drain. I'd rather have a sweet tea, if you don't mind."

"Wow. A little popularity and you become some kind of diva," she replied with sarcasm.

"If it's not a Mountain Dew, it's not good enough for Will Sayre," replied Glen with a British accent.

"Some things never change," said Gary. "You're still a spoiled brat."

"No, I just prefer it over the other drinks," added Will.

"No problem, Mr. Sayre. One sweet tea on its way," said the waitress as she disappeared into the crowd.

Ken said, "Will, you should come out and play more often. Your fans need you."

"It is fun, but I don't usually have the time to practice and play. Plus I can't really keep a steady schedule since I have to go out of town at different times in the month. Tonight just happened to work out."

"You're certainly welcome to join us whenever you're

available," added Greg.

"I appreciate that."

The waitress returned with a bottle of Mountain Dew and Will just stared at it. "I thought you didn't serve this here."

"We don't, so I went next door and picked one up for you. Nothing but the best for you, Will."

He grabbed her shoulders and gave her a kiss on the cheek, then took the precious nectar with relief. "You will get quite a tip from me tonight. Thank you so much."

A hulk of a man approached Will and spoke down to him. "Do you know Renee Woodson?"

Will looked up and instantly recognized him as the man who hit Rebecca. His defenses were on full alert as he nodded. "I think you know the answer already." He stood his ground and wondered if he was going to have to fight this huge man again. The man didn't seem drunk this time, and that's probably what helped Will overpower this guy last time. Fighting him now was the last thing Will needed. A lot of abusive guys don't want to let go of someone they think belongs to them. Will's concern that this was one of those cases increased his heart rate as he faced this man in front of the crowd.

"I want to apologize for what I did. I had way too much to drink and made some bad choices that night. Tell Renee I don't want any trouble, and let her know I'm sorry it ended the way it did."

Surprised, Will nodded again. "I'll do that."

"For what it's worth, you guys sound great," said the man before he hulked back into the crowd, parting the people like Moses and the Red Sea. Will breathed a sigh of relief, thanking God he didn't have to go another round with the big guy.

"Will, is everything okay?" asked Greg with real concern.

"Oh, yeah. It's fine."

"I thought that guy was going to crush you."

"I was wondering about it myself," Will replied. "Remember that night at the Ratskeller when we accidentally caught the stage on fire?"

"That was awesome! I thought one guy was going to kill Glen when he kicked over his flaming drink next to Gary. I've never seen Gary move so fast."

They laughed for a few minutes and then rejoined the rest of the band.

They talked with the crowd for several more minutes before getting back to the stage area and playing another collection of songs that drove the crowd wild. Not many bands played side two of 'Abbey Road' by the Beatles, note for note, so it turned out to be a real treat for this audience. Will enjoyed this bunch of guys and they all appeared to have fun the rest of the evening, as did the audience. Finally, after the third set of songs, Will left the band as they packed up their equipment.

He drove home with his head in the clouds, ears ringing from the decibels he and the band had played. This had been a remarkable ending to a perfect night. Thinking about Renee left him in such a positive mood and he couldn't get her out of his mind. He wanted to keep focusing on his time with her, but he had to get some sleep over the next few hours in case he couldn't get any over the Atlantic. His adrenaline was still pumping so that would be a challenge.

# Chapter Sixteen

WILL STARED OUT OF THE WINdow, daydreaming. Looking down at the clouds at 30,000 feet was breathtaking, with the bluest skies in the background and the impressive cotton sculptures all around to be seen by anyone who noticed. Above the clouds, it seemed to be just a short jump up into outer space, and if a person looked closely, it was as though he could actually see space. There was a soft, dark section of the sky that hinted of the black, vast expanse outside of Earth's atmosphere, and it was easy to imagine seeing stars in this little region beyond the blue. Below that, however, was endless white carpeting of cotton candy. It was tempting to step out and walk across it, strolling over ever-changing, rolling hills.

A small mountain of clouds was soon blown into a new shape, resembling a tree. Within a few minutes, it could have been an animal. These winds at this altitude weren't noticeable inside the airplane, but the effects of the winds were beautiful works of art that were constantly reformed for their spectators staring out their windows. Someone once told him God was like the wind. You can't see the wind but you can see the effects of the wind. This was very apparent today.

What an incredible job, to be like a master glass-blower, creating millions and millions of shapes every day with this palette of clouds. There's a massive supply of material up here in the sky, and the only tool needed was a breath of wind. The imagination of the audience would be pleased every single day with the results of each masterpiece, only to be surprised by the newest change that occurred with the next glance of the viewer. Not everyone saw the same design in this art form, but everyone inevitably saw something in the clouds. Staring at these cotton forms was like going to a museum, where a person could just sit for hours gazing at the beauty being displayed for all to see. It's especially easy to do as a captive audience inside a flight over the Atlantic Ocean before the sun went down.

*****

"Would you like the pasta or the chicken for dinner, Mr. Sayre?"

He looked up at the stewardess. "Oh, hi. The pasta, please."

"Thank you, sir."

"Please call me, Will. I haven't seen you on this flight before. Do you usually work a different section of the plane?"

"Actually, I just moved to Atlanta and this is my first flight to Europe. My name is Anne. If you need anything, just let me know."

"Thanks. I'll do that."

The stewardess made her way down the aisle and back to two of her co-workers, who seemed to be waiting to ambush her.

One stewardess asked, "What did he say to you, Anne?"

"Who?"

The other stewardess answered, "Will Sayre, the sharp dresser by the window."

"He said he wants the pasta, why do you ask?"

The first stewardess bargained, "I'll trade sections with

you."

"What? I don't want to trade. What is it about Mr. Sayre that's making you two so giggly?"

The other stewardess replied, "He's quite a gentleman. After a flight last year, he took me out to dinner and a play in London and it was a wonderful evening. I wouldn't mind getting invited again for tomorrow night, if you know what I mean."

The first stewardess added, "He took me to breakfast at a great café, then sightseeing around town, and lunch at a quaint restaurant before he had to leave for a meeting. He was the best date I've ever had."

Anne hesitated, then replied, "Well, I think I'll just keep my assignments and may get to know this guy a little better, if you don't mind."

"You lucky dog," said one of her friends.

"Okay, you'll have to tell us all about it in a few days," added the other.

*****

Will stared off into space again as he sipped coffee at the outdoor café on one of the streets in London the next morning. Sunshine and blue skies were a pleasant surprise as he started out his day, but there was something missing. He craved time with Renee and wished he had passed on this project so he could have stayed home with her. His co-worker could have taken this one for him and given him a break from traveling. That may be the plan next time he's asked to visit a customer site in a couple of weeks.

"It really is a coincidence you and I are staying at the same hotel this trip," said Anne.

Will turned to her and commented, "You look better today than you did in your stewardess outfit last night. I like your hair better this way. Did you say this is your first time to

London?"

"Yes, it is. I'm so excited."

"I usually try to avoid the crowds and visit places that aren't the typical tourist areas. What are you interested in?"

Anne thought for a moment, then looked him in the eyes. "I would love to see a play, but I'm open to anything. I don't have to go back to work until tomorrow, so I have all day."

"We're almost to Buckingham Palace, so let's walk this way a little further and you can see where the queen lives. I have two tickets to go inside on a tour today."

"Groovy," replied Anne, which made Will laugh for the first time this trip.

"So you're already back to the swinging sixties, I see."

They stood up and continued down the street, and toured the palace. After that, they spent the day exploring the shops on Carnaby Street, walking by the Thames near the Tower Bridge, and Will gave in and took her into the Tower of London, since it wasn't very busy. He always enjoyed walking around inside Westminster Abbey, so since he went to the Tower of London for her, he insisted they go there as part of a trade. She wasn't familiar with the Beatles, so Will would take his historical Beatles walk the next day. He did take her to a play later in the evening, which she seemed to enjoy, but he couldn't wait for some alone time. Things were definitely different since he had met Renee, and he actually thought of her more than he did this young stewardess he had just met.

He got the impression that Anne would have let him stay in her hotel room the previous night, but that wasn't Will's style. He didn't mind spending time with them in public, but he didn't want to take these dates any further. Since he had been enamored by Renee, he didn't even want to spend time with anyone else now. The way her hair framed her face, her smile, the way she kidded with him, the sound of her laugh, her voice, and the way she looked into his eyes. Everything about her was exactly what he needed in his life and he was at a point where he was ready for a change. He could do without dating other women and would be happy spending all of his time with Renee. Was he really prepared for this kind of commitment, the first he had been in for almost five years?

The next morning Will walked to several of his target destinations, including the locations for several scenes from four of the Beatles' movies. He stopped at several office buildings where they worked in the sixties, and came up to the clothing boutique that used to be painted with colorful designs before the city made them re-paint it all white. If only he could have been allowed to go inside and explore each one. He paused at several of the private nightclubs that were popular hangouts where the Beatles could relax and watch other bands without getting swarmed by their fans. So much had changed over the past forty years. It was almost as though he was still chasing ghosts that haunted him, with no chance of catching up with them. Only memories remained. Many of the people he passed on the sidewalks probably didn't even realize the significance these historic buildings had all those years ago, but it didn't matter. This was important to him.

After rambling around the colorful area in Knotting Hill where some scenes from their first movie were filmed, he came back to a restaurant which was used in their second movie and took a lunch break there. It didn't appear the same as it did in 1965, but he didn't expect it to. The food was good and he had a few minutes to think about his life. What it would be like to let Renee get more involved and actually let her in to his lonely personal space where no woman had been allowed since …

Things were different now. He had been holding on to ghosts of the past for too long and it was time to release them and move on with his life. He needed to escape. If Renee turned out to be everything she seemed to be, he would even release this unnamed girl from his past and look forward to a new soul mate. Maybe this girl from years ago truly wasn't his soul mate and Renee was the real one. Is it possible to have more than one? Everyone says there's only that one person who we're meant to be with. Will had always believed he found her and lost her, but maybe he was wrong. Maybe he had searched long enough and finally found the one.

He was pulled back from daydreaming as the waitress came up to collect the payment. He stood up from the long bench, and headed out the door for his next stop. He had been searching for this kind of happiness for a long time, never convinced he would ever find it. Just the thought of discovering the end of the rainbow was overwhelming, but it made him walk a little faster and smile a bit more now. Things really were different for him after getting to know Renee, and he hoped she felt the same about him. He would have to make sure of that. He didn't want any surprises like the last time.

His next stops were from old promotional photos of the famous group, although the areas didn't look like they did back in the sixties. Still, standing in these spots and walking in their footsteps was haunting and eerie, especially since he was alone in his trek, with only a few people around him at any particular site. Didn't today's locals even know what had happened in these locations back then? Maybe nobody else cared, which was probably the case. As he made it to Chapel Street, he stopped in front of an apartment at the end of the street, where the manager of the Beatles lived and died in 1967. This was certainly the most melancholy of all the places Will had visited today, and there was a feeling of sadness thinking about what happened here. In his mind, Will scrolled through all of the photos he could remember that were taken at this flat, most of them in full color, filled with joy and laughter, but unfortunately the one which stood out had two men carrying a lifeless body covered in a sheet on a stretcher out of his apartment. This picture was black and white with no happiness. It was time to move on and remember something more positive.

The recording studio on Abbey Road and the crosswalk out front were interesting to visit, and the front door of the building was open. Someone walked toward the entrance, so Will followed him into the studio briefly before being asked politely to leave. He put on a fake British accent to argue with one of the roadies he had followed, and enjoyed the banter as he exited the front door. Feeling good about himself, he checked the time and called Renee on his cell phone.

"How are you this morning?"

"Hi, Will. Are you working hard today or hardly working?" she asked.

"No, actually, I'm in London still and I just had lunch. I'm five hours ahead of you. Remember, I wanted you to go to that website I mentioned before I left. Are you already there?"

"Yes, actually I already have it up on the screen. Let me sit down. What should I be seeing here? Oh, here comes my princess."

"Hi," said the little girl.

"Hi, Rebecca. So this is the crossing where the Beatles had their pictures taken for one of their last albums and I'm about to cross it. You may be able to see me on the sidewalk now with the wall behind me."

"Yes, I see you waving. This is amazing. Oh, I see you walking across the street. Very cool. Now I need to find a picture of this album cover you keep talking about."

"I have a copy you can borrow when I get home."

"Will, do a silly walk across the road." Rebecca asked.

"I'll probably get arrested, but here goes," Will replied as he looked around.

The girls erupted with laughter into the phone as this

crazy man walked like a monkey waving his arms back across Abbey Road, toward the studio. How foolish would that have looked on their computer screen?

"Hey, I forgot to tell you I was just thrown out of the studio since I didn't have reservations and wasn't actually recording there today. While I stood outside, I thought of you. I hope you didn't mind me calling. I couldn't stop thinking about you."

There was silence on the phone for a couple of seconds.

"Renee, are you still there?"

"Yes, I'm here. It's just nice to hear that you couldn't stop thinking about me. I miss you too."

"I miss you too, Will," added Rebecca.

"Anyway, I'm walking around London on a mission today, so I'll talk to you later, okay?"

"Have a good time. Don't pick up any stray girls."

"Well, if one follows me, can I keep her?"

"Don't even think about it. Thanks for calling."

It was great to hear her voice and let her be part of this moment. It would be even better to take a picture of Renee and Rebecca crossing this street someday.

Will met with his customers that week and finished his work in London quickly. On his last day there, he found a wonderful aroma which led him to a great sweets shop, and he picked out some tasty looking chocolates for Renee and Rebecca, as well as for Kim and Nicole. He couldn't wait to see their faces when he gave these to the girls, and he looked forward to his trip being over with soon.

# Chapter Seventeen

THERE WAS A LOT TO THINK ABOUT on the long return flight over the Atlantic. What would it be like for Rebecca, having never seen her father? His heart ached for her. This man had served in the military and gave his life so others could live in freedom, and Will had a tremendous amount of respect for him without ever having the chance to meet him. However, Renee felt betrayed by this man for leaving her and dying while she was pregnant. She couldn't realize just how proud she should be of her husband. He died heroically, buried in Arlington Cemetery, yet he was not given a place of honor in his own home by his own family.

With his latest business trip complete, Will arranged to stop overnight in the nation's capital and visit Arlington Cemetery the next morning to pay his respects to the father of his new friend's little girl, the husband of this girl he wanted to spend every day with. It was almost as though he needed permission to date this woman, permission from her dead husband, as crazy as that sounded. He had just about called her his 'girlfriend' and liked the sound of it. Did she feel the same way about him? He made that mistake years ago, and didn't want to follow his own footsteps down that path again. Time to focus on his surroundings now and push aside his past experiences. This was a new day. He had to take a chance and put his feelings out there, despite the risk he could be hurt again.

He loved being in Washington D.C., especially in the spring, and was surrounded by flowers of every color as he walked through the cemetery. The aromas carried through almost every area he went, and he relished breathing them in. Renee was allergic to gardenias, jasmine, and lavender, so she might have a problem here this time of year, but the powerful scents intoxicated Will. He wished she was here with him today. He would offer her a mint and enjoy seeing her sneeze.

He found out where the man's grave was before he left for London, but stopped by the visitor's center of the cemetery to make sure he knew exactly where it was positioned in this considerable collection of white headstones. Although it was not a bad thing to walk aimlessly in this burial ground, today was not the day for it. He would come back here another time with Renee and Rebecca. He was sure of it.

With a map to his destination in hand, Will strolled past the red tulips as they reached up through the ground and opened slightly toward the sky. They were Renee's favorite flower, and it seemed as though every color imaginable was represented. It was a humbling experience being in the middle of so many thousands of graves. The number of graves was comparable to the number of flowers. Here were the remains of men so much greater and braver than he could ever imagine being, and he paused momentarily, knowing they had died so he could have the freedoms he enjoyed every day. Will wept openly for a few seconds before drying his eyes. Why was he so emotional here? He didn't feel worthy of their sacrifice and it humbled him as he gazed upon the vastness of Arlington.

He wandered near a group of white and pink cherry blossom trees and sat down on the bench across the walkway from them. Turning his head slowly so he could take in the colors, he regained his composure, unable to stop his eyes from witnessing the many white stones that decorated the green grass for what looked like miles. This was certainly the most peaceful place in the world to be buried and these men deserved the best. Closing his eyes but keeping his face toward the sun, he absorbed the warmth and smiled at how perfect this day had turned out.

His own relatives had fought in Colonial battles, the Revolutionary War, Civil War, World War II, and Vietnam, and some had been killed in battle. All of them were either buried near the battlefield or in a small church cemetery in their hometowns, but none were buried here. Yet, there were so many headstones at Arlington. Was it possible this many people could have died for their country? He certainly lived in a country that valued freedom for the whole more than individual life itself.

Will stood up and walked toward the next section and suspected he was about to find what he came here for. Stepping off the walkway, he followed a row of stones until he read the name he had come all this way to see. This was it. He stood by the gravesite of the man who left two beautiful ladies behind. It just didn't seem fair that Will was now able to spend time with both Renee and Rebecca, while it should have been this man. He broke down again, immediately going to one knee, and put one hand on the white stone just inches in front of him. With his other hand, he covered his eyes. Should he be embarrassed by this display of emotion? This was so unusual for him but he couldn't help it.

Just days before, Will had read how this man heroically sacrificed everything for his fellow soldiers and local residents in a faraway country. He was taken by surprise while on a mission to clear the area from terrorists who attacked their own citizens, including women and children, and was killed instantly. Will's favorite picture was one he found of Renee's husband offering a local Afghan child some food, while both soldier and child staring into each other's faces. It was taken only hours before his last mission, but a great lasting testimony for this man. Renee should be proud of her husband. Maybe Rebecca had never seen this photo of her dad, but Will wanted to show her. It was his obituary photo and said more about him than all of the words combined.

He wished Renee could see it the same way and hoped that someday she would pass on these and other details to Rebecca. The little girl deserved to hear what kind of man her father really had been. Instead, Renee kept her memories to herself and didn't share them with her daughter. Hopefully, things would change after this trip.

Will was the only living person within this entire section of the cemetery, so it made no sense for him to strike up a conversation with the dead soldier. Renee's husband wouldn't be able to hear him, yet it was somehow satisfying to be here in front of a specific headstone, kneeling on this sacred ground. He wished he could tell this man face to face how proud he was and how thankful he was for serving his country with honor, even to the point of death.

After several minutes, Will finally stood up and glanced around. He stared at the red, yellow, and purple flowers as he wiped his eyes once again, then looked down to read the headstone one last time. He nodded as he walked back down the row and was soon on the sidewalk again. He followed it around to the eternal flame where John F. Kennedy was interred, and glanced up at Robert E. Lee's old house at the top of the hill. That's where he headed as the sidewalk circled around and uphill. He had several ancestors who fought under General Lee, and was somehow drawn to the integrity of this man, even though he was the one who led the great rebellion dividing the nation. There was something rewarding about walking through this man's house and reflecting on Lee's personal life.

Once outside again, the view of the city was remarkable, with the Washington Monument on the left, the US Capitol building in the middle, the Jefferson Memorial on the right, and thousands of white gravestones in the foreground below.

Will turned his wrist to see the time, looked up at the panorama again, then ambled down toward the tomb of the unknown soldier. He passed so many flowers and cherry blossom trees along the way and was surprised to see the black tulips where the lone marine stood at attention. He had never seen black flowers before but they were striking as they also seemed to stand guard. The marine marched in front of the tomb, and Will contemplated the honor being given to all those who served this great country. He had to catch a flight, so he walked back into the midst of the rows of white stones to visualize it all again. Gazing up at the cloudless sky, he smiled as the sun shone brightly on his face, then walked back through the cemetery toward the entrance. It was an emotional, yet powerful experience that every American should go through at least once in his life.

# Chapter Eighteen

**F**INALLY BACK HOME THAT EVENING, Will fought to contain his excitement, even though he wanted to drive over and see Renee right away. It was after 11PM, so he would have to wait another day to see her. Would she mind if he called her this late, or would she be sound asleep already in preparation for the next day? He had paid her several surprise visits, one in which she hadn't even crawled out of bed, so his next visit would definitely be preceded with a phone call.

He showered and unpacked, then lay on his bed in the dark, unable to stop his mind from plastering images of Renee all over the backs of his eyelids. She had a good heart, personality, and sense of humor. He wanted to be with her more than any of the women he had met over the past five years or so, and he'd been with a lot. She had to be the one. He was determined to keep dating her and get to know her even more. Yet, the back of his mind kept reminding him he had been here once before, and it turned out the opposite of what he had expected. It was a painful part of his life and he had spent years trying to escape from that era of his past. This time it was different. She was special. He knew it.

Almost immediately after that thought, the alarm went off and it was the next morning already. Excellent. He must have finally fallen asleep and the rest of the night seemed to go quickly. Should he call her before she left to drop off Rebecca at school? Maybe they could get together sometime today. He picked up his cell phone and punched in some numbers.

"Hello, world traveler," said Renee. "Are you back in town?"

Hearing her voice instantly brought a smile to Will's face, as he replied, "Yes, I am. I want to meet you for lunch today, so even if you only get 30 minutes, I can pick you up and have you back in time."

"Well, I'll have to think about it." She paused for a second, then added, "Okay, sounds good."

"You didn't have to think too much, I guess."

"No, I'd like to see you so pick me up on the corner of Thistle and Dogwood Avenue at 11:30, and I'll be waiting for you."

"Perfect. See you then."

It was funny to hear a woman tell him to pick her up at a specific time and place. Usually he was the one telling his date when and where he would get her. He didn't mind though. He would do anything for this one. He put the boxes of chocolates with his briefcase and finished getting ready for the day.

He arrived at his office in the downtown area, greeted by his personal assistant. "Welcome back. Did the trip go well?"

"Hi, Sue. Yes it did, but I'm getting too old to be gone for so long at a time."

"Oh, yes," she replied sarcastically. "What will you be this year? Twenty six or twenty seven?"

"I used to be able to take off for a month at a time and I didn't mind it at all. But now things are different. I don't even want to be away for a week, even if it's in London."

Sue playfully added, "It wouldn't be that you miss a certain blonde named Renee, would it?"

"It's possible. Hey, don't you have some work to do? I

sent you those reports I needed you to prepare for me."

"Yes, sir," she saluted. "Have you looked on your desk yet?"

He laughed at her serious demeanor and glanced to his desk. Sure enough, a new stack of papers sat on the left corner, and she added, "I also e-mailed you a soft copy in case you find you'd like to change anything."

She walked away smugly, and he replied, "Thanks. You are awesome. And don't say it. I know that you know you're awesome too."

She just glanced back at him with a smirk, not saying a word.

He sat down and spent the rest of the morning at his desk finalizing the work he needed to do as follow-up from his recent trip, and kept watching the time slowly crawl as he waited for his lunch date with his new favorite woman. He tried to review his notes from the trip to see if he had missed anything, but his mind was miles away in his thoughts of Renee as he let her distract him from his tasks.

At one point, he spent a few minutes loading the photos he took of Renee and Rebecca in the Indian dresses onto his computer, and he watched the slideshow of the two of them posing for him. He couldn't take his eyes off of these new photos, along with the ones from the zoo, and he just sat there with a smile on his face.

"I made some coffee. Do you want any?"

Sue's voice snapped him to reality again and he looked up at her as she stood near his desk. "Yes, thank you. Plenty of sugar, please."

"Don't I always?" she replied while her eyes gave him an attitude. "Oh, ye of little faith."

Will tasted it and said, "Perfect, of course. What would I do without you?"

"Maybe you'd learn how to use some of this fancy equipment that you have around here, like the coffee maker and the printer. Oh, and by the way you keep checking the clock, I assume you must be meeting someone important for lunch. Do you want me to make any reservations?"

He looked at her and shook his head. "How do you know everything?"

"Women's intuition." She saw his screensaver and continued, "I have to admit Renee seems like a lot of fun. She has quite a personality in her Indian sari."

"Oh really? I hadn't noticed."

She slapped him on the back of the head and walked back to her desk near the front door. "So would you like me to make reservations for two?"

"If you insist. I was thinking about going to that little café near Dogwood at 11:30."

"Consider it done. She works at the distribution center right there at Dogwood Avenue, so you should probably head over there now so pick her up on time. Women don't like to be left waiting, you know."

Standing up quickly, he kissed her on the cheek and said, "Thanks again. See you in a bit."

He started toward the door, but was interrupted before he reached it. "Aren't you forgetting a special gift for that special someone?"

Will snapped his fingers and turned back to his desk, where Sue handed him a package. He grinned, returned to the lobby area and disappeared through the front door. It was only a few minutes' drive to where Renee worked and he immediately saw her standing on the sidewalk when he turned the corner.

"Hey, stranger. Are you going my way?" she asked.

"Well, actually I am, so hop in. We can eat over there and it'll be quick."

She stepped into the convertible, which was low to the

ground, and several faces in the glass window of the distribution center watched them drive off.

"Who were those people?" Will asked.

"Oh, those were probably my co-workers. It's not every day that a handsome man picks me up in a sports car and whisks me away for lunch, so it was like headline news there. I'm sorry."

"No problem. Maybe I can meet them sometime and see if they would tell me what you're really like."

"Yeah, I'm sure you'd be so thrilled you wouldn't ask me out again."

"Not a chance, Renee. Not a chance."

She smirked as he parked at the curb, then ran around to open the door for her and helped her out of the car. He said something to the waitress and she led them both to an outside table in the shade.

"I hope you don't mind sitting out here. The weather is so nice and you probably need to see some sunshine and feel the light breeze about now."

"It's beautiful out here."

"I picked up something for you and Rebecca in London. I hope you like chocolate."

"Are you kidding? That's similar to asking if I like air. Ooh. These look fancy. I can't even pronounce these words."

"They say something about chocolate with creamy stuff inside. You'll like them. I have a small box for Rebecca too."

"That was so thoughtful," and she leaned over and kissed him on the cheek.

The waitress came and Will ordered drinks and sandwiches for both of them.

"How was your trip? Did you meet any nice girls?"

Will stammered and replied, "Well, I did meet a young stewardess on the plane out there."

"Hmm. Did you spend time with her in London too?"

"Yeah, we did walk around London one day, but it wasn't the same without you."

She paused and looked away. Did he say something wrong?

"Did you spend time with a girl in India too?" she asked

"Uh, yes, I went out a few times with one of the girls from the hotel, but it was different. She was an old friend and we just went around town."

This wasn't heading the direction he had planned. Renee had become like the ice queen within a minute. The waitress came by with their sweet iced teas, which helped to ease the tension that had engulfed their meeting.

"Renee, these girls are only friends. I've met them to pass the time away while I'm traveling."

"Do you consider those girls as dates?"

"No, not really. Well, I guess some of them could be. I don't know. Why does it matter?"

"Are you just passing the time away with me now or are we on a real date?"

"No, I want to be with you. This is definitely a real date. I had hoped to tell you about some of the things I discovered in London, what I realized while I was over there."

"Oh, you did just give me some ideas about what you did over there and who you spent it with. I understand."

"No, that's not what I meant."

The waitress returned again and Will had to stop for a few minutes while she set out their sandwiches and asked if there was anything else they needed. Will shook his head, but there was nothing behind his fake smile. Things were not going well at all. Renee looked hurt for some reason, but she took a bite out of her sandwich and turned away, as though she was trying to hide her feelings.

As soon as the waitress walked away, Will continued, "I've dated a lot of girls, but I haven't found someone I really connected with."

"So you also met different girls when you've traveled to other countries?"

"What? You're not listening to me."

"Well, have you?"

"Yes I have, but if you'll just listen, I'm trying to tell you something."

"How many girls do you think you've dated in the past couple of years? How about the past year?"

"I have no idea. Why does this even matter now?"

"Oh, it matters. Would you say more than ten?"

"Come on. This isn't even relevant. It should just be about you and me."

"More than twenty?"

"Yes, but that was in the past."

"More than fifty?"

"Yes, but I want to focus on you now," Will said emphatically.

"More than a hundred?"

"Listen. Let's stop this and start over again. There's something very important I wanted to tell you."

"You really have been around, haven't you?"

She kept eating, never looking at Will for a second, and that wasn't like her.

"Renee, what is going on here? I can't understand how you could be so different today than the last time we went out. I'm still the same person, but you're not. What's changed?"

Finally, she turned at him, but there were tears in her eyes. She spoke softly, "I think you're a great guy, Will, and you made me feel very special when we've been together."

"You are special," he interrupted, and she held up her hand.

"Let me finish. I just can't compete with your overseas dream girls who you seem to like so much. I am a one-man woman and I put all of my heart into that one man. You just don't appear to be able to do this with me and that's the way you are. I don't want to try to change you, but I just can't be with someone like that."

"I've dated a lot of girls but it doesn't mean I want to spend the rest of my life with any of them."

"Will, I need to get back to work now. I'm sorry I can't be added to your list of conquests. I've had fun with you, but it's just not right for me."

She stood up and started walking toward the distribution center where she worked, and Will stared at her in disbelief. "I can drive you back. Just wait a minute."

"No, I need the walk right now. Bye Will."

He sat there as she marched away. It was as though he was back in time, when another girl had walked out of his life and his heart pounded relentlessly. He was frozen to his chair. It was a panic attack and he didn't know what to do as Renee continued walking, leaving another painful void in his life. Just get up and run after her. No, his body wouldn't listen. This was too much for him. He needed to get his arms around the situation.

He had planned to tell her that a moment of decision came to him this past week and he wanted to devote all of his waking hours to her and her alone. How could that decision have just been washed away a few minutes ago? Did this really just happen or was he actually in bed at home, getting ready to wake up and call Renee to meet her for lunch? The cool breeze moved his hair across his forehead and he reached up to brush it back. This was real.

# Chapter Nineteen

RENEE RUBBED HER EYES AS SHE walked in the front door at work and she hoped none of her friends would be there waiting for her. The sun shone in through the front windows and she stared at her shadow for a moment on the opposite wall. She made sure she didn't turn around and look back to see Will, although she wanted to know if he had chased after her. She waited, but nobody came rushing through the door. It didn't matter anyway. It sounded like he chased just about any girl he saw.

She didn't want to talk to anyone now and really wished she could go home. It was that time of the month, and her emotions were on a roller coaster. The joys of being a woman. Her stomach felt uneasy and she probably could have taken the rest of the day off as a sick day, but she stayed. She wanted to get busy soon and try to take her mind off of you-know-who. Besides, her boss probably wouldn't be pleased if she left now. She couldn't believe the turn of events so far. She had been so excited to see Will for lunch, but once he started talking about his other women, her day was ruined. That's not what she wanted to hear from him at all.

"So how was your lunch date with Mr. Right?" MaryAnn asked from the doorway across the hall.

Renee didn't even look up and tried to ignore the question as she continued down the opposite end of the corridor, pretending not to hear her friend.

"Hey, Renee. What's wrong?" MaryAnn asked as she caught up with her.

"I'm sorry. I just don't want to talk about it."

"Did something happen during lunch? You were so happy a half hour ago."

"I knew he was too good to be true," she blurted out and the tears came uncontrollably. "I'm sorry. My hormones are driving me crazy."

MaryAnn put her arm around Renee and led her into the break room. A few people were in there, so they found an isolated table in the corner and sat down. Retta and Lisa saw them both walk in and came over right away.

"What's going on?" Retta asked.

Renee took a deep breath and tried to calm herself. "You all were right about Will."

"What do you mean?" asked Lisa.

"He has a girl in every country, and met with one in London a few days ago, and one in India a couple of weeks ago. Both since he and I had started dating."

Her friends looked at each other and Renee watched their expressions through teary eyes.

"It's probably best that you found out now. There's no telling what diseases he might be carrying," replied Lisa.

"He probably knows all kinds of tricks and you'd always be wondering who he last tried them with," added MaryAnn.

"Well, he admitted he spent time with these women, so he certainly gets around. I just thought we had something special going on and he wouldn't be like that," said Renee.

"Men can be so dense. They're just barely above the level of rocks and tree stumps when it comes to intelligence," added Lisa. "Don't they even have feelings? Can't they see when their actions hurt other people?"

"Maybe you just need to show him you're so much more than these women he meets during his travels and you'll win him over," added Retta.

"Yeah, but I'd always be wondering if he's going to meet someone during every trip and I can't deal with that," replied Renee.

Lisa asked, "Where does he meet these girls? Are they escorts or …"

"No, he said one was a flight attendant and one was at the hotel where he stayed."

"Well, two girls isn't too bad, right?" asked MaryAnn.

"When I asked him how many there had been, he stopped answering when I got to a hundred, so I'm sure it's more than that."

"Wow. He definitely gets around," said Retta.

"He made me feel so good over the past few weeks and I really was convinced he was the right man for me. He's so much better than any other man I've ever met," said Renee as she broke down again.

"If he made you feel so special, then how can you give up on him now?" Retta asked. "You should let him know you really like him, but you can't put up with him going out with other girls. If he really cares for you, he'll stop it."

"No, once a man's been dating like that for years, you won't be able to change him," said MaryAnn. "Especially if he's had the taste for a different girl in every city. He's probably set in his ways."

"Well, if you're through with him, do you mind if I go out with him once, just to see what he's like?" asked Lisa.

"What?" exclaimed the other girls at the same time.

"That's just not right," said Retta.

"I'm only kidding," said Lisa. "Well, maybe a little. I've never dated someone who made me feel as special as this guy made Renee feel and I want some of that."

"He did make me feel like a queen, every time I saw him," replied Renee. "Even at lunch today, he picked me up in his convertible and pulled the chair out for me. He's a perfect gentleman. I felt like a poor girl being courted by a prince."

"Yes, but that's how he can pick up so many girls on his trips," added MaryAnn. "He's a gentleman, he's a smooth talker, and they all fall for it."

"No, but with me, it was different. I think I really touched him somehow too. We clicked in a way that was so perfect. I just don't understand why he would keep going out with other women."

Lisa commented, "He may have made every one of his girls feel the same way. Maybe he's just a love 'em and leave 'em kind of guy."

"But what about the way he treated Rebecca? She's only six and he spent time with her as well. If he was just after a conquest of me, then why would he have bought flowers and chocolates for her too?"

"That's sneaky," said Lisa. "He lured you in by buttering up your daughter."

"He bought you both flowers and chocolates?" asked Retta.

"Yes, plus an amazing fruit bouquet, clothes from India, and more."

"You can't give up on him, girl," demanded Retta. "He's a keeper."

"What about his other women?" asked Renee.

"Once you've won him over, there won't be any other women," Retta continued.

"I don't think so," Lisa replied. "He's more like a wolf on the prowl for a little kitten like you. Hey, what if you played more like the competition and planned a romantic evening alone with him at your apartment?"

"What do you mean?" asked MaryAnn.

"Maybe lure him over with a special dessert, only to greet him at the door in a slinky negligee," replied Lisa. "He couldn't resist your charm."

"I'm not like that. I haven't had a physical relationship with any man since before my husband was killed. I'm really just a goody-two-shoe. I don't think I could put on such an act ."

"Plus it might backfire and scare him off," added Retta.

"No man could resist Renee in a revealing outfit with her hair down," continued Lisa. "Trust me. It's probably what he's used to anyway."

"Well, it seems that all of my other dates give up on me because I don't give in, so they end up cheating on me," Renee replied.

"See? This could help prevent Mr. Right from going else-where," said Lisa.

"I don't know what to do," Renee said. "I walked away from him at lunch today and I don't think he even knew why I was upset."

MaryAnn touched her hand and said, "You just lay low today and wait until he calls you again, and he will call you."

Renee looked at her inquisitively. "But what if he does call? I wouldn't even know what to say."

Retta replied, "Let's not think about it all afternoon, okay? Why don't we just keep busy and stay positive. Things have a way of working themselves out."

Renee nodded and glanced at each of her friends, still maintaining her enchanting smile, and took a deep breath. Thinking about Lisa's suggestion, she questioned whether that was the right direction to take to make Will forget about other women.

# Chapter Twenty

**W**ILL STARED DOWN THE ROAD in disbelief, wondering if he should have ran after Renee when she walked back to the distribution center. No, maybe she needed some time to think. He got back in his car and drove toward his office. Of course the first song on the radio was 'Yesterday' by the Beatles, but he immediately changed the channel. He certainly didn't want to hear a sad song like that right now. The other channel played 'More Than a Feeling' by Boston, and he changed the channel again. He didn't want to hear about a girl walking out of his life. The third radio station played 'Missing You' by John Waite, and he turned the radio off and drove to his office.

Is it possible the same thing he went through years ago had happened to him again? Could another girl he cared so much about have just walked out of his life for the second time? What was wrong with these women? He had done everything he could to make these girls feel special, yet in both instances, they moved on without him. It made no sense. He pulled up to the curb and parked, then walked into his office.

"Hi, boss," said Sue cheerfully.

"Hi, Sue. Please take a message on any calls. I have some work to do and can't be disturbed for a while."

"Is everything alright?"

"Not really, but we'll have to talk about it later."

Will went to his office and shut the door. He stared out the window for a minute or two before sitting down and picked up the phone to call one of his friends. The blue sky was inviting and the sweet sounds of the birds relaxing, but Will didn't take the time like he usually did to enjoy the outside. He turned his back on the window.

"Hi, Patrick. This is Will. Do you have a few minutes to talk?"

"Sure. What's up?"

"Do you ever wonder if women speak the same language as men?"

"No, I know for a fact they don't. Women are the most likely descendants of aliens, so they're a completely different kind of animal. Why do you ask?"

"I feel better now. For a minute, I thought it was just me."

"I'm glad I could help. Let me know if you need any other words of wisdom."

"No wait, Patrick. I actually was going somewhere with this conversation and wanted some of your lessons learned now, if you don't mind."

"Oh, that's fine. You may continue."

"I just returned from a business trip and planned a nice lunch with Renee."

"Is that the girl you met in India or Europe on your last trip?"

"No, No, No. This is the one I met here in town. The one with the daughter."

"Yes, I remember now. Very nice. I'll have to meet her sometime."

"Well, she started asking if I ever went out with other girls on trips and took me by surprise."

"Wow, you didn't lie about them, I hope."

"No, of course not. I told her I had, but she got upset and

wanted to know how many girls I've dated in the past year. Why is that such a big deal?"

"Most of mankind has a few dates a year, but you have a few dates every week, Will. I can see how that would bother any normal girl."

"But none of them meant anything to me. I went out with each of these girls once or twice when I was traveling and that's it. Just passing the time away, but instead of doing it alone, I've passed time with other women. It helps to make the time go by faster. Don't you see?"

Patrick gave a hearty laugh and replied, "You should know better than to think any woman is going to be okay with knowing you've been spending time with another woman or two or a hundred. It's just not reality."

"You're not hearing what I've been saying. I've only gone out with these girls once or twice, and even then only sightseeing around the city, going out to dinner, or something simple. Nothing more. No long term commitments."

"It doesn't matter. Some women can be selfish and don't want to share their man with other women. I know, it's a strange possessive thing they have, but it's true. They can be vicious toward one another and are jealous of other women. It can be a nasty situation to be in the middle of."

"No, Renee's not like that. She's a friendly person and wouldn't be jealous over nothing. We've only gone out a few times and I haven't really given her any signals that we're officially an item."

"Over nothing? What about all the other girls? It doesn't matter if you haven't given her signals because you probably already have without realizing it. In her eyes, you might be an item and by mentioning you've been with her competition, then you've just become a traitor to her."

"What? Her competition? What do you mean?"

"Half of Earth's population is her competition and now

she knows you've been with almost every one of them on your business trips. She might be planning to some kind of revenge on you."

"No, that's not her at all."

"Listen. Didn't you say you really liked her?"

"Yes, of course. I was just planning to tell her I wanted to date her exclusively when she basically said, 'Have a nice life' and walked away." Will paused for a moment, then continued, "Something like this happened to me several years ago and I feel like I'm in a recurring nightmare. Why is it that just when I think I've found the most fantastic girl in the world, the one I want to spend the rest of my life with, she walks out of my life?"

"Is it possible you were wrong back then and you might be wrong now?"

"No to both. The one I fell for years ago was in a league above the rest. I had dated other girls, but this one was beautiful inside and out. She made me laugh, she made me feel good about myself, and I wanted to be with her all the time. I wanted to give her flowers every day and smell her perfume on the letters she wrote to me."

"Sounds like puppy love to me," said Patrick. "You must have thought it was more serious than it really was, and she was ready to move on."

"Yeah, you're probably right about that. I can still see her playing the piano and listening to the sound she could get out of it." Will paused as though he watched this mystery girl from his past bringing life to some distant piano. "She was the first girl I ever knew who was drop-dead gorgeous in every way. I must not have been in the same league."

"So, is it possible your recent crush is nothing more than infatuation?"

"No, I'm certain it's not just a crush. I would want to get to know her as a friend as well, since she's the most interesting and enjoyable person I've been around in a long time."

"More interesting than that girl you met at the gym a couple of weeks ago?"

"Patrick, she was just someone to help pass the time away at the gym. Nothing long term."

"But that's not how women think. Remember, their brains are wired differently from ours, probably something the aliens did centuries ago to try to drive men to extinction. Every woman sees every other woman as her competitor. If you really care for this girl, you need to understand that and be more careful about spending time with anyone else."

"It doesn't make much sense to me, but I'll work on it. How can I get her to realize that anyone I've ever dated is a thing of the past?"

"Do you ever get calls from these women? Do you have pictures of any of them? Do they stop by and visit you?"

"No, why?"

"That's the kind of stuff women look for in their men. They hate it when you have any hint of a life with someone other than themselves. You have to burn your little black book and any photos you might have of women of the past, even those as recent as in the past week. Romantic letters with perfume on them can be especially condemning if she finds them."

"Shouldn't be a problem. I don't really keep up with any of them and I don't save photos or old letters any more. I'm good there."

"That's nice to hear. What about on social media? Do any of them stalk you?"

"What? No, not at all. I don't have time to get on those things. I couldn't imagine what that would be like. What if even half of the girls I've met over the years started contacting me? I shudder at the thought."

"It's probably not too bad. Besides, maybe you flatter

yourself too much by thinking those girls from your past would even remember you."

"You're right. They probably only went out with me to help the time go by faster on their trips too, so I helped them in the same way they helped me. Makes sense."

"Wrong. These are women we're talking about, remember? They are programmed to put a great deal of importance on relationships, even a simple dinner or night at the theater. You might have done the same thing to some of those women that your mystery girlfriend did to you, only in your case it's multiplied exponentially."

"No, they wouldn't have thought anything more than just a simple night out with a friend."

"If you really believe that, you haven't been listening to me at all. You have to be careful about leading those of the opposite gender on, even unknowingly. It happens all the time and I can see it happening to you, my friend. The same way you were devastated by that girl from your past, these other women you've dated may have been shattered when you didn't call them back or meet with them again."

"I wish we had talked about this several years ago. I may have done a lot of things differently."

"Actually, I believe we did talk about this with you years ago, but you just brushed it aside. Hey, one more thing. How do you really feel about this girl?"

"I was certain I found my soul mate once before and I let her slip away. Now it's too late for me to do anything about her, since she married and moved on with her life. I think I've found my soul mate again, a second one if that's possible, and I'm not going to let her slip away."

"You know we're all behind you and we'll help you in any way possible. If you want any of us to talk to her, just let me know and we'll be glad to fill her in on what you're really like."

"I may just take you up on that. Well, it's been good talking with you. I'll let you know how things work out."

Will turned his chair to face the window. The sky appeared to be brighter than it had a few minutes earlier, and the birds sang with even more melody. Maybe this wasn't the end of the world. Not if he could help it.

# Chapter Twenty-One

REFLECTIONS OF LIGHT CHANGES caught Will's eyes as he turned toward his office door and he moved his head to see his screensaver alternating photos of Renee and Rebecca. He could never tire from watching the memories from the zoo or the fashion show of outfits from India. Renee's hair was stunning and her eyes captivated him like no other woman. Her lips revealed a personality Will just didn't want to live without. She made him feel as though he was the most special man in the world. She was so much fun to be with and these photos made him wish he was with her right now.

Why would she be so hung up over his past and upset about women who were only friends, nothing more? Were all women like this? He watched the slideshow with sadness and confusion and couldn't help but wonder if Renee was really finished with him. It hurt to think about that, especially since he had already experienced this same rejection by someone he adored years ago. He didn't understand it then and he couldn't make sense of it now. Just when it seemed as though two people were perfect for each other, why would one of them choose to end it, ruining what could be a lifetime of happiness?

Women appeared to be the one group of people who made the worst choices and could very well be the cause of half of all marriages ending in divorce. Well, maybe that was an exaggeration, since there were probably a lot of men who were idiots and caused problems between happy couples too. It was just odd that in the two closest relationships he had ever had, both were ended by the female-half of the relationship. Even stranger, in both instances he couldn't figure out why the other half would have ended it.

It occurred to Will that he should have followed up with the girl in each case and tried to understand why each one would have felt that way. Maybe it was a misunderstanding which could have been cleared up with a simple conversation and he blew it by not even asking why. It's just so overwhelming to hear that the one person who was his entire world didn't want to be with him anymore. He had collapsed into his shell to internalize his feelings and kept going with his life back then, not even doing a thing to restore what meant so much to him. He had continued as though nothing happened, except that his better half was no longer part of his life.

This caused so much pain years ago. Will was not about to let it happen again. He needed to call Renee and clear everything up before she was out of reach.

A knock at the door snapped Will out of his painful memories and Sue peeked in. "Will, you have some visitors I think you should see."

"Who is it?" Will asked, but as he stood up, he recognized their voices.

Sue opened the door and Patrick, Gregory, Frank, and Daniel walked through and greeted Will with handshakes and hugs. Sue quietly slipped back out and shut the door.

Daniel said, "Patrick called and said you needed us right away, so here we are."

"When you're hurting, we're hurting," Frank added.

Will looked at Patrick and nodded. "I appreciate your concern, guys. I'm having some relationship problems, but I don't know if there's anything you can do."

"We thought we could talk about some of our experiences," Patrick replied, "and let you know you're not alone. Women are not the easiest creatures to understand, but if you have the right one, then she's worth giving everything you've got in order to keep her."

"Words of wisdom from the elders of the tribe?" Will asked.

"We're not that much older than you, pal," replied Daniel with a finger in Will's chest.

"But yes, we have years more experience dealing with the one who means the most to us," added Patrick.

"We don't have more experience with as many different girls as you have, but that could be part of your problem," said Gregory.

"First of all, you need to know that women don't make sense much of the time," Daniel said. "You just need to go along and pretend you understand and that you agree with them."

"Yes, if you try to reason with them as you would with a man, then you could be seen as the enemy and she may automatically build up a wall and not let you in," added Patrick. "Remember, she is a different kind of animal and doesn't think like we do."

"My problem now is that Renee doesn't think I put her above any other woman I meet," said Will, "but it's just not true."

"No, your problem is she's not the only woman in your life," replied Frank. "You might have dated hundreds of girls, but it just takes one competitor to drive a wedge between you and Renee. If she's that important to you, then you need to let her know there's only one, and cut out 100% of the other dates."

"But the other girls were only ..."

"It doesn't matter," Patrick interrupted. "All it takes is one girl to make your little lady jealous, and then you're toast. Never even give her a reason to feel that way."

"I get it," Will responded.

"You're a great guy and I think you'd make a fine husband to some lucky lady," said Gregory.

"Well, thanks. I'm flattered."

Gregory gave his friends a strange look, then added, "No, I didn't mean it like that. I'm just saying you're not a scumbag and I believe you deserve to find your love for a lifetime. She's out there and if you think Renee is the one, then don't let her go so easily. Call her or visit her and straighten things up between you two before it's too late."

"I'm glad you think I'm not a scumbag. It means a lot to me," Will replied. "Actually, just before you barged in here, I came to the same conclusion."

"That you're not a scumbag?" asked Patrick.

"No, that I need to call Renee today and do whatever it takes to get back with her."

"Remember, a woman needs to hear you say she's special and that she's the only one," added Daniel. "It's not enough to assume she knows it. You have to tell her, and not just once. Let her know regularly."

"You know, I thought I've done a pretty good job with the girls I've dated, but it's different when you want to be with the same one day after day. I wish there was a manual on how to understand women."

"It would be volumes and you'd never have time to read it all before you die," said Gregory. "These creatures are complex organisms that were never meant to be understood. They're like calculus or trigonometry. They make no sense and when you think you understand them, you realize just how wrong you really are."

"Watching men trying to figure out women is actually like

watching a comedy of errors," added Frank. "There's very little chance of finding the answer. We just have to go along with it, realizing that they are a much higher intelligence than we could ever hope to be."

Patrick added, "Let her know you'll never abandon her or hurt her, and that you really care for her. Women need to feel secure. It sounds like Renee thinks she plays second fiddle to other women in your life and she's probably afraid you're not going to be with her in the long run. That she's just one of many. If you're thinking long term with this one, then let her know it."

"You guys are smarter than you appear to be," Will replied.

"I wish we could say the same for you," Frank added. "The deer in the headlight look just doesn't work for you."

"I don't have that look," replied Will with exasperation.

"Some men just feel like they're walking on eggshells when their lady is going through that time of the month," continued Daniel. "Talk about it with her and let her know you want to help her get through it."

"So you think that's what it was?" asked Will.

"Sure sounds like it might have played a part," said Gregory.

"It's not that easy," said Will. "With Renee, it just seems to come out of nowhere and blindsides me when I least expect it, and it takes me off guard. My first response is to be defensive, but…"

"Wrong," they all replied in unison.

"Remember, she's on your team and you need to help her through every difficulty she faces," said Patrick. "She'll probably tell you what she needs when she starts to feel like that, and then you'll know what to do."

"And it works every time?" asked Will.

"When it doesn't, then pray," replied Patrick.

Everyone else laughed, but Will had just learned an important part of making a relationship work in difficult situations. Women were more complicated than he ever realized.

# Chapter Twenty-Two

**C**LASSICAL MUSIC PLAYED QUIETLY as Kim sat at the coffee shop sipping her usual café mocha and relaxing in her stress-free zone. Once a week, Doug helped Nicole get ready for school and drove her there so she could unwind before going to work. The dimmed lights here provided a peaceful environment before she handled a busy day with six-year olds and she could unwind for a half-hour with a good novel. Her cellphone interrupted her tranquility.

"I'm sorry to bother you, but I need to talk to you about your brother."

This didn't sound like something that could be resolved in a minute or two, and Kim hesitated before deciding her peace this afternoon had ended.

"Hi, Renee. What do you want to know about Will?"

"We had lunch and started talking about his trip to England, but I asked him about seeing other girls in his travels."

Oh boy. This would be an interesting discussion. She looked around the room, already coming out of her zone, even though the relaxing paintings and music still surrounded her.

"What did he say?" Kim asked, already knowing he wouldn't hide the fact that he enjoyed the company of other women.

"I don't know if you realize it, but Will goes out with a lot of different women."

"Don't worry, Renee. He has dated a lot but he's not a player. He's spent time with other ladies here and there, but doesn't take it any further than that, if you know what I mean."

"How can you be so sure?"

"I know Will and he's a good man. He's not the sleeping around kind-of-guy. I believe he truly wants to settle down and have a family and he has spent the past few years sampling as many girls as he can in order to find the right one."

Kim couldn't believe she said it like that and made a face as the words came out.

"He still sounds like a player," Renee replied with some frustration in her voice. "How can someone like that ever settle down?"

"Trust me. He's a good man who desperately wants to find the right woman to spend the rest of his life with."

Silence filled the conversation for a moment as Kim briefly listened to the classical music playing overhead. A beautiful Mozart composition. It would be nice to close her eyes and enjoy it now, but she wanted to help clear up any misconceptions Renee had about Will.

"How can I compete with all of these other women?"

"You just need to be yourself and you've already won him over. Will really likes you. It's even more than that. I think once he realizes you're the one he enjoys spending time with, and he may have already made that decision, he'll stop dating other girls completely."

"I'm not so sure. He told me he went out with other girls on his last couple of trips, including the one he just returned from."

That rat! He should have known better than doing something like this. "Renee, if you let him know you expect him to put you first and not go out with other girls, I believe he'll do it."

"I still don't know. I'd be afraid he's going to compare me to one of his European or Asian girls."

"He's already done that and made the choice that he likes you better than all of the girls he's ever dated. Since he's gone out with you several times, it's a sign you're the one he wants to spend time with. Not any of the girls from his past. You can't change what's already happened and you shouldn't want to. All that matters is what you do now and what he does now, from here on forward."

"Well, I may have blown it already. When he told me about these girls, I walked away from him and told him I couldn't deal with it."

"Oh, I see. This could be a problem."

"Do you think he'd still be interested in seeing me after that?"

"He may think you're a possessive, jealous witch, but by making such a statement now, it may help him to realize he needs to change his lifestyle if he wants to spend more time with you."

"I like that. Not the witchy part, but the other part. I don't think I was a witch, but I may have let my hormones cause me to overreact. It's PMS time and I always turn into a monster for a few days every month. Should I call him and apologize or wait to see if he's going to call me?"

"Remember when I told you he lost the only girl he ever felt could be his soul mate? I'll bet he's thinking about that right now and he's determined to never let it happen again."

"So, what do you mean?"

"My guess is that you made him forget about how much he missed her, and you've already replaced this girl as his potential one and only. If that's true, then he's not going to let you slip away like he did with his mystery girl and he'll call you soon."

"I don't like to keep hearing about this perfect girl from his past. How can I deal with her?"

"She's long gone and has been married for several years. She's out of the picture. Only a memory. You have the opportunity to replace her once and for all and take her place as the sole owner of Will's heart. Forget about all of the girls from his past. You are already the winner if Will is dating you, alright?"

If only Renee wasn't so obsessed with other women in Will's life. That may be easier said than done. Most women would probably feel the same way. Why were men so obsessed with attractive girls? That's the bigger problem. If Will wanted to keep her, he had better control himself around other women.

"It's not easy to do, Kim."

"I know. If it was anyone other than Will, I'd be jealous too, but I know Will and I hope you'll get to know him better. Hey, how about if you and I get together to talk more in person tomorrow afternoon? I know a great place you'll enjoy."

"I don't know. I don't have anyone to watch Rebecca and it's not much notice."

"That's the fun part. I'll get Will to babysit Nicole and Rebecca, so you can see him before we leave and watch his reaction. Plus it'll give Rebecca a chance to be with him for a while too."

"Do you really think he'll do it?"

"I do. What do you think? We'll have fun."

"Yeah, let's do it. Thanks again, Kim."

"Great. I have to get going, so I'll call you later to finalize plans. See you tomorrow."

Kim laughed at her plan and couldn't wait to talk to Will about babysitting the girls. She would have no problem convincing him to do it. Somehow, she had a way with him and could convince him to do anything for her. It wasn't always like that when they were kids, but since they've been adults, she had him wrapped around her finger.

Since their parents died a few years ago, Will had been a protective big brother to Kim, drawing closer than ever to her and her family. He would do practically anything for her, and this was the time to take full advantage of that.

Another nice classical piece came on, a wonderful Debussy called 'Clair de Lune,' and she sipped her favorite coffee once again while slipping back into her relaxed mode for a few more minutes. Kim followed the piano melody with her head, slightly moving it side to side as if she were playing the song herself. Picking up her mystery novel about a romantic young couple on vacation in Upper Michigan in the winter, she drifted back into the story, captivated by the author's imagery. She momentarily let the rapidly changing lives of her brother and Renee escape from her mind once again.

# Chapter Twenty-Three

THE COOL MORNING INVIGORATED Will as he loaded his kayak on top of his SUV. This was the best time to relax on top of the water, especially watching the sun come up over the river's shoreline. Once he verified that several cans of Mountain Dew were in the cooler, he put it in the back seat and drove off into the darkness to his secret destination.

Fortunately, not many people came out to this spot, so the isolation was heavenly. There was a lot on his mind and he needed to sort out a few things in his life. What better place to be alone with God than in the middle of a calm river with a scenic shoreline? He parked, unloaded the little six-foot kayak from its perch, and set the miniature cooler inside. The boat silently slid into the black water with only a few ripples visible from Will's flashlight. He stepped in, turned off the light, and paddled away from the riverbank toward his sanctuary. His only audience included a few deer and some smaller critters he could only hear walking through the bushes.

People who had never been on the river before sunrise didn't know what they were missing. He sat still for some time and floated with the gentle current, drinking from a can of his favorite liquid. In a few hours, he would meet at his sister's house to babysit Nicole and Rebecca while their mother's went out for lunch. He wasn't sure what that was all about but he hoped it would turn out for the better. Thoughts went through his mind as he cleared his head from the worries of the day. He closed his eyes and listened to the sounds of nature.

The morning light barely hinted that the sun would be joining him within the hour. He drifted close to the shoreline, taking in the shapes of the full trees nearby as they came into view. The sounds of birds filled the air with a music that stirred his soul. He listened, paddled a little more, then drifted and listened once again. His presence didn't seem to disturb his unseen friends, since they kept whistling the entire time.

He alternated paddling on both sides, leaving only a slight movement in the water behind him as he steered toward the center of the river. There was a spot up ahead of Will that would soon be the point where the sun would make its presence known. His eyes kept going back to that spot as the daylight crept out of the darkness, sending it retreating behind him on the other side of the earth. He rested his paddles on the kayak and leaned back to take a break. The movement of the light contrasted with his stillness and he watched as the curtain steadily rose on an incredible show.

Mist rose from the surface of the water, matching his cool breath as it escaped from his mouth each time he exhaled. The sky was clear with no clouds in sight and would provide an unspoiled backdrop as the sun eventually made its way out of hiding. The chilly air felt good against Will's face. He had dressed in flannel and a light jacket and was prepared for the comfortable North Carolina morning on the water.

The only movement he saw was the sunlight as it raced to cover the entire river and all of the trees on both sides. Occasionally, a few birds flew into the new light, probably welcoming the morning. This was a show worth getting up early for. He faced the point where the rays came from, but his eyes caught the light's motion all around him. Suddenly, the sun seemed to explode above the horizon as the warmth touched his face and he closed his eyes. The sunrise was complete and the day had begun with more splendor than he had seen in a long time.

*****

Kim's doorbell rang and Will's smiling face peeked in the window by the door. She let him in and watched Renee's reaction as he came through the entry way. Renee's eyes lit up, but she was hesitant to go and greet him. What was going on in her friend's head?

"You both look great," said Will as he kissed Kim on the cheek and walked over to hug Renee, who seemed to enjoy it but again didn't provide any expression of emotion for Will. "That dress is awesome on you, Renee."

She tilted her head but then went back to Nicole's room, probably to say 'bye' to Rebecca.

"Doug had to work today, but the girls are in Nicole's room playing. We're going out for lunch and will be back in a little while. Do you need anything before we leave?"

"No, I think I can handle these two for a couple of hours. I get the feeling you're plotting something against me. What's up?"

Kim laughed and said, "Silly boy. Do you still think the world revolves around you, big brother? Come on, Renee. I'll drive."

Nicole and Rebecca ran in to the living room with squeals of delight when they saw Will, both hugging him as he squatted down to their level. Renee followed them and walked out the front door with his sister, looking back at her daughter.

"They'll be fine ladies. Have a good time together."

Kim drove to her and Doug's favorite restaurant and expected the discussions would be focused on Will the entire time. A young hostess greeted them almost immediately and seated them by the window. Kim smiled about what Will said regarding Renee in her dress. Renee had on one of the outfits she had loaned her and commented, "Will was right. You really do look great in that dress."

"You think so? There's something about it that makes me feel special, like I'm somebody, but I wonder if I should even be wearing it."

"Nonsense. I could get used to seeing you dress like this more often. It really accentuates your hair and your curves, and it makes you look classy."

Renee blushed and her eyes caught Kim's briefly before glancing around the restaurant. "It's strange not having our daughters with us."

"Yes, but it's nice for us to be able to get together and talk, don't you think?"

"I know, but I don't get to do it very often. I feel guilty leaving her with someone else on a Saturday when I have the day off. How did you talk Will into babysitting?"

"I told him we were in a bind and needed his help today. He stepped up, as usual, and offered to help. Rebecca will have a fun time with Will and Nicole, so relax and enjoy the time we have now. Will is great with kids and he'll enjoy being with them."

"You're right. It's so good to have a friend like you. I don't know what I'd do without you."

"You'd manage, but it wouldn't be as fun without me."

They both laughed and she saw the hesitation in Renee's eyes. Something was on her mind and Kim was about to find out.

"Do your parents live in town?" Renee asked.

Kim paused, then responded. "No, mine and Will's parents were killed in a plane crash several years ago while on vacation."

"I'm so sorry. My mom died of cancer and my dad had a

stroke. I'm an only child."

"So we have that in common. I won't even step one foot on a plane, but Will has probably flown over three million miles. It's almost as though he's tempting fate with every flight. After the accident happened, Will took his inheritance and invested recklessly, but he seems to have done very well with it. I'm more conservative, yet Doug, Nicole, and I live comfortably. Will and I are similar on most everything else."

"Why hasn't Will married someone by now?" Renee blurted out. "What's the real reason? He's everything a girl could possibly want and he doesn't appear to have any faults. What's going on with him?"

Kim considered the questions and thought for a moment. "He's met a lot of girls over the years but he has this impossibly high standard that none of them can live up to."

"What do you mean?"

She paused. How much would Will want her to discuss about his personal life? This was important enough to share with her friend at this point in their relationship so she continued.

"I told you that years ago, he met a girl and they hit it off perfectly. Over time, he felt she was everything he had ever dreamed of and he really believed she was the one girl that was meant for him. I believe he was even planning to ask this girl to marry him, but something happened."

"What was it?"

"I don't know the details, but he stopped seeing her and has never been the same. His life changed at that moment and I think he compares every girl he meets to the one girl who made such an impression on his life. The problem is he put that girl on a pedestal and nobody can compare to what he saw in her."

"Wow. How romantic and how sad."

"Yeah, and if he keeps this idealized image of this first

true love, he may never find someone who will meet up to those standards. I don't remember if she was really as perfect as he thought she was, since I was still a young teen-ager at the time, but even if she was, he needs to get over it and move on with his life."

"Was she pretty?"

"Oh, yeah. She was a knockout. I remember thinking she looked better than any movie actress I'd ever seen."

"How can I compete with that?"

"Renee, I've seen the way he is since he's started going out with you and I've heard the things he says about you. You make him feel like he did with this dream girl and I believe you are the one who can replace this girl from his past."

"I don't know about that."

"I do. His personality has changed for the better since he's met you and I honestly think you're the one he's been searching for all these years."

Tears streamed from Renee's eyes as she considered these words. Kim had just given her a lot to think about. Maybe she had never made anyone feel the way Will felt and it would give her the confidence to continue pursuing her brother at all costs. She didn't know why, but she was convinced that Will's life was better with Renee in it. She was indeed the woman Will needed and he was the perfect match for her. Kim hoped it wasn't too late for them to get back together and make things work.

"What was her name," asked Renee without looking up.

"Ah, we don't go there. Just call her, 'She-who-must-not-be-named' and leave it at that. Will stops me if I even start to mention it."

They both laughed, but then Renee became serious. "I have my own faults and my own issues to deal with and I don't think it's fair to put them on your brother."

"Will has talked to me about that and he wants to help you

deal with whatever issues you face. He is a team player and would never let you face them by yourself. Give him a chance and you'll see what he can do for you."

Renee shook her head, her face still wet with tears. "I'm sure he would but I just don't think it's right for me to expect him to take care of my problems."

"Don't expect him to take care of your problems but let him if he wants to, okay?"

"He's in a class by himself and I'm a single-mom with strings attached. I would only be holding him down from what he really could be doing. I'm not the one."

"Will has faults of his own. He's been a bachelor for so long he's set in his ways. It may frustrate you sometimes but you can also have fun with it. Plus he's so used to getting everything he wants that he can be a spoiled brat. He can get anything he ever wanted, except for one thing. This dream girl who has eluded him for years is now within his grasp and he knows it. You're a gorgeous young woman with a beautiful daughter and despite what you think about yourself, you are a great catch for any guy, especially my big brother. You are that dream girl he wants so desperately. I wish you would realize it."

Renee looked away, wiping her eyes again. Kim had reached into her friend's heart. Hopefully, her insecurities would go away once and for all so she could live up to her potential.

# Chapter Twenty-Four

"**H**AVE YOU TWO EATEN LUNCH yet, or did your moms leave that for me?"

"No, we haven't had anything to eat, Uncle Will, and we're starving."

Rebecca added, "I'm so hungry I could eat an elephant," and both girls giggled.

"I'll bet you are. Well, I think I heard your mother say she had picked up some elephant for you both to eat for lunch, so we'll have that."

Rebecca said, "Eww! We're not really going to eat an elephant, are we?"

"No, if my mommy picked up an elephant, it would be a present for you, since you like elephants so much. Plus, I don't think anyone can pick up an elephant. They're too heavy."

Rebecca added, "And we wouldn't eat it either."

"Hmm. Whatever you say." Examining the contents of the refrigerator, Will asked, "Doesn't your mom buy anything good to eat, Nicole? I don't see any snake, frog, lizard, bear, squirrel, or possum. Did she forget to go grocery shopping?"

"You're gross, Uncle Will. We don't eat those kinds of animals," and both girls laughed.

"Then I guess you're stuck with a squid sandwich and worm pancakes again."

"We're not eating that!" exclaimed Rebecca, while making a face to help express her dislike of squids and worms.

"Wait a minute. She does have some chocolate chips in the pantry. That's one of the food groups, isn't it?"

Nicole and Rebecca looked at each other with wide eyes, both nodding their head in agreement and saying, "Yes."

"Wow, she has a bottle of Mountain Dew. That's my favorite drink. Your mother has better taste than I realized, Nicole."

"Yes, it's Mommy's favorite drink too, but she doesn't let us have any."

"What? Haven't you ever wondered why it's her favorite drink? You should try it and see for yourselves."

The girls looked at each other with smiles and Nicole said, "Okay."

Rummaging through the freezer, Will added, "Hey, there's bacon and hash browns here. Do you like those?"

"Those are for breakfast, Uncle Will. Don't you know anything?"

"On the contrary, my young know-it-all niece. I could make you bacon and chocolate chips for lunch and you could wash it down with Mountain Dew. What would you think of that?"

"Could we have a scrambled egg with it too?" asked Rebecca.

"Of course, my dear. Anything for you. Do you want to help me get everything ready for lunch?"

Nicole replied, "Sure. What can we do?"

"I can't remember where the plates are so if you two can set the table, I'll work some magic on the stovetop."

Nicole and Rebecca met and whispered something together, then went to work getting a step ladder out of the closet. Nicole positioned it and climbed up to get plates out of the cabinet and Rebecca set the table. They also found forks and put them out as well, while Will watched them proudly. He prepared his healthy lunch while his audience stood on the step ladder by the stove to see everything he did, Nicole on the top step and Rebecca on the bottom step, and within a few minutes, it was ready to eat.

The girls sat in their seats while Will scooped eggs onto each plate, put out several slices of bacon, then dished out some hash browns for everyone. He then opened a bag of chocolate chips and poured a bunch next to everyone's eggs while the girls turned to each other and laughed.

"I've never had bacon and eggs for lunch," said Rebecca.

"I've never had chocolate chips poured out on my plate either," added Nicole.

"If someone tells you that you can't eat bacon and eggs for lunch, now you can just tell them you've done it before," said Will.

"And if someone tells us we can't eat chocolate chips before they go into cookies, we can tell them we can," said Rebecca.

"Yes, and how do you like your drinks?" asked Will.

"Mountain Dew is my new favorite drink," replied Nicole.

"Mine too," added Rebecca.

"You have excellent taste, young ladies."

Nicole asked about some of the interesting things Will had eaten in China, Malaysia, and Sweden, and Will gladly told them about his adventures on the other side of the world. Every once in a while, the girls erupted with laughter or responded simultaneously with "Eww." Will acted as though everyone ate duck tongue, reindeer sausage, insects, fish cheeks, or tuna belly, and pretended to be surprised when they revealed that neither of them had ever tried these delicacies. It was a fun lunch, and it seemed as though the girls liked Will's cooking as well as his company.

The resemblance each of the girls had with their respective mothers was amazing. Nicole had long straight dark brown hair, just like her Kim, while Rebecca had long wavy blonde hair just like Renee. Even the facial structure and eyes of each girl were duplicates of their mothers'. The science of passing certain genes down through generations was indeed fascinating. Maybe someday he would be able to pass some of his genes and traits down to a little boy or girl of his own.

When they finished eating, Will said, "Now, I need to clean up our mess so we don't leave it for your mother to take care of. Do you think all of this can go into the dishwasher?"

"I think so," said Nicole.

Will proceeded to scrape off the plates and pans, then put them into the dishwasher.

"How much soap needs to go in here?"

Nicole asked, "Don't you use a dishwasher at your house?"

"No, I've never tried it. Ms. Sue always does it for me. It can't be that hard to figure out, right?"

"Who is Ms. Sue?" asked Rebecca.

"She's my assistant at my office and she helps me with a lot of things I don't have time to do. You'd like her."

"She's one of my mom's friends," added Nicole. "She has a little girl in pre-school."

Will added some soap, shut the door, and Nicole pushed a few buttons. Almost immediately, the dishwasher made noise and Will nodded at their accomplishment.

"See, anyone can do it."

The girls clapped excitedly as he bowed and he led them into the living room.

"You should come over more often, Uncle Will."

"I'd like that, Nicole. You two are great helpers. I couldn't have figured out all that without your help."

"You knew how to use the stove," Rebecca added.

"Well, I have to be able to cook myself something, don't

I? If I didn't, I would starve since I don't have anyone else to cook things for me. That's one of the few appliances I do know how to use."

Rebecca asked, "Would you read us some books?" as she climbed up on the couch.

Will sat next to her, and said, "Of course I would."

Nicole climbed up beside him as Rebecca handed him the first book.

He read to them with excitement in his voice and they laughed at his expressions and accents. Some characters had a deep voice, while others had the voice of a child. The girls laughed the most at his goofy voice, as well as the faces he made when he created some of the silly voices. He tried to get them to look at the pictures instead of watching his expressions, but they wouldn't listen.

Suddenly, Nicole screamed and pointed toward the kitchen. It was a mountain of bubbles, slowly oozing across the floor. Will put the book down and went to investigate, with the girls right behind him.

"I think you put too much bubble juice in the dishwasher," said Rebecca.

They all just stared at the advancing bubbles as Will stood there contemplating his options. Just then, the front door opened, while Kim and Renee walked in.

"Great timing," said Will sarcastically.

Nicole and Rebecca ran to them, full of squeals and laughter. Their mothers probably couldn't even understand what the girls said as they both filled in the details of the afternoon at the same time. They led Kim and Renee toward the kitchen where Will stood smiling.

"I can explain everything," said Will calmly as both ladies stared past him and gasped. "I think I put a little too much bubble juice in the dishwasher. I know you can't see the dishwasher but that's where these bubbles are coming from."

"Haven't you ever used a dishwasher, Will?" asked Kim.

"Uh, no I haven't."

"He said Ms. Sue always washes the dishes for him," commented Rebecca.

"Who is Ms. Sue?" asked Renee with a hint of anger.

"Don't worry," replied Kim. "She's Will's assistant at the office. I've known her and her husband for years. Will, you need to stop having someone else do everything for you. Sue is not your servant."

"Hey, I did this myself, didn't I?"

"Yes, but look what happened."

The girls giggled and ran around in the bubbles, while his sister gave Will the evil eye.

"Don't worry, I can fix this," said Will as he walked through the waist-high pile of bubbles to find the dishwasher. He slipped and disappeared for a second, but stood back up quickly and smiled.

Rebecca and Nicole squealed again and ran through the bubbles where Will stood trying to figure out how to stop the dishwasher.

"What's gotten into these girls?" Kim asked. "They're like wild animals."

"Uncle Will cooked us breakfast for lunch and let us have chocolate chips," said Nicole as she ran around the kitchen through the bubbles.

"And Mountain Dew is our new favorite drink," added Rebecca as she followed her friend.

Kim closed her eyes and covered them with her hand, as Will found the button that stopped the dishwasher.

"There we are. That turned it off," said Will as he looked sheepishly at Renee and Kim. "Why don't you two go sit in the other room for a minute with the girls and read them a book or two? I'll clean up the bubbles."

Kim watched the girls running around slipping hysterically on the floor and said, "I think they're so wired they won't be able to sit still to read a book right now, Will."

He watched the little girls zip around the kitchen and said, "I didn't think caffeine and sugar really affected kids like this. It doesn't seem to do anything to me."

Renee's face was plastered with a big smile, but she covered it up with her hand and turned to walk out of the kitchen so nobody could see it. Kim, however, didn't smile or even look at him as she took the hands of Rebecca and Nicole led them into the living room.

Alone in the kitchen, he stared at the roomful of suds.

"Another fine mess I've gotten myself into," he mumbled to himself.

# Chapter Twenty-Five

WILL ARRIVED BACK AT HIS OF-fice and Sue asked, "So, how did every-thing go this afternoon?"

"Don't ask."

"Too late. I already did. What happened?"

"The kids and I had a good time."

"Well, that's great news, isn't it?"

"Yeah, we had fun, but right before Kim and Renee re-turned home, the dishwasher practically exploded. I've never seen anything like it before."

"What do you mean? They don't just explode."

Will sat on the edge of Sue's desk and looked her in the eyes. "We had put the dishes in and started the beast, but after we had gone in the other room to read some books, one of the kids screamed. Bubbles poured out and filled up the kitchen."

Sue laughed. "You must have put way too much dish-washer soap in it."

"It's not that funny. Kim is really mad at me."

"I'll give her a call and straighten things out."

"No, she also said I need to stop relying on you to bail me out of things and do everything for me."

"Well, well, well. That's exactly what I've been telling you for a long time."

"Do I treat you like a servant?"

"Interesting question. Did it come from your sister?"

"Yes, but I don't treat you that way, do I?"

"Uh, yes. Sometimes I feel like you think you're a little too important to handle the daily things that need to be done."

"What do you mean?"

"Who makes all of your travel reservations, dinner reservations, buys cards and gifts for your dates, takes care of your coffee, everything in your office, schedules home repairs, office repairs, …"

"Alright, I get your point. But you're a highly paid personal assistant. Much more than an executive secretary. It's all in your job description."

"I realize that, but a lot of this stuff you could do yourself. When you go overseas, you always hire drivers rather than drive yourself around. I'm surprised you don't have a chauffeur here in town."

"Actually, I was going to ask you to start looking into chauffeurs next week."

"I knew it."

"I'm only kidding. I like driving my own car around here. It's just that I have a busy schedule and I don't have time for these little inconveniences."

"These little inconveniences are what most people have to deal with every day. You should come down off of your pedestal and try it sometime."

"Are you saying you want a raise?"

"No, I'm just saying you need to be able to figure out how to do some of these things yourself and not rely on me to be there to take care of your every need. I've told you I might start to stay home more with my daughter in the afternoons after school and where would that leave you?" Will sat there staring at the floor for a few seconds. "You're right. I'll start doing some of these things myself."

Just then, Renee walked in the front door with Rebecca.

Will stood up and walked toward them.

"What brings my two favorite ladies to my humble office this fine afternoon?"

"We were in the neighborhood and wanted to see where you worked," replied Renee. Looking at his assistant, she asked, "Are you Sue?"

"Yes, I'm Will's personal assistant. You must be Renee and Rebecca?"

"Yes. It's nice to meet you. I've heard a lot about you, especially that you usually take care of the dishwasher for Will."

Sue laughed and turned to Will, who pretended to smile, while Renee glanced up at him and laughed as well.

"Well, you may be interested to know that I plan to learn how to properly fill a dishwasher with bubble juice so it won't happen again," Will replied.

"Your sister was mad for a little while but once you left, we all had a good laugh about it."

"I'm glad to hear it. It could have happened to anyone, you know."

"No, that could only happen to you," Sue said to Will.

"Never again."

"Anyway, Kim said I'd find you at work today." She caught Sue's eye and asked, "Does he usually make you work on a Saturday?"

Sue laughed. "No, Will has a big presentation to make on Monday, so I'm helping him get it ready today. He pays me extra for these kinds of inconveniences."

"Do I?" Will asked, as Sue slapped his arm.

"You'd better."

"Ms. Kim asked Nicole how chocolate chips got into the peanut butter jar," blurted out little Rebecca.

"Oh? And what did Nicole tell her mother?" Will asked.

"We all laughed and then Nicole said it was you."

"That tattle tale. I'll get her next time I see her."

"Actually, Nicole justified it very well," Renee added. "She said the peanut butter factory must have forgotten to add the chocolate chips, so you did it for them."

"Good for her. She's absolutely right," replied Will with a nod.

Renee put her hand on Will's arm. "Will, I wanted to see if you would like to go shopping with me tomorrow. I need to find a few dresses like this one I'm wearing, and thought you might like to help me pick them out."

"I'd love to. This really is a great looking dress, by the way. I wanted to say more about it when I saw you at Kim's house, but…"

"That's fine. I forgive you. You did mention it earlier and I appreciated it."

Those words were music to Will's ears. She wasn't mad at him anymore. He still had a chance with her after their lunch experience.

"What time do you want me to pick you up?"

"How about 1:00?"

"Perfect."

"Rebecca and I need to get going. Besides, I can see how busy you are today so you can get back to work. See you tomorrow. Nice meeting you, Sue."

"It's good to meet you too. Bye Rebecca."

Rebecca waved as she looked at Sue and Will, and he waved back at her.

As they exited through the front door, Will said, "Life is good."

"Would you like me to call and remind you about tomorrow's 1:00 appointment?" Sue asked.

"Yes, wait, no. I can do it myself." He picked up his phone and stared at it for a moment, then handed it to Sue. "Would you setup something on my phone to alarm about 12:00? That will remind me I need to get ready to pick up

Renee by 1:00."

"Here, let me show you how to do it, then you can do it yourself the next time."

"Great idea."

"Are you sure there's not a meeting after church tomorrow that would cause you to be late?"

Will paused for a moment, but replied, "No, nothing this week. I think we're good."

Sue pushed some buttons and within a few seconds, she had a reminder set for him.

"Excellent. I need to get some work done this afternoon before Monday's presentation. Would you mind picking up something for Renee?"

"You must be kidding."

"No, just this once. I really have a lot to finish up and I could use your help. You know what girls like."

"Yes, I do. Consider it done," she said as he walked to his office and shut the door. Under her breath she added, "I'll make sure this will be the last time you ever ask me to buy a present for one of your girls."

# Chapter Twenty-Six

**R**ENEE HAD EASILY TALKED **WILL** into going shopping and he initially wondered if it would be something he'd regret. He had been shopping with women before and had some ideas, all negative, about what it would be like today. Maybe she would be different.

The first clothes store was not too bad, and he watched as she picked out dresses and shoes to try on. She seemed excited to have him there with her and he enjoyed experiencing her animated expressions. She was gorgeous to look at, and he nodded, staring at her in admiration as she went through outfit after outfit.

"That one looks great Renee. Let's get it."

She examined her prize, frowning and tilting her head slightly, but replied without even turning to Will, "No, I think I'd like to check another store to see if they have anything better than this."

Will shook his head, surprised she wouldn't buy that dress, but went along with her as she strolled out of the store. She appeared to walk on air, as if she was in a fairy tale, and he didn't want to rain on her parade. He just followed behind as she flitted between the clothes racks and out the front door and then caught up to walk beside her. She grabbed his arm and wrapped her arms around it as she almost danced with every step.

He glanced up and saw another woman's clothes store and felt her leading him toward the entrance. She talked continuously, but it was challenging for him to make out everything she said. Her conversations bounced from one topic to the next so it was always difficult to follow her train of thought. She was in such a great mood that he enjoyed watching her chatter away without paying attention to the words. She smiled, talked, looked at him, talked, and her eyes sparkled the whole time. He only hoped she hadn't asked him a question which expected a response, since he had just tuned her out and only heard a few words here and there. She seemed happy so he grinned and kept walking with her.

Inside the store, she let go and walked to a section of clothes that must have caught her attention and he slowed down to see what she selected. Everything she picked out would have been great on her, but for some unknown reason, she wouldn't go try all of the outfits on.

"Why don't you see how it looks on you?"

"I don't know. The colors on it make me appear washed out. Let me go over there and see how that one is."

He followed her to the next section and she excitedly held up part of a red dress to examine.

"Aren't you going to buy anything today?"

"If I find the right one, I'll buy it."

"Well what's wrong with this dress?"

"It's a bit too far below the knees. I like it to stop right at the knee."

She kept exploring and holding up dresses against her while Will eagerly nodded, but each one had some unknown flaw that caused it to be put back on the rack. If she did try one on, there was something she didn't like about how it made her look, and she moved on to the next outfit, the next rack, the next store.

"How about if we stop and get an ice cream? Are you ready for a break?"

She gazed into his eyes and gave him a smile that made him forget about his frustrations over the past couple of hours regarding her inability to find a dress to purchase.

"Alright, I could use some chocolate."

She gave him a kiss on the cheek and they headed toward the sweet shop.

"I'm sorry if I seem too choosy. I just feel self-conscious about my appearance and I'm afraid these dresses won't look good on me."

Will stood in front of her and locked eyes. "You are the most beautiful girl in this entire mall and you were a knockout in everything you tried on today." She glanced away briefly, then stared into his eyes again. "I would have been happy with the first outfit you picked out."

She hugged him and he returned the hug.

"You must have poor eyesight or forgot to wear contacts today."

"I have perfect vision and I don't wear contacts. I wish you'd believe me when I tell you how great you look."

She stepped back to see his face again and replied, "It's just that nobody has ever told me those things so it's hard for me to believe you're not just saying them to make me feel good."

He put his hands on each of her cheeks, then put his face close to hers and kissed her on the lips. "All you have to do is look in the mirror and you'll see what I mean."

They stepped up to the counter and he said, "She'll have a hot fudge sundae with chocolate ice cream and marshmallow, and I'll have a two scoop cone of chocolate chip ice cream."

She held onto his arm and said, "You ordered for me again?"

"Yes, my dear. I know exactly what you wanted and

you'll eat it whether you like it or not."

"Yes, sir."

The ice cream lady handed them their treats and Will led Renee to an empty table by the wall. She sampled a spoonful of her ice cream, closed her eyes, and made "Mmmmm" noises, so he assumed she must have enjoyed his selection.

Will tasted his ice cream and noticed an older couple standing in the mall between stores. The older woman kissed her husband then went into the store by herself, leaving the man to find a seat in the middle of the mall. He sat and watched people walk by and considered the man's plan.

Renee looked at him and said, "I want to apologize for walking away from you the other day."

Will was elated, but held in his feelings. "I understand. I really haven't had many long-term relationships, and with my travels, I've just dated here and there. I'm sorry if I made you feel as though you weren't the most important person in the world to me."

She hesitated, but added, "I have some extreme mood changes sometimes, and I let my hormones get the best of me that day. I shouldn't have overreacted."

"No, I understand. I was inconsiderate of your feelings, and I'll never let it happen again."

What did her silence mean at this moment? It seemed to be positive, since she had a smile and took another bite of her sundae. What he wouldn't give to be inside her mind right now.

"Will, look at that store. I've wanted to go there, so let's check it out next."

Will glanced over his shoulder, while stuffing the ice cream in his mouth and he nodded to her. He then pointed to her left and asked, "Have you ever been in that one there?"

When she turned, he stole a scoop of her hot fudge before she turned back and he quickly covered his mouth with his cone so she couldn't tell he had just swiped some of her treat.

"Which one? The painting store?"

"Yes, they have some reproductions of the classic impressionist art that I have in my office."

"No, I don't think I've ever stepped inside. Once I saw the prices, I just kept on walking."

They finished eating, stood up, and meandered into the middle of the mall. Will saw the old man relaxing in peace on a cushioned chair. It was inspiring.

"You go ahead and check out the clothes shop. I'm going to just sit here and wait for you. Do you mind?"

She looked up at him and said, "Oh, okay. No, I don't mind. I'll be back in a few minutes."

It was like celebrating a victory, but he held it in as she kissed him on the cheek. He couldn't help but think about how he saw the same scene with the older couple just a few minutes ago, and he went over to sit down beside the older man. Obviously, this man knew what he was doing and had some experience dealing with women's shopping habits. Maybe he could learn something from this guy.

"Mind if I join you here?"

The older man turned to Will and shook his head. "Not at all. I find that my wife can wander around aimlessly but if I sit here in the middle, she always comes back. She's like a boomerang. She gets it all out of her system and I don't feel like I've been dragged around all day."

"Good plan."

"Plus, I get to enjoy the scenery here until she returns."

Will glanced around at the different shops and noticed one store in particular seemed to be exceptionally busy. It was called, 'The Purple Giraffe.' He compared the crowds going into the other shops with that one but there was no comparison. That store had the most people's attention by far. He took out his cell phone and punched some numbers.

"Hi, this is Will Sayre. What can you tell me about a clothes store called 'The Purple Giraffe'? Is it a chain?" He waited a few seconds, and then replied, "Really? What do the shares sell for now?" Another pause, then "Very interesting. Go ahead and buy me a thousand shares." He listened for a minute, then responded, "Great. I appreciate it. Talk to you later."

The two men sat in silence for a while and Will asked his elder some questions. Will laughed as the older gentleman explained some of the things he had learned about women over the years, and it was obvious this man had a great understanding of their behaviors. It was an enjoyable discussion as the man shared his gleaned wisdom with the rookie. Twenty years from now, this man would be long gone, but Will would not forget him and his humor. The more they talked, the more Will pictured himself with Renee thirty years into the future. Maybe he would be the older man someday, sitting on a bench in a mall and explaining to a young newlywed how to have a long happy marriage with a woman.

Soon enough, the man's wife walked toward them and the older man stood up to hold her hand. He kissed her cheek, waved back at Will, and then walked side by side with his wife. Will had just learned an important life lesson about how to go shopping with a woman, plus several more tips that may come in handy with Renee down the road. He looked at the various stores around him, noticing the crowds flocking in to one specific entrance and feeling good about his recent purchase.

He relaxed, sitting there as the rest of the world seemed rush to get somewhere and then out of the crowd came Renee. She beamed and headed directly for him, by far the most amazing woman he had ever seen. He stood up and took her hand, then kissed her on the cheek just like the old man did with his wife.

"Hey, you must have found something you like."

Her eyes sparkled and she held up two bags, "Yes, they have the best selection and everything was on sale."

Will said, "Well if you're happy, I'm happy," and merged arm and arm into the stream of people walking through the mall.

Stepping outside into the sunlight felt good with the cool wind blowing the new green leaves in the trees, and he squeezed her hand as they walked to his convertible and climbed in.

"It's a great day to drive with the top down, isn't it?" she asked.

"Yes, it is."

He drove from the mall toward Renee's apartment and picked up speed to merge with the Interstate traffic that flew by them. As soon as he reached the speed limit and steadied the car, the nightmarish sound of squealing tires and crunching metal filled the air. Will instinctively slammed his brakes in response to the car in front of him doing the same. Renee screamed and closed her eyes as more crash sounds took over the peaceful drive for several seconds. It appeared to go on forever, but an eerie silence soon took over as all traffic stopped.

"Are you okay?" Will asked as smoke hovered above their heads.

She slowly opened her eyes and said, "I think so. How did we miss the red car that hit the brakes?"

He looked up and the car in front of him was only inches from his bumper. Will jumped out to see what happened on the road. The car behind him had barely missed his rear bumper. Will's car was untouched.

"Are you sure you're not hurt, Renee?"

"I'm fine. I just can't believe you didn't get hit by the car behind us either."

"I'm going to see if anyone needs help. I'll be right back."

Will walked up to the car in front of him and as far as he could see, the road was filled with cars and trucks that crashed into each other. People stepped out of their vehicles to check out the damage, but it seemed as though nobody up there was seriously hurt. He turned to Renee, who gave him a weak smile, and he walked to the car behind him. Back there, probably a dozen more cars had crashed, some with steam pouring out of the hood. Fortunately, none of those people appeared to be injured either, but the damage to the front and rear of these cars was extensive.

A policeman drove up on the side of the road and slowed to a stop beside Will's car.

"How did you manage to not get hit? You're right in the middle of this pile up."

"Hi, Officer. I really don't know. Just lucky I guess," Will replied.

The policeman glanced at Renee, then looked up ahead at the line of cars wrecked in front of them. "I think someone was watching out for you, man. You're the only one in this mess that didn't get hit. I need to get a statement from you, but then you're free to go."

"No problem."

Will answered several questions while Renee listened and nodded when asked if she agreed with some of Will's comments. Then the officer talked to another policeman who had checked to see if anyone needed medical attention.

"Thanks for your time, Mr. Sayre," the policeman said. "If you can drive around these vehicles, you can turn off at Brentwood Avenue by the black truck up there and be on your way."

Will nodded and slowly pulled around the car in front, driving cautiously beside the line of damaged automobiles. He looked over at Renee, who stared at each one they went by and he said, "Sorry for the excitement on the way home. Hopefully, it will be an uneventful trip the rest of the way."

Without turning to him, Renee replied, "There must have been at least twenty cars in this crash. How did you not even get a scratch?"

"I guess that policeman was right. Someone's watching out for us," Will said with a laugh, but he noticed Renee's return gaze remained very serious.

# Chapter Twenty-Seven

**T**HE TAPPING OF SUE'S KEYBOARD filled the air as Will concentrated on the presentation he planned to give to one of his customers later in the week. She was much better at typing up reports and putting together slide shows, so it was good to have her help with this one. So far, he had only found a few things that needed to be changed, so the day was off to a great start. His cell phone interrupted his focus, but it could only be someone he wouldn't mind talking to now.

"Good morning, Renee. What can I do for you?"

"Good morning. You have to be the most romantic man I have ever met."

"I'll bet you say that to all the guys," Will replied with a toothy grin as he turned his chair to gaze out his window. "What did I do this time?"

"I just received something in the mail from you and it appears to be very special."

"It is special and you're very welcome. I wanted to let you know how much I enjoy being with you."

"I've never done anything like this before. Are you sure I can do it?"

Will paused for a moment. What was she talking about? "Not sure you can do what?"

"I've never gone ballroom dancing before. I'm afraid I

might have two left feet and will embarrass you."

The smile left Will's face as he turned to look at Sue. She seemed to be trying to hide her face but was clearly laughing hysterically at her desk.

"Ballroom dancing. Is that right?" replied Will with no emotion.

"It sure sounds like a lot of fun though, so I can't wait to take lessons with you tonight."

"Tonight. Ballroom dancing. Sounds like fun," muttered Will as he glared at Sue while she kept her face turned away from him. He crinkled up a piece of paper and stood up, walking to his office doorway.

"Do I need to wear some kind of special shoes or just regular heels?"

"I'm not sure. I guess I'll have to call and find out. Do you have the phone number handy?" asked Will just before throwing the wad of paper at Sue. She ducked and quickly made her way to the ladies room before Will could reach her.

"No, but I'll text it to you in a few minutes. I can't wait. I've always wanted to learn how to waltz."

"Well, I guess this will be your lucky day," said Will, who had walked past Sue's desk and now stood beside the bathroom door. "I'll give you a call as soon as I find out more about these ballroom dancing lessons." Will placed heavy emphasis on 'ballroom dancing' to make sure Sue heard him clearly through the door. "I have to work a little later tonight, so I won't be able to pick you up for dinner beforehand, so I'll just have to come over about 6:30 to get you."

"So you do actually work. That's fine. I'll arrange for a babysitter to come over about 6:15 and be with Rebecca tonight. Thanks again. I really look forward to waltzing with you."

"Yes, it should be a blast. Talk to you later."

Will stood silently, listening for any sounds coming from

inside the restroom. It was quiet. Had she slipped out some-how? "Oh, Sue. Do you know anything about me giving Renee some ballroom dancing lessons?"

She calmly came out of the ladies room with no expres-sion and walked past Will on her way back to the reception desk. "Yes, I believe you had asked me to send her something women would like, so I did."

"I meant something like chocolates or flowers, not dance lessons."

"Gee, I guess this is one example where it would have been better if you had picked out your own gift for your date rather than ask me to do it."

"Oh, I see where this is heading. Well, you got me with this one and I won't let it happen again. Ballroom dancing. How can I get out of this?"

Sue looked up at Will and said, "Just do it, and I guarantee you two will enjoy dancing together. It doesn't matter what anyone thinks. Have fun with her."

Will turned and walked back to his desk as he received a text from Renee. He stared at his phone and called the num-ber to find out what kind of shoes they needed to wear for their lessons. He texted the answer back to Renee, reminding her that he would pick her up at 6:30.

He had never even considered ballroom dancing as a pos-sibility, but it might not be too bad. As long as he wasn't so terrible they asked him to leave, he would be able to hold Renee close to him, face to face. They may actually have a good time together. With these thoughts, how could he focus on his presentation? All he could picture now was Renee in a colorful short dress and heels while he waltzed her around the room.

It took everything he had to block out these images to spend the rest of the day concentrating on his job. This never used to be a problem, but she was the biggest distraction he had ever known. Not in a bad way, of course, but he realized more and more that he couldn't focus on work now that Renee was in his life. She affected him like no other woman, at least in the past five years, and he liked it.

Will wrapped up his presentation by 5:30 and Sue was on her way out. She said, "Have a great time tonight. Remember to make it fun for you both."

"In the morning, I'll let you know how things went. You'll either get a raise or you'll be fired."

Sue laughed and waved to him as she walked through the front door toward her car.

Will went upstairs to get freshened up. He turned on a CD player and listened to a collection of old songs from the 1960's while changing clothes. He forgot to ask if he needed to dress up, but figured casual business clothes would do. He took his Miata convertible since it would just be the two of them and a Beatles song immediately played when he started up the car. That was not so unusual, since Will always had one of their CD's in his car. He almost opened the roof but presumed that Renee might have done something fancy with her hair and wouldn't want it messed up.

He parked and walked to her apartment, knocking on the door. Should he have brought flowers? No, dance lessons should be enough. Renee opened the door and stood there for a moment while Will's eyes took in her appearance. Something was different.

"Is anything wrong?" she asked.

"No, I just can't believe you can look better and better every time I see you."

"I decided on a classy look tonight, with a new hairstyle and a longer skirt. I hope you don't mind."

"Not at all. It fits you perfectly." Will couldn't take his eyes off of her as she led him into her living room. He looked forward to spending the rest of the evening with her even more now. How could she change her styles and be so good in every one?

"This is Debbie. She's going to be with Rebecca while we go out.

"Hi, I'm Will."

"Hi, Mr. Sayre. They've told me all about you," replied Debbie.

Rebecca ran out of her bedroom and said to Will, "Have fun dancing with my mommy."

"I sure will. And when I learn how to do it, I'm going to dance with you. Be good while we're out."

"I'm always good," said Rebecca.

Renee said something to Debbie, kissed her daughter, and then led Will to the front door, waving at the two girls.

Will opened the car door for Renee, eyeing the patterns on her dress as she sat down inside. As Will sat in the driver's seat and started driving, he said, "I love your hair. And that dress is great on you. The colors are perfect."

"Thanks. This is one of the outfits we bought Sunday. I knew you liked some of the styles from the sixties, so I almost went with a retro theme from the sixties. I borrowed a mini-skirt and go-go boots from Kim, but changed my mind at the last minute."

"My little sister has a miniskirt and go-go boots? I've never seen her wear anything like that before. She has good taste."

"You'd be surprised at how similar you two are. I can certainly tell you're related."

Will glanced at her as she looked back at him and he was mesmerized. He had better keep his eyes on the road though. He could just imagine her in a sixties outfit and it drove him wild. It didn't take long to get to the dance studio and he quickly went around the car to help her out. He offered his arm to escort her across the parking lot and into the studio, feeling good about being here with her. He would probably make a fool out of himself, but it didn't matter. She was spectacular and he wanted to hold her tonight.

They were paired up together with a young lady who gave them some of the basics in private lessons. She demonstrated some steps, then had Will and Renee try them. Standing so close together, the alluring aroma of Renee's perfume captivated Will and he kept moving his face closer to her hair whenever he got the opportunity. With every attempt, she smiled and pushed him back into dance position. This was proving to be an enjoyable experience.

The dance instructor was talented and actually made Will feel as if he could waltz with Renee. He had problems figuring out how to properly lead and make them move together smoothly, but the instructor helped him learn some useful techniques. Being an engineer, he had a logical left-brain tendency, so dancing didn't come natural for him. He kept forgetting his steps and was a little stiff while Renee performed gracefully. Hopefully, she wouldn't be discouraged with his failures. At least he hadn't stepped on her feet at all. He just couldn't remember his steps.

After an hour of lessons, Will had improved and the two of them waltzed beautifully together. He would probably forget how to do this the next week when they returned for their second out of four lessons. They thanked their instructor and laughed all the way out to Will's car.

"This was so much fun. Thanks for planning this out for us. I can't wait to come back next week."

Should he tell her it was Sue's idea and not his? He stayed silent as he opened the door for Renee.

"I have to admit I had a great time," Will revealed. "I wasn't so sure at first."

His date talked all the way home but as usual, Will couldn't follow the conversation very well. She seemed to bounce from one topic to another, so he just listened and waited for her to sound like she expected a response from him. He was getting pretty good at trying to follow her discussions and responding at the right time.

At Renee's apartment, Will walked her to the door and she turned to face him under the porch light.

"I was so proud to be with you tonight," said Will. "You did such a great job on the dance floor and it made me feel good to be seen with you. You look incredible."

"I'm glad you like it. I haven't had this much fun, since…" she paused. "Probably never."

The dim porch light on her makeup made her seem like a movie star from the 1940's and he lost himself for a moment as he stared at her face. She was certainly a keeper. He pulled her close and kissed her ruby lips, breathing in her perfume. This was the most passionate kiss he had experienced in years. He wrapped his arms around her and squeezed her body close to his, moving his lips along hers as he adjusted his head. It would be easy to just keep doing this but he had to stop. He pulled away from her, standing face to face, while she gazed up at him.

"I'd better get going. You have too much power over me when you make yourself up like this and give me such a great evening."

"I guess I don't have enough power over you if you're able to just leave like that," she replied, captivating him with sad eyes.

He kissed her on the lips one last time. "I'll be over for dinner tomorrow night, okay?"

"I can't wait. I look forward to cooking a meal for you before you have to go out of town."

He ran out to his car as she stood at her front door waving at him. Sue definitely deserved a promotion for this.

# Chapter Twenty-Eight

**R**ENEE HAD CONCERNS ABOUT talking to Will regarding his past, especially mentioning other women again, and wanted to make sure she didn't come across as a jealous witch like she did the last time she drilled him about his past relationships. After learning about the unmentionable girl from Will's sister, it intrigued her and she wanted to find out if Will would ever truly be able to have a close relationship with another woman. It's possible Will wouldn't even entertain the thought of sharing these details with her and she expected that. However, she had to try. It sure seemed as though he wanted to be in a close relationship with her.

She raced around her apartment, picking up clutter and cleaning up minor messes, while she hummed to a song on the CD player to get her mind off of her nerves. The last thing she wanted to do was scare off this man who appeared to be so perfect for her, but she needed to understand what made him tick.

The doorbell rang as her heart stopped momentarily before her heart rate increased dramatically. She glanced toward the door, but ran to the mirror in her room to check her face. Smiling at how good her new dress made her feel, she wiped her eyes to make sure they weren't moist before greeting him at the door. This could either be the last time he wanted to see her or the beginning of something special in her life.

Renee ran to the front door, footsteps not even keeping up with the drumming of her heart. Opening the door with excitement, she stared up into his eyes and melted when he returned her smile. Why did he have such power over her? He's just another man, isn't he? No, he's more than any other man. This one had to be Mr. Right.

"You look unbelievable! Let me see the whole presentation."

He took her hand and spun her around as her dress spread out like a flower and his eyes took it all in. He stared at her shoes, her dress, her hair, and finally into her eyes, never removing the smile from his face. He was obviously extremely pleased and that made Renee's day. Maybe she had it after all.

He hugged her and gave her a wonderful kiss that warmed up her entire body while she kept her eyes closed to savor the moment. When he stopped and stood back, she didn't want to open them, but forced herself to look up at him again. He gazed around the room and she automatically did the same to see if he would find anything out of place. The apartment was great, so she had nothing to be concerned about.

"You're just in time because dinner will be ready in a couple of minutes. I didn't leave you any time to be late."

"What if I was stuck in traffic?"

"Doesn't matter. You'd be in the doghouse, boy!"

He laughed and asked, "Is there anything I can do to help you get ready?"

"The only thing I'll let you do is sit on the couch and wait for me to call you. If you're in the kitchen, you'll see all of my secret recipes and hidden techniques I used to prepare a wonderful dinner, and I'd have to kill you."

Will made his way to the couch, sitting down as he stared at her with great interest. "Well, I certainly wouldn't want to put you in that kind of position. I'll wait here. But for the record, I want you to remember I offered to help."

"Duly noted, but offer is declined. Stay seated until I call you. Sit, boy, sit. Good boy."

He glanced around the room. The music in the background was a familiar Beatles song and she sang along quietly while setting the table. People told her she had a good singing voice, but this was the first time she had sung out loud in front of him. Hopefully, he wouldn't mind. Somehow, she seemed to know the words to that classic song. Maybe it had been in her subconscious mind after hearing it many years ago but had been shut out.

"You have better taste than I realized," Will commented. "This song isn't the typical garbage played on the radio these days. And your voice is awesome."

"Yes, well I do appreciate great music when I hear it. Actually, I listened this CD you gave me after you lectured me about my tastes in music, and I honestly agree with you. They did write some beautiful music."

"Wow! Will you marry me?"

Renee held her breath as she considered what she had just heard. "What?"

"I'm just kidding. It's just so difficult to find someone who appreciates the classics, and I figured if I ever found someone who had these same tastes as me, I'd better marry her and keep her for the rest of my life."

What had Will's sister had told her about Will's search for the right girl all these years? She smiled at the fact that she had just won points with him in her taste of music and quickly finished setting the table to get the meal ready for them.

"Dinner is served."

He stood up, but his eyes didn't connect with hers. He appeared to take in the aromas, closing his eyes, and finally looked directly into hers as he walked close to her.

"This smells delicious. I am really impressed with everything you've done today."

"What, this old thing? It's just something I throw together when I don't care who's coming to dinner."

He laughed and held her hand as he leaned over and kissed her on the cheek. "Well, I'm glad you invited me."

They both sat down and had a perfect dinner together. When they finished, she led him into her living room.

"You sit here and watch a baseball game or whatever you guys like to do, while I clean up the kitchen."

Will protested, "I can help you clean up. It's no problem."

"No, I insist. You relax here and I'll be back in a few minutes. It won't take long."

"Okay, but I want to go on record that I offered to help."

"Duly noted, but offer denied. Again."

★★★★★

Will sat on the sofa and clicked on the TV, scrolling through the channels for a few seconds before leaving it one with an old movie. Hmm. Sean Connery and Natalie Wood. What a unique combination. He watched it for a few moments, while glancing over at Renee in the kitchen. Was she testing him about the cleanup and he failed by not insisting he help her? She whistled a happy tune, so that was good.

The movie wasn't a classic, but it kept him interested while he waited. He didn't realize Natalie Wood spoke Russian. Renee walked in and sat beside him as he reached to turn off the TV.

"You don't have to turn it off. It looks interesting. Do you want to watch it for a few minutes? I like Natalie Wood."

"You like old movies?" Will asked.

"Oh yes, those are my favorites."

Wow. A very good sign. Old movies were about the only ones he liked. "Fine. We'll watch it for a few minutes."

They both sat back, arm to arm, and she leaned her head

over onto his shoulder.

The movie had some characters who spoke Russian and the English translation appeared in tiny lettering at the bottom of the screen. Will had never seen a TV this small and had a difficult time reading the subtitles, even with his good vision.

"What do you think they're saying?" he asked.

"You don't know? Here, let me translate for you." Renee gave it her best Russian accent and continued. "Ivan, do you want glass of milk?"

Will laughed and peeked at her, but she kept staring at the TV with a hint of a tight-lipped smile. He responded back with his own translation in a deep Russian accent. "This not good time for milk. These men are trying to kill me."

"But you look thirsty," Renee continued.

"What do you mean? This is my scared look because they almost shot my face off."

Renee laughed and replied, "I'll bring you some anyway."

"No, milk is sissy drink. Real man drinks Mountain Dew."

She laughed again and responded with a seductive Russian voice, "Milk makes you handsome and strong. I would very much like to see you drink glass of milk."

Will laughed and shook his head. In his normal voice, Will asked, "Why are you talking so much about milk?"

"I'm just translating as I hear it," Renee responded, still with a Russian accent.

"Oh, okay."

"I really am thirsty for tall glass of chocolate milk," she continued in Russian form. "Would you like one too?"

"Ya, if you insist," Will replied with his best Russian accent.

Renee quickly got up and went to the kitchen, made some noise stirring the milk, and returned with two tall glasses of chocolate milk. Before sitting down, she shut off the TV.

"Will, I need to know more about you, but if I get too personal, please let me know."

"It's already too personal. I'm leaving," said Will as he stood up. "No, just kidding," he continued as he sat down and was punched in the arm by his host. "You can ask me anything about me, and if I don't know the answer, you can ask my personal assistant, my sister, or my friend Patrick. They all know me better than I do."

"Have you ever been serious with a girl?"

"Well. Straight to the point." Will looked down for a moment, then continued. "As you know, I've dated a few times," to which she punched him again.

"More than a few times, buster."

"As I said, I have dated, but there's only been one time when I honestly felt like I had found the right girl for me."

"What was she like?"

"I had crushes growing up, but she was the first girl who really grabbed my attention. While other girls were cute, she was stunning, like a movie star from the Forties."

"Okay, that's enough. I get it."

"I was like the poor deer in *Bambi* when he found that female deer."

"What do you mean?"

"You know, I was 'twitterpated' by this girl."

"Twitterpated. Alright. Interesting description."

"Everything about her was magical and I wanted to be with her all the time."

"What happened?"

He paused and his thoughts carried him to a painful place. "For some reason, she didn't want to be with me anymore. It shattered me to pieces."

"What was the problem?"

"I never even asked her. I thought we would be together forever, and when she told me that, I was crushed. What could

I say to her? She must have had a good reason, but I didn't make an effort to find out what it was."

"You must know now what her reasons were, right?"

"No. I just figured she was in a league of her own and I wasn't worthy of being with someone as perfect as her."

"Will, that's ridiculous. You're the most amazing man I've ever met, and I feel as though I don't deserve being with a man like you."

"I appreciate the compliment, but back then I was probably just an immature boy who didn't impress the ladies very much. Today, I'm a little more refined, but I want you to know you are easily in the same class as her. You are as beautiful as an actress from the Forties and Fifties and just as classy."

"Give me a break. I'm not even …"

"Renee, don't say it. I've been a connoisseur of women for several years, and I see in you more than you can see in yourself. In addition to your physical beauty, you have a beauty in your heart that I haven't seen in any woman."

"You're a smooth talker, Will Sayre, but you overestimate me."

"I can't even begin to describe how you've affected me. Everything I've said so far is only the tip of the iceberg, and I look forward to getting to know you more and more."

"What if your mystery woman came back to you tomorrow? Would you jump at the opportunity?"

"Not a chance. She was once my dreamboat, but she married and moved on with her life. I carried on as well and have been guided to you. I can't even see myself with anyone other than you. I don't want to even imagine my life without you."

"How can you be so sure? There are a lot of women more attractive and witty than I."

"No, you're like a rare flower to which no other can compare. I don't want to even search elsewhere."

"Wow. What can I say to that? You make me feel more

special than anyone has ever tried, and I have to pinch myself sometimes to make sure I'm not dreaming."

"I feel the same way with you. I've been searching so long for someone who could make me feel 'twitterpated' again, and you are the only one."

She laughed. "It sounds so scientific it's over my head. I guess I need to watch *Bambi* again."

"Yes, then you'll understand what you do to me. Does that answer your questions?"

"For now."

She gave him a kiss on the lips, then stood up and walked into the kitchen with her empty glass. The more he thought about her, the more he realized he was truly falling for this woman.

# Chapter Twenty-Nine

**S**UE WALKED IN TO **W**ILL'S OFFICE and handed him a document he had asked for. He skimmed through it, satisfied all of the changes he requested had been made. She waited next to his desk when the door slammed and someone came in the front door, causing her peek around the corner to investigate.

"Oh, it's only you," she said when Chuck strolled by her desk.

"It's nice to see you too, Sue," he replied without stopping on his way to Will's office. "So are you sure you don't want me to make the trip to Amsterdam?"

"Hey, Chuck. No, I'll take care of that one since it's a quick trip. Sue made airline reservations for one of us to go to Seoul Saturday, and it's not me. I need you to work on the proposal for South Korea. You'll be out there for a week."

"Oh, right. That looks like a good one."

Sue stood in the doorway and asked Will, "Did you remember you're picking up Renee for dance lessons?"

Will cringed when she said that in front of Chuck. "I didn't forget. Thanks for the reminder."

Laughter came from deep within Chuck's insides but Will ignored it. "You've stooped to taking dance lessons with your dates now?"

"If you must know, yes, I've taken her dancing. She enjoys it, and I want to make her happy."

Sue gave them a smirk then headed back to her desk.

"It's just not very manly, my friend."

"Maybe that's why you've never married and have no prospects for a long term relationship."

"The last I checked," replied Chuck, "you hadn't married either and it seems you've dated more women than me this year."

Without looking up from writing Will replied, "Well, that was before I met Renee and started dating her exclusively."

"Good for you. Just don't get too close to me, though. I don't want any of it rubbing off in case it's contagious."

"No problem. I sent you the schedule for the Korea project so check it out and see if you notice any discrepancies."

"Alright. Thanks." Chuck stepped out of Will's office and went to his own office, closing the door behind him.

With Sue's help, Will finished up his presentation after lunch, verified his airline and hotel plans, then wrapped up his work for the week before 5:00.

Knocking on Chuck's door he said, "I'm out for most of this week. See you next Monday."

Chuck opened his door. "No, I need to leave for Seoul Saturday, so I'll be out all of next week. Maybe even the following week if I find myself a nice Korean comfort woman to keep me company over there."

Will shook his head. "Okay. See you when you get back. Remember, I'm only paying for one week."

"Have a good trip, Will," replied Chuck.

"You too."

Sue whispered to Will, "How do you get along with that guy? He's just the opposite of you."

"I appreciate the complement," replied Will and they both laughed. "Actually, he does have a good work ethic and he's really not such a bad guy. Unfortunately, I see some similarities between us, and I think deep down he may be searching for the right woman to settle down with. He'd never admit it, of course."

"Chuck just goes about it a little sleazier than you do. He gives me the creeps sometimes."

"If he ever gives you any problems, let me know."

"Don't worry. I have some mace that works very well, and I've been hoping to use it on him. Maybe someday."

Will laughed, ran upstairs to get freshened up, then rushed out the door with a quick wave to Sue as she finished up for the day as well. He sped over to Renee's and picked her up for a quick meal before the dance lessons started.

"Are you sure you want the top down?" asked Will. "It'll mess up your hair."

"No, I love the way it feels. Let's drive with it down tonight."

"Okay. I enjoy seeing your hair blowing in the wind, but I just wanted to make sure."

They stopped at another outdoor café before sunset and parked at the curb. Will escorted her from the car to the table and they sat down to order. They talked together about waltzing and laughed when they remembered getting all tangled up the last time. In almost no time, the waitress brought out their food.

"Where are you going Tuesday night?" she asked as they ate their soup and sandwiches. The wind had picked up and cooled off the city.

"Just a progress meeting in Amsterdam to see where the project's at. One month the customers come here for the meeting, and the next month I go out there."

She pulled a sweater over her shoulder to keep out the wind and watched his eyes. "Do you think you'll have time to take in some of the sights?"

"No, not this trip. I've been to Anne Frank's house on

Prinsengracht, and of course the Van Gogh and Rembrandt museums. It's a great city to walk or bicycle along the canals or take a canal tour by boat."

"Yeah, I've heard about what else goes on there," she replied with some bite in her voice as she looked away and sipped her drink.

"Every city has its dark side. The key is to just stay away from those areas and only spend time in the historic parts."

"So you haven't been to the red light districts or sampled some of the …"

"Renee, you should know me better than that by now. Of course not. I'm a history fanatic and I wouldn't be caught dead in those places you've heard about."

She smiled at him and nodded while he ate another bite of his sandwich. He checked his watch. "Relax, Will. We have plenty of time."

"I'm sorry. Things have been busy at work, and I've been rushed all day. I'll try to slow it down a notch and focus on you rather than the time."

"Sounds perfect. I won't let you down," she said with raised eyebrows.

They finished their meals and he asked her, "Do you want to drive the Miata?"

"The what?"

"That's what the car is. A Mazda Miata. Why don't you take the wheel?"

She gave him a crazed look and shook her head. "I'd be afraid I'd crash it, and a year of my paychecks probably wouldn't cover the costs."

"No, you'll do fine. The dance studio is only a few blocks away. Give it a try. I know you've wanted to give it a test drive."

"It would be fun, but …"

"No buts. Just do it."

She bit her lip, but turned it into a smile as her eyes sparkled and she walked to the driver's side. He opened the door and handed her the keys, then went to the other side to get it. She started the car and revved up the gas a bit too much, making a face and glancing at Will out of the corner of her eye. She shifted gears and slowly moved out onto the road, cautiously accelerating to join the traffic.

He stared at Renee as her hair blew in the wind with the open top. She seemed to be enjoying this. At the first traffic light, she hit the brakes too hard, causing them to lurch forward when the car stopped suddenly. The people in the car next to them stared at her and shook their heads. She laughed uncontrollably but moved forward with no problems when the light turned green. The fading light of the sunset made her hair glow and he visualized her as an actress in a movie from the 1950's. She made everything a fun adventure.

Her driving lesson in his car soon ended and she parked in a spot that had no other cars nearby, probably afraid she'd scratch it up if she parked too close to another.

"You did superb."

"As long as you don't count hitting the gas too hard or that first stop."

He pressed a button which caused the top to come up and close, then got out and walked around to the driver's side. Opening the door and offering Renee his hand, he helped her out and kept holding her hand as they strolled together to their lesson. He couldn't wait to stand close to her and hold her as they moved in unison on the dance floor.

# Chapter Thirty

AT A LITTLE CORNER CAFÉ, WILL and his friends sat outside under an umbrella.

"So what's the occasion?" Patrick asked.

"Do we really need a reason to get together, or can't we just get coffee because we have some spare time?" Will replied.

"I think you've got something up your sleeve," added Daniel.

"Blah. This is the worst coffee I've ever had," said Will after tasting his drink and staring intently at the cup.

"That would be your usual girly drink, wouldn't it?" asked Gregory.

"I don't drink girly drinks and this is certainly not my usual," commented Will, holding up the cup to examine it more closely. "This one is so bad I wouldn't even give this to my dog."

"You don't even have a dog," said Patrick with a laugh.

"Someday I plan to settle down and get a dog, and when that happens, I won't make him drink this slop."

"Hey," interrupted Gregory. "This isn't my coffee. This tastes too chocolaty."

"Aha. After a few drinks, I think this chicken scratch on the outside of my cup could be interpreted as 'Gregory' so I'll bet she gave you mine and I have yours."

"You're right. The writing on my cup looks like 'Will' if you tilt your head and squint your eyes." replied Gregory as they traded cups.

They both tasted the contents of the swapped cups and nodded.

Will glared at Gregory. "You actually like coffee that tastes like this?"

"What? This is exactly how I like it," replied Gregory indignantly.

"It was so bad I thought they left out a key ingredient," said Will, still staring at his friend.

"So you wouldn't give Gregory's coffee to your imaginary dog?" asked Daniel.

"Not a chance. That's the worst coffee I've ever tasted," said Will. "And I don't mean an imaginary dog. I really plan to retire someday, settle down, and get a dog. Maybe two. Kim and I had both dogs and cats when we grew up, but college, jobs, and my travel schedule have kept me away from home a lot."

Patrick pointed at Will. "That's right. You're plan was to retire by the time you were thirty, so you only have a few more years."

"Yep. I'm thinking it's about time," Will said before sipping his coffee.

They all laughed while Will sat back and gazed across the street, breathing in the pleasant aromas from the flower beds around the trees that lined both sides of the street. "No, I mean it. I'm tired of all the travel. I've made more money than I ever imagined and the stock market helped it to grow tremendously. I could sell my business and actually live in my house for a change rather than camping out in the rooms over my office."

Patrick raised his cup in a toast. "Great idea. We're all behind you 100%," and the other men touched their cups to his. "To Will and his retirement plans. If there's anything we can do to help, let us know."

"I appreciate that."

Daniel put his cup down and looked at Will. "Don't tell me you plan to marry Renee and stay home while she works."

Will raised his eyebrows. "Hmm. Not a bad idea. Although I don't think she likes her current job. I'd have to help her setup her own business. She's a genius with decorating. I think she would really enjoy something like that. I mentioned it to her once but she seemed intimidated. I could help her get over it."

"So you would actually retire and live off of her income?" asked Gregory.

"I could retire but we wouldn't have to live off of her income. We could donate hers to charity and live off of my investments. Plus I wouldn't sit idle. I'd want to get more involved with disaster relief. Maybe join the Peace Corps or go on more missionary trips."

"Sounds like a good plan," added Patrick.

"You must have done well for yourself," commented Daniel.

Will stared at his drink. "More than I ever dreamed possible."

"Good for you," said Gregory. "I hope it works out for you."

"Another toast," said Daniel as he raised his cup. "To Will and his dogs."

Their coffee cups met again amid laughter, and they made plans for another basketball game.

*****

A shadow painted a specific parking spot outside Renee's apartment, and Will targeted that one as he zipped his SUV around the corner and slowed down. The little shady spot wouldn't really cool off his car much, but psychologically it was the best place to park. He stood up and walked toward her front door but stopped in mid-step. He had better call first to give her an advanced warning of his visit. Why couldn't he ever remember to call her ahead of time?

His call to her cell phone went unanswered so he checked the number. Oh well. He tried. Maybe she was out shopping with Rebecca. He turned to search for Renee's little blue compact car. Good. There it was. She must be here but just couldn't get to the phone. Will continued his march to Renee's apartment, checking to make sure he wasn't about to get hit by a careless driver on the way to the door.

He knocked politely and stepped back to examine the overcast sky as he waited. There was some movement of the curtains and the door unlocked and opened quietly, revealing Rebecca in a cute little sundress with one sandal on and one sandal in her hand.

"Hi, Beautiful. Is your mother here?"

"Yes, but she's napping. You can come in though, since she'll be getting up soon."

Will hesitated. It might be considered inappropriate to come in while Renee slept. "Maybe I should stop by in a little while when she's finished with her nap."

"Nope. She'd want to see you anyway so come on in now."

"Alright, if you insist but it was your idea," Will responded as he followed her through the door. "Why would she be sleeping in the middle of the day? Doesn't she sleep at night?"

"She always takes a nap on the week-ends and sometimes she takes one after work if she had a bad day."

"Wow. That seems like a waste of some good daylight. Personally, I prefer to sleep at night."

"So do I," replied Rebecca. "Once in a while, she makes me try to take a nap too, but I can't sleep. I'm just not tired during the day."

Will came in and smiled as he walked near the couch and saw Rebecca's mother. Renee slept on her back there, not even moving as he stared at her for a moment before settling into a chair nearby. "Do you ever draw mustaches on her while she sleeps?" he asked.

She giggled quietly as she sat down but shook her head. She put on her other sandal and worked on the strap for a few seconds. "Will, are your toes the same size on both feet?" she whispered.

"What?"

"The middle toe on my right foot is bigger than the middle toe on my left foot. Are yours like that?"

"Uh, I've never really noticed. I think they're probably the same."

"Look at mine," she said as she stretched out her legs to let him compare.

"I see what you mean. My guess is you inherited that from your mother. Have you checked to see if she has the same difference?"

Rebecca stared at Will with wide eyes, then got up and went to the end of the couch. She examined her mother's toes, going back and forth from one foot to another, then ran back to Will with a big smile. She whispered excitedly, "Hers are exactly the same as mine. Her right middle toe is bigger than her left middle toe."

"See? What did I tell you? I'll bet if you looked closely, you'll find other special things she passed down to you also."

"What do you mean?"

"Check out my hand," Will said, holding out his hand for her to see. "You know how everyone has their own special fingerprint? The lines on your hand are unique also, and your mom may have the same lines as you."

She stared at Will's hand, then compared it with her open

hand. "Can you show me?"

He pointed to his hand and she studied it. "These lines don't touch on my hand, but on yours they do. And see where this line connects with that big line on my hand? Look where it connects on your hand."

"And the lines on my hand might match my mom's?"

"It's possible. Check for yourself."

Rebecca walked back to the couch without a sound and explored her mother's hand. It wasn't opened all the way so Rebecca gently positioned it until the palm was open. It was funny to watch the little girl gaze between her hand and Renee's hand and Will couldn't help but enjoy the scene. The fact that Renee was asleep made it even funnier but he had to be careful not to laugh too loud and wake her up.

Rebecca ran back to Will and whispered, "You're right. The lines on her hand match mine perfectly, but they're different from yours. What else might be the same?"

"Oh, I'm not sure. I think I've heard that ears could be unique. It's kind of hard to see your own ears and compare though."

"If I put my ear up to Mommy's ear, would you see if they're the same?"

"I don't think so. She's sleeping and might get the wrong idea."

"She wouldn't mind. Please, Will? Just see if they're the same. It won't take long."

He shook his head and laughed but gave in to her enthusiasm and stood up as she tugged on his arm. "Okay, but just for a few seconds."

Rebecca placed her head next to her mother's and Will came up close to examine their ears. He had never looked this closely at Renee and casually pushed hair away from her face so he could see her ear better. "Well, what do you know? Your ear lobe and the curves in your ear match your mother's perfectly. You are a little clone after all."

Renee stirred and opened her eyes, giving Will a strange expression as she turned her head to face him. "What are you doing?"

"Mommy, you and I have the same toes, hands, and ears."

"That's nice, dear. What's Will doing?"

Will laughed and replied, "Hi, Sleepyhead. Your daughter asked me to compare her ear with yours to see if they looked the same or different, and … I'm sorry. I honestly didn't want to disturb you while you slept."

"Yet you did it anyway," Renee said as she sat up.

"Yes, I really shouldn't have even come in while you were napping the day away. It's my fault."

"I told him he could come in and wait for you to wake up, so it's really my fault," added Rebecca.

"You did, but I should have known better and come back later."

"So did you enjoy watching me while I slept?"

"Immensely, but I feel guilty now."

"Good. You should feel guilty," replied Renee with raised eyebrows as her tight lips upturned into a beautiful smile.

"Anyway, I came to ask you if you two would like to go ice skating this afternoon."

"Ice skating? Are you crazy?" Renee replied.

"No, it's a lot of fun. I could help you, and Rebecca can use a walker to help her balance. We'd have a blast."

"It sounds like a great idea," added Rebecca.

"Yeah, is this something you've done with girls in Sweden or Finland?" she asked with a little bite in her voice.

"Uh, I have, yes, but this would just be you and me and Rebecca."

"I'm sorry. I just have a difficult time with your reputation."

"My reputation?" he responded, shaking his head. "Okay,

I understand. No, really I don't. Are you going to hold it against me for everything I've ever done in my past?"

"I know it doesn't make sense to you, Will, but sometimes I do. It's just the way I am."

"Alright. I had hoped to offer you something enjoyable we could do together today since I'll be out of town the rest of the week. I'm sorry."

Will stood up and turned toward the front door with a dejected expression on his face, making eye-contact with Renee briefly. Rebecca gave her mother a mean look and Will struggled to keep from laughing. He turned his face away.

"I'm trying to understand your past and deal with it," said Renee as she stood up. "I want to be part of your life but I want to be the only one."

He turned back to her and walked up right in front of her, gently cupping her face in his hands. Her demeanor changed as her eyes gave in to him. "You are the only woman I want to spend time with anymore. I've searched all over the world for that one person who could make my life complete and you are that woman. You sure seem to be the only one for me. Forever."

Renee closed her eyes and tears crept silently down her cheeks as he kissed her on the lips. She put her arms around him and leaned into his shoulder. He wrapped his arms around her as well, and they stayed like that for several seconds.

"Awkward," said Rebecca, as both her mother and Will released each other and stepped back. Renee wiped her eyes and they all laughed at Rebecca's comment.

"We would love to go ice skating with you, wouldn't we Rebecca?"

"Yes," replied her daughter, dancing around the two of them.

"Great," said Will. You'll need to dress for some cold weather since they keep it a bit frosty inside the rink."

It seemed as though Renee had finally overcome her jealousies, which was a relief. This was a major obstacle to their relationship that hopefully would never come up again.

# Chapter Thirty-One

**A**FTER BUNDLING UP IN THEIR WIN-
ter jackets, the three of them piled into Will's
SUV and drive to the indoor skating rink. They
went inside and Will selected skates for them all.

"If I break my arm and have to miss weeks of work, I'm
coming after you," said Renee to Will's laughter and they put
on the skates.

He then rolled a modified walker for elderly people up to
Rebecca. "Here, try standing up, then hold on to this. It will
help keep you from falling."

She gave him a grin and followed his directions. Her eyes
registered surprise as she moved across the ice without falling. "Look, I'm ice skating, Mommy."

Will helped her get started out on the rink and let the little
girl go out on her own. He watched her for a few seconds but
she moved with confidence and speed. Not a lot of grace, but
that would come later. He came back to Renee and admired
her long hair protruding from her winter hat as he skated near
her. She had the presence of a true Scandinavian and was the
most attractive woman in the whole place.

Renee appeared to be nervous, so Will kneeled down to
where she still sat. "Take my hands. I'll pull you up and try
to help you balance."

She did so, but her face reflected fear despite an artificial grin. "Oh boy."

"You're doing fine. Let's slowly go out into the rink. We'll stay close to the edge so you can hold on to the rail if you feel you need to."

She did well with his guidance, and they made their way around the circle of ice. "You're a natural," he commented.

"Only until you let go of me. Then I'm going straight down on my bottom."

He moved in front of her, still holding her hands, and skated backward so he could see

her eyes. "If you'll have me, I'll never let go of you."

Her lips formed the incomparable smile that had mesmerized him since he first met Renee, and his heart pounded.

"I've waited so long to find someone who I could share my life with," started Will, "and I really want that person to be you. I don't want to date anyone else. You're the one I hope to spend my time with."

Her eyes fixed on his as he led her around the rink several times, only glancing away occasionally to make sure he didn't bump into someone. He could spend the rest of his life staring into those wonderful eyes.

"Look who's coming up beside us," he said as Rebecca and her walker came up next to them.

Renee turned her face to the little girl. "You're doing so well. Can you believe we're really ice skating?"

"This is fun. I can go fast too," she said to her mother and skated away again.

"You and Rebecca are such a special pair. I really want to be a part of your family if you'll let me."

"What are you saying, Will?"

He turned to make sure he wouldn't run into someone, then returned his gaze to her. "I'm not perfect, but I'm crazy about you and I love the way I feel when I'm with you. I'd even give up my travel if you wanted me too."

"You don't need to do that."

"If it would help you not to be so jealous, it would be worth it. Plus I'm getting tired of airports, airplanes, and hotels."

She just stared back into his eyes. What was she thinking now? From what he had been told, PMS was similar to bi-polar, and she might be happy and friendly one minute then rip his head off the next. He had seen the downside of Renee's hormones already and he didn't look forward to that coming back again. This seemed to be a positive day, except when she briefly scolded him for going skating with Finnish girls in his past. He couldn't change his past, so she would have to accept that he had dated other women over the past few years.

Just then, the back of Will's skate hit someone else's skate and he went down on his rear-end, pulling Renee on top of him. They both laughed hysterically as they lay there, and Rebecca skated up next to them with the happiest laughter Will had ever heard. His eyes met Renee's again, and he immediately locked his lips with hers for a moment. Never waste such an opportunity. He then helped her up and led her off the rink and to the benches.

"I'm sorry. I was lost in your eyes for a moment too long and didn't see that kid at all. Are you hurt?"

"Not at all. I don't think I've laughed that hard in a long time."

Rebecca walked up to them and Will said, "You're doing great on the ice. Are you thirsty?"

She nodded and Will looked at Renee inquisitively. "I could use a drink too," she replied, and Will went to get something for them while they sat at one of the tables. He soon returned with a tray of drinks and joined them.

"I have to admit you are the funnest person I've ever met," Renee told him. "You're always full of surprises, and you treat my daughter and I like a princess and a queen."

"Well, thank you ma'am," he replied. "You both deserve the best, and I want to make sure you always feel special. That's part of my job."

She laughed and glanced down at Rebecca. She appeared to be enthralled by the skaters that went around the rink and was in her own little world. "Are you having fun?"

Rebecca gazed up at her mom, nodded enthusiastically, and took another sip. "Can I go back out on the ice again?"

"Of course. Just finish your drink." She did, then stood up with her walker and made her way back out to the circle of ice.

"Could you ever forget about what I've done in the past and focus on you and I?" asked Will.

She looked toward the rink for a moment. "If you're really the same person you show me when we're together, I could accept it. Are you going to change someday and show me that you're not really the Prince Charming I've been seeing in you these past few months?"

"What do you mean? What you see is what you get. This is the real me."

"It just doesn't seem that anyone could be as nice as you make yourself out to be."

"You know my sister, right? Is she a nice person? We're very similar. We had a great upbringing, and we make good choices. If I appear to be a nice guy, it's because I really am a nice guy. Ask Kim. She knows me pretty well."

"Yeah, but sometimes when something seems too good to be true, it is too good to be true. I don't want to be hurt again and I don't want Rebecca to get hurt."

"I'm not the hurting kind. If I make a commitment, I will follow through with it. You have my word."

She glanced at his eyes briefly, then turned away. Her eyes were moist and red. She had been hurt before. He could tell. How could anyone hurt such a delicate, precious flower?

A moment of anger came up when that big guy at her apartment came to his mind. He wished he had pounded the monster a few more times, but scolded himself for that thought. If she'll let him be part of her family, he would never let anyone hurt her or her daughter again.

"Let's skate some more, Will. Would you guide me again?"

"Sure." He helped her up and led her to the rink again. She waved at Rebecca as she skated by again with the walker. "Are you ready?" he asked Renee.

She nodded and he held her hand in his. They skated side by side for a long time and Renee kept getting better and better as the afternoon went on. Maybe they could double date here with Kim and Doug in the future, giving Rebecca some skating time with Nicole. They skated with the little girl for a little while, and other times it was as though Will and Renee were the only ones on the ice. This was the life he had always wanted.

# Chapter Thirty-Two

**M**USIC PLAYED FROM RENEE'S CD player as her and Rebecca rearranged some of her decorations at the apartment. Will had given her a few paintings she liked and bought her some rustic pieces from the antique shop in town to hang on her wall. She loved the antique style of his office yet she preferred a more modern décor. The excitement of new color for her walls gave her energy. With Rebecca's help, she took advantage of it.

They occasionally danced around the room together when a song came on with a good beat, causing her daughter to release a fountain of giggles each time as she tried to keep up with her silly mother. Cleaning the house, straightening up for company, and adding new decorations to her apartment had become some of Renee's favorite activities lately. Rebecca appeared to have a lot of fun and they gave them both opportunities to bond with a special mother-daughter time. These experiences were second only to her dates with Will, which had become the most rewarding times of her entire life. This was the best her life had been since...

"I'd like to put this one over the couch, okay?" Renee said to her daughter as she showed her the painting. "If I hold it up, would you make sure it's straight?"

"Alright. I like the colors but the people look all smudged

up."

Renee laughed as she stepped onto the couch and lifted the painting up against the wall. She found where it seemed best and turned back toward Rebecca. "Is this centered?"

The little girl stood behind her mother and studied it for a moment. She closed one eye, tilted her head, raised her thumb and moved it back and forth. "No, I think it needs to go to the right just a bit."

Renee slid it slightly and leaned back to see. "You're right. This is better." She took a pencil and lightly marked on the wall on each side of the frame before setting it down and stepping to the floor.

"Mommy, I just realized if I stand back from the painting, it doesn't seem as bad as it does up close."

"That's right. If you look at it from a distance, then only glance at it and turn away again, it appears a lot like something real you've seen momentarily. If you look up close, you'll see a lot of smudged paint."

"Hmm. I've changed my mind. I like it now."

"I'm glad. These are Will's favorite kinds of paintings and I've decided I like them now too."

"Is Will ever going to be my daddy?"

Wow. What a question. "Honey, that's out of our control. We'll just have to wait and see what happens between him and me."

"I think he would make a good daddy."

"So do I," Renee replied as she gazed off into her bedroom. Will told her that Rebecca deserved to learn about her biological father. Maybe now was the time. "Wait here. I have something to show you."

Renee stood up and went into her bedroom, pulling a large box out of her closet. She hadn't opened it for several years, but this was something Rebecca needed to know about. She carried it out into the living room and joined her daughter on the couch, setting the box on the coffee table in front of them.

"I've never really told you about your father, but Will said you should know what happened to him." She looked into her daughter's inquisitive eyes while Rebecca sat speechless. She should have never waited this long to explain these details. "I always thought he was a bad man for leaving us, but that was a big mistake. He was a good man who loved me and was so excited to be your daddy."

As she spoke these words, Renee choked up but smiled in an effort to keep her daughter from crying. "I'm sorry, Sweetie. It's just that when I told him I had you in my belly, he wanted so much to be here when you were born. He would have made a good daddy."

"What happened?"

"He was with a group of soldiers who had just rescued some families from evil men in a country overseas. He wrote me a letter to tell me about how good he felt about what they had done. He said the children there hugged him and he couldn't wait to have kids of his own."

"So he was in a war?"

Renee nodded. She opened the box and rummaged around for a few seconds before pulling out a photograph. She stared at it, wiping her eyes, and handed it to Rebecca. She accepted it cautiously, gazing intently at it. This was the first time she had ever seen a picture of her father. It showed a handsome young man in an army uniform, holding a little girl. The girl was dirty with ragged clothes. Maybe three years old.

"Why didn't he ever come home to be with me?"

Renee sobbed again and lifted out a flag that was folded into a triangle. Without turning to her daughter, she continued, "I've always told people that he left us, without mentioning he was in the army. In my mind, he chose to go off to war rather than stay home and be part of our family. I didn't want him to go, but he had a sense of duty to fight the bad people in the world and make it a better place to live. I've been selfish and wanted him home with us, holding you rather than holding that little girl he didn't even know on the other side of the world."

"Why are you showing me a flag?"

Renee set the flag on the table next to the box while Rebecca held on to the photo. "He and some other soldiers were killed outside of the village where that picture was taken. This was the flag that covered his casket at your father's funeral. Soldiers gave it to me. I still had you in my belly."

She hugged her daughter as tears streamed down both of their cheeks. Renee sat up and pulled some medals out of the box.

"What are those?" asked the little girl.

"These medals were given to your father for his bravery in the war. The surviving soldiers in his group said he was a true hero and that we should be proud of him. Yet I hated him because he never came back to be with you and me." She looked at Rebecca and added, "I'm so sorry for keeping him out of your life all these years. Will was right. He was a hero and deserves so much more than being shut up in this box forever."

Renee held up an envelope and showed it to her daughter.

"This letter is the one he wrote that day. It arrived in the mail after you were born."

"We could put out his flag and the medals to help decorate the apartment," said Rebecca.

"You're right. I'm going to get a special box to put them in, and we'll hang them up for everyone to see. Great idea."

"Won't Will be sad if we put something about my father on the wall?"

"No, Will's not like that. He thinks we should celebrate your father's memory since he really was a hero. It will make him very happy."

"Did he talk about God like Will does?"

Renee let pleasant memories come back to her. "Yes, I guess I'm truly attracted to men who have faith in God. I've turned my back on God for years, but I think we should go to church with Will sometime when he's in town."

"What else do you remember about him?"

It felt good to release these thoughts that had been locked up for so long. "He liked to laugh and he knew how to make me laugh. That's what made me want to spend time with him. And he also was very protective of me."

"Like the way Will is protective of both of us?"

"Yes, I suppose so. I never really put those together, but Will is like him in many ways."

Renee couldn't stop the tears that flowed freely as she remembered her husband, when they first met, what they did on dates, why she loved this man. This was the first time she had thought of him without hating him since he died, and she just hugged her daughter as the joy surrounded them both. Rebecca cried too, but she probably didn't know why.

"So now I know about my daddy. I'd still like to have Will be my second daddy."

Renee laughed and leaned over to tickle Rebecca, who squealed and squirmed on the couch. "Maybe someday, my little princess."

# Chapter Thirty-Three

WILL PULLED INTO HIS USUAL parking spot across from Renee's apartment, and ran across the lot to get his date for the evening. Ringing the doorbell, he waited with anticipation for Renee to answer. She told him about a surprise she had for him this evening, but wouldn't give any hints. When she finally opened the door, his eyes widened and his jaw dropped.

"Are you okay, Will?" Renee asked.

"You seem like a dream," was all he could mutter.

"A good dream, I hope. Come on in. For a second, I didn't think you liked it."

"I still can't believe you borrowed this from my sister."

"Yes, we're almost exactly the same size so I can wear a lot of her clothes."

"I can't picture her in sixties psychedelic miniskirts and go-go boots."

"She said it was for a party she went to, but she hasn't worn it since."

"Well, I have to admit I sure like seeing you in it."

"I'm glad," said Renee. "How was Amsterdam?"

"The trip was exhausting, but everything went well. Airport to hotel to the office to the hotel to restaurant to hotel to airport. I'm glad to be back in town with you."

Rebecca ran up to him and he knelt down to hug her and lift her up to his level. "Do you like Mommy's dress?" she asked.

"I sure do, sweetheart. She makes it look incredible."

"I helped with her hair."

"I can tell. You always do a great job with it," he said while kissing her cheek and causing the little girl to giggle and squirm. "We have to be on our way, so be good for Debbie," he added.

"Hi, Mr. Sayre," said Debbie as he waved to Rebecca's babysitter. Have fun at your ballroom dance lessons."

"Yeah, this is the last one, then there's a party afterword, where I'll embarrass myself in front of a lot of people," said Will as he watched Renee kiss her daughter.

"No, you'll be fine," replied Renee as they headed out the front door.

As they walked toward Will's convertible, he stared at her outfit.

"What are you looking at?"

"I'm going to seem a little boring tonight, but you're spectacular."

"You really like it that much?"

"Oh, yeah," he said as he opened the door for her to get in. "I think we're going to have fun tonight."

They drove in silence for a few minutes, while Will glanced at her every chance he could. She must have caught his sneak peeks, since she smiled without returning his gaze. How could she be so much fun to spend time with? She's fun without even saying a word.

The dance lessons went well and were just as enjoyable as the other ones they had attended. When they were finished, they walked out to the main room where a large group of people had already gathered. Will wasn't the nervous kind so it really didn't bother him too much. He stayed focused on his date, which was easy to do, and danced as though she was the only person in the room with him. Their time together was so enjoyable, yet he never suspected he would have this much fun waltzing with a woman.

When the party was over, they strolled out into the moonlight to find his car. She laughed and talked non-stop, giving him the impression that she had a great time. He didn't want the evening to end.

"Do you feel like going out to eat?" he asked as he held the door for her.

"Are you kidding? I'm dressed like a go-go dancer."

"It would be perfect for the place I'm thinking about. There's a band there that plays a lot of classic sixties music. You'd fit right in."

"I don't know. Although, I don't want to go home yet. I guess we could slip in quickly and get seated."

"Great," said Will as he drove to the restaurant.

She appeared a little self-conscious as they walked up to the hostess, so he kept encouraging her and complementing her on how well she looked.

"Hi, Will," said the hostess. "Just two tonight?"

This could be a problem. He avoided Renee's glare. "Yes, and can we get a table close to the stage?"

She nodded and led them down the aisle.

"So you know her?" Renee whispered.

"Yeah, I know the guys in the band and have been here several times."

"Hmm," she replied. "She's cute."

"There's nothing to be jealous about. She's just a friend and that's all."

"I know. I'm just giving you a hard time," she said with a sneaky grin, which set his mind at ease.

"Here you go. Enjoy," said the hostess, handing them each a menu.

They took the menus and Will held her hand as she sat in the booth. He sat across from her, and turned to see the band. "It's not too loud here, is it?"

"What? I can't here you. It's too loud," she replied. "Just kidding. It's fine."

They checked out the menu and Will pointed out one of the items. "I think you'd love this."

"Okay, I'll trust your judgment. You seem to know what you're talking about most of the time."

"Only most of the time?" he asked, as the waitress came up to their table.

"Hi, Will," said the waitress, as Will quickly looked at his date apologetically. Renee scolded him with an expression of raised eyebrows.

"Hi, we'll both have water with lemon," said Will. "She'd like the salmon with asparagus and I'll take the shrimp scampi with rice."

"Sounds good," replied the waitress. "I'll be right back with your drinks."

Will watched her walk toward the kitchen and said to Renee, "I'm sorry about that. I've seen her here before …"

"Don't worry, Will. I understand that you know a lot of women and I'm dealing with it. Let's just have fun tonight."

Will stared into her eyes for a moment as the band finished playing.

The keyboard player in the band thanked the audience, then stared at their table. "I see we have a special guest here tonight with his amazing date."

Will pretended not to hear the man and started talking to Renee. She shushed him and nodded to the stage.

The man at the microphone pointed to their table and clapped, which caused others in the restaurant to clap. Will tried to ignore it again. "Did I embarrass you too much at the dance studio?" he asked, but she shook her head.

"Do you know this guy, Will? He's talking to you."

Will glanced over his shoulder and waved, but tried to get back into his conversation with Renee. "I really had fun waltzing you around the room, especially when we tried the Austrian waltz and tripped as we spun around and around."

The man onstage kept talking and trying to get Will's attention. "One of the most zealous British Invasion players in North Carolina, Mr. Will Sayre. Let's give him a hand to see if we can entice him to come onstage," as the restaurant erupted in applause.

"What is he talking about?" she asked.

"Maybe this wasn't such a good idea," he said to himself.

"He wants you to go up on the stage, Will. See what he wants."

Will reluctantly turned to see the entire band encouraging him to come up with them, and he looked at Renee. "Do you mind?"

She shook her head but had a confused expression on her face.

Will stood up and walked toward the small stage, climbing up to shake hands with the guys in the band. The applause took a while to die down, but once it was quieter, Will stepped up to the microphone. "Hi, I'm here with a gorgeous woman and she's all decked out from a party we just came from. Please stand up and show everyone your outfit, Renee."

She gave him the evil eye as he laughed, but stood gracefully as the applause erupted again, this time with whistling and much more intensity than before. She spun around at Will's direction and sat down with a princess-like wave of her hand. He had embarrassed her, but he'd make it up.

The guitar player in the band spoke to Will, then pointed to a guitar at the back of the stage. The anticipation in the air filled the entire room. He walked back to pick up the extra guitar, then pushed a few buttons and quietly tested out the sound. Turning the knobs, he walked forward and said something to the guitar player. They both nodded, looked around at the other guys in the band, and the sound exploded from the stage as the band launched into a classic sixties song by the Kinks. Will started, "Girl, you really got me now…"

He sang lead on the song and enjoyed seeing the expressions of surprise on Renee's face as the band brought down the house. He must have forgotten to tell her that he sometimes filled in for a couple of local bands. There would be some explaining to do. Hopefully, she wouldn't hold it against him as something else secretive from his past.

The band finished the song and the dozens of people who had moved out to the dance floor screamed their approval.

"Thanks everyone. In honor of my beautiful sixties date and her stunning outfit, I'd like to do another classic from that era."

Will glanced over at Renee to make sure she hadn't walked out on him. She was more attractive than ever, with her hair just right and her ruby lips in a perfect smile. He stepped back, checked with the other guys in the band, and went right into another winner from The Beatles. Will sang 'I Feel Fine' with surprising intensity. The crowd grew around the stage and Will checked on Renee periodically. He caught her dancing in her seat, bopping her head to the music. It seemed as though she was enjoying herself so that was very good. To his surprise, she stood up to join the group on the dance floor.

After the song ended and the applause quieted, Will stepped up to the microphone again. "You're an awesome crowd tonight. I'm going to do one more song, then turn it back over to these guys."

The audience showed their disapproval but Will interrupted. "Hey, remember these guys are excellent. They're going to play some more sixties music after their break. Besides, I can see that the waitress has brought my dinner and I don't want it to get cold."

Will looked right at Renee and pointed to her as the band started the next song. Will sang the slower tune from 1970, 'Maybe I'm Amazed,' and spectators didn't seem to mind that it wasn't another fast song. The keyboard player did a great job with the music. Will sang directly to her and she wiped her eyes a few times as she listened to him pour out his heart. This was one of the songs on the CD's he had given to her, so he was certain she knew this song. When it was over, the crowd gave a standing ovation as Will struggled to make out off the stage and back to his seat. He recognized a lot of the people who wanted to stop and talk with him, but many he didn't know. He kept popping his head up to see Renee over the heads of the people on the dance floor, and eventually arrived at his seat.

"I'm sorry about that Renee. I didn't even think about them asking me to go onstage tonight."

"Well, you're quite the celebrity. What other secrets should I know about?"

"I didn't mean for it to be a secret. It just never came up in conversation that I sometimes played in a band."

"Very interesting. I wonder what else about you might have never come up in conversation."

"There's no telling. How's your salmon?"

"Changing the subject, eh?"

"No, I just don't want our food to get cold," said Will as he took a bite of his meal.

"Well, I was certainly entertained watching you do what you enjoy."

"I'm glad."

"It was also entertaining watching some of the girls going crazy over your performance and good looks," added Renee as she ate some of her salmon without glancing up at him.

"I don't have any control over that. You'll just have to trust me …"

"Don't worry. I'm just trying to make you sweat a little. I trust you."

Will stared into her playful eyes as she took another bite, and she raised her eyebrows. She drove him wild. The more he got to know her, the more he wanted to be with her. She was definitely a keeper.

# Chapter Thirty-Four

**A**S **WILL SCRAMBLED TO FINISH** getting several presentations ready for his next business trip, his mind danced with thoughts of Renee. He would much rather spend the next two weeks with her than to go to India alone for his job. He hated being alone. It would be challenging for him to avoid going out with some of the ladies he met on the way or while he was in Bangalore, but he was determined to keep his word. He had proven he could do it in Amsterdam, so it was possible.

There was one woman who seemed to constantly check with the hotel in Bangalore to find out when he had reservations there. She must have known someone who worked at the front desk who informed her. Vijaya certainly wouldn't let that person know when he arrived. He would have to make sure this woman knew he wouldn't be spending time with her this trip. Maybe he should tell her he's engaged. Maybe he would stay at a different hotel. No, he would just face her and tell her the truth. He was no longer available. Wow. What an interesting revelation.

Sue walked up to his door and said, "I've booked your airline reservations and the hotel. Let me know if you need anything else."

"Thanks. I have some more to finish up tomorrow, so I'll have to come in to wrap it up in the morning."

"Do you need me to help with anything tomorrow? I'd be glad to come in too."

"No, just take the day off. It's just a few minor updates I can handle myself."

"Call me if you need me."

"Will do. I appreciate all of your help with this today."

She nodded with a smile and walked back to her desk. Will reached a stopping point then glanced at an antique clock on the fireplace across from his desk. He needed to get to Renee's apartment soon. She had invited him over for a special dessert and he didn't want to be late. He put some papers and a laptop into his briefcase and closed the lid, then walked up to Sue's desk.

"I'm going over to Renee's now. I appreciate you staying late to make those changes for me. Tell your hubby I owe him dinner at that seafood restaurant he likes on the river."

"What for?"

"For letting me keep you later than usual tonight."

"Sounds good. We'll take you up on it when you get back."

"See you in a couple of weeks."

Stepping outside, he let the door close with a bang as he rushed to his car and drove away. He didn't like being so tied up with work that he wasn't able to have dinner with Renee. It was nice she agreed to wait for him to finish his work, then just have a dessert waiting for him. Maybe tomorrow wouldn't be so busy and he could spend more time with her then, before leaving for India.

He was drained. If he sat down for long, he would probably fall asleep, but that wouldn't be polite to his host. He needed to stay awake and not appear to be so worn out. Gulping down another Mountain Dew, he pulled into the parking lot and found a spot. Hopefully his eyes didn't look too tired. He glanced at the mirror, then shook his head and got out. Oh well.

His knuckles rapped lightly on the door so he wouldn't wake Rebecca. She was probably in bed by now. The door opened slightly to reveal Renee's pretty eyes and bright red lips. Why would she have done up her lips so late? Her eye shadow was captivating as she blinked at him a few times to tease him. She motioned for him to come in, so he stepped into her apartment. She only had a short night gown on with that lipstick. There couldn't have been much else underneath. He would love to come home to this every night after he got married, but not tonight. Strange. He never expected her to behave like this.

"Rebecca is spending the night with one of her friends tonight, so it's just you and me."

"I'm sorry to get here so late. I was hoping to see Rebecca before going out of town."

"Aren't you glad to see me?" she asked, giving him a seductive pose. Although her eyes were captivating, it wasn't easy to keep his eyes on them.

"Of course," he replied. "But I would've been glad to see you even in jeans and a flannel shirt as well."

She led him to the couch and encouraged him to sit. "I'll bring your dessert in just a minute." She walked into the kitchen as he forced his eyes to go elsewhere in the apartment. He gave in and glanced back at her. She seemed to be tempting him, moving her hips much more than usual. This really wasn't like Renee. He glanced away again.

"I hope you're in the mood for some chocolate mousse," she said as she carried a small plate to the couch and sat down very close to him.

"It looks delicious. I should have known you were so good with sweets."

"You have no idea."

She sat down and kicked her legs up beside her as she fed

him from the plate. "This tastes even better than it looks," said Will.

"You sound surprised," she replied while giving him another bite.

Will swallowed the mousse and said, "No, you had just done so well with the presentation that I couldn't believe it would taste good also."

"I'm glad you like it," she said as she wiped some chocolate from his upper lip and licked it off. "Wait. Are you talking about me or the mousse?"

Will didn't know how to respond to that. "You seem cold. Are you sure you don't want to put a blanket around you?"

She raised her eyebrows and slowly shook her head. He opened his mouth as she gave him the last bite, and his eyes glanced momentarily at her little nightgown. He quickly stared up into her eyes as she smiled and put the plate down on the table next to the couch.

She leaned into him and spoke softly. "You've worked too much today. I could help you relax."

"No, I just need to get a good night's sleep and I'll be fine."

She took that opportunity to reach up and kiss him on the lips, which he accepted for the moment. He wanted to kiss her, but not like this. She was getting a little too intimate and it made him feel uncomfortable. He would welcome this kind of behavior from her if they were married, but at this moment, she wasn't his wife. She sat up and slid on top of him, putting both hands over his ears. He pulled his head away, but she tried to follow his movement.

"Renee, I can't do this." He squirmed his way out from under her and she was left on the couch with a confused expression. "You look so incredible, but we shouldn't be doing this now. I need to stop while I have some self-control."

"I thought you liked me, Will."

He moved closer to her pouting lips. "I like you so much that I have to leave now. You're the most interesting woman I've ever met, and I want to make sure we don't do something that..."

"Like walking out on me when I'm trying to show you how much I like you?"

"Yes. No, I don't mean to appear that I'm not crazy about you. I just don't think we should be doing something like this, since it could lead to something we would both regret."

"I wouldn't regret it."

"Yes, I think you would. This kind of kissing and whatever else you have in mind really isn't the real Renee."

"What do you mean? Look closely. This is me."

"I'm sorry. This isn't something I do. I have made some commitments to myself and I have strict rules about this. Maybe someday, but not now."

Will stood up as she stared at him with disbelief. Her eyes were red and tears formed at the corners. Why didn't she say anything more? He reached down and kissed her on the cheek. "The mousse was delicious. I'm just sorry we're not on the same page tonight. I have to get home and start getting ready for my trip. I leave tomorrow in the late afternoon, so I'll call you for lunch."

He walked by himself to the door, turning back to see Renee still sitting in the same place on the couch. Hopefully, she would understand and would be okay. This wasn't how he expected the evening to go. Streetlights illuminated his walk to the car, giving him the company of shadows all the way. This had to be an ominous sign. Nothing felt right at the moment. He gave his dark companion one last stern glare before getting into his car and sitting down in silence.

Will wanted to get out of there since escape was what he desperately needed, but his hand wouldn't move to turn the key. Thoughts flooded his mind, but he couldn't make them stop. His dream girl would have never come on to him like that. She would have played hard to get and would never be so forward. Maybe he had been wrong about Renee all of this time.

No, she must have made a mistake and thought it's what he wanted out of a woman. She never gave any hint of being like this, so it had to be a one-time thing. She certainly wouldn't be like that again. Although, if she came on to him like that tonight, how many times had she behaved in the same way in the past with other men? Could this have been the real Renee?

Will gazed at her front door for a few seconds, hoping she would come running out to him and apologize, but that didn't happen. He finally turned the key and drove off into the blackness of a cloudy evening.

# Chapter Thirty-Five

THE DAY BEGAN WITH A DRIZZLING rain and no sunshine. Renee stayed in bed longer than she should have, hitting the snooze at least three times. This would have been a perfect day to stay home and sleep longer while listening to the depressing rain patter outside. If only she didn't have to get up and go to work.

Her whole world had crashed on her the night before. Would Will ever consider going out with her again? Why was he thrown off by her attention? He said she was attractive but had he been lying? He dated a lot of other women in his past, but he wouldn't treat any of them like he did her. Something had to be wrong with him. Or maybe it was her?

The annoying buzzer went off again and she slammed her fingers down on it to get it to stop. Struggling to crawl out of bed, she made sure it wouldn't alarm again. She stood up and walked to the bathroom mirror to see how unappealing she really was. Hmm. Messy hair, tired eyes. Yet Will told her he found her attractive even in this exact same state just a few months ago. She burst into tears covered her face with her hands as she left her reflection alone.

Renee went to her closet to pick out the least interesting clothes she could find and got dressed. The tears eased but her mood didn't improve. She must have made Will feel uncomfortable by throwing herself at him in nothing but a skimpy nightgown. Why would she have done that anyway? It was a bad idea. She should have never listened to her friends. Who was it that told her to plan that kind of romantic surprise for him? It was Lisa. Renee should have known better. Lisa never kept a boyfriend for more than a few months. Maybe she could apologize to Will and tell him it would never happen again.

Yet he had been with other women before. This couldn't have been the first time one of them came on strong to him, especially the European girls. Surely he couldn't resist some of their charms. How could he have resisted her charms last night? He had never made a move on her in the months they had known each other. Maybe Will truly was the gentleman he appeared to be and would never consider that kind of relationship before marriage. No, it wasn't possible in today's world.

She finished getting dressed and the phone rang. Maybe it was Will.

"Hi, Mommy."

"Hi, Sweetie. Did you have a fun slumber party?"

"Yes. We all had a great time. Are you getting ready for work?"

"Yep, I'm almost ready to leave. I'll see you in a few hours at school, okay?"

"Okay. I love you."

"I love you too, Rebecca. Have a great day."

There's nothing like a child to bring a person up from feeling sorry for oneself. Tears came again, but this time from the love of her daughter. Renee hung up the phone with a smile as she wiped the moisture from her eyes. No matter how bad things were with her and Will, she still had her precious little girl. She wasn't going to feel sorry for herself.

Renee drove to work and fought to control her emotions.

She had gone from depression to extreme joy in just a few minutes, and the mood swing had been overwhelming. Talking to her friends about last night was inevitable, although she didn't look forward to those discussions. They might come sooner than she expected. MaryAnn stepped out of her car in the parking lot at work. Renee parked next to her and tried to clear her mind. She could handle this. The light rain snapped her back to reality.

"Good morning, Renee. How was your 'dessert' with Will?"

MaryAnn beamed with excitement as she walked around her car. Renee hated to burst her bubble with the truth. How could she respond? "Well, it didn't quite turn out how I expected."

"What do you mean? Did he like your surprise?"

"He liked the chocolate mousse dessert, but once I offered him the main course, he turned and ran."

"What?" MaryAnn's expression of disbelief said it all. Exactly how Renee felt last night. The rain quickened so she picked up the pace, forcing MaryAnn to catch up.

"He said he wasn't that kind of guy and had to go. I gave him the impression I was too easy and he didn't like it."

"I'm so sorry, Renee. Are you going to work it out with him and let him know it was all a mistake? You should have never listened to Lisa!"

"I don't know. He's getting ready to go on a business trip for almost two weeks."

"Hmm. I wonder if he gives in to some of the girls he meets on his trips," replied MaryAnn with an angry tone.

"Will said that he never did more than a dinner or a boat ride or a play. He also said he hasn't gone out with anyone else since we've been serious."

"How can a guy entertain so many different girls, on the other side of the world and not cross the line? I don't know that I can believe it. Isn't it a man's goal in life, to conquer women in bed?"

Renee stared down as they walked into the employee entrance at the distribution center, and considered MaryAnn's comments. Was she right? Had Will lied to her all of these months? Her other friends greeted her with bright eyes but MaryAnn cut them short with her expression and a hand gesture across the neck. She was a good friend. Now wasn't the time to talk about Will with her friends. MaryAnn did the talking and filled them in on the details of the failed 'dessert' scheme.

Renee tried to get into the rhythm of packing boxes and didn't really hear the discussions between her friends about her personal business. Their mouths moved, their arms waved, their expressions showed anger. It didn't matter. She just wanted the day to go by quickly so she could get Rebecca at school. That wonderful child was her saving grace, despite Renee's relationship troubles. Every few months, she seemed to be in this same position, so she just needed to get used to it. Her friends were either divorced or in a bad relationship and she was doomed to the same fate.

Lisa came up and hugged Renee. "I'm sorry it didn't work out for you. It was a bad idea. I'm going to stop using that tactic myself."

"Yeah, it's just not like me to be so forward with a guy. I thought I wanted our relationship to go to the next level, but now I'm sure it was wrong."

"Even so, I think you're dreamboat is pulling your leg," added Lisa. "No man can resist the temptation of a beautiful woman over and over again. Especially someone like you. Your dreamboat is trying to make you think he's perfect."

"I don't know about perfect, but he's sure going to a lot of trouble to prove to you that he can say 'No' to a woman's attentions," replied Retta. "What was he like when you finished eating the mousse and you started to make the move on him?"

Renee paused for a second. "He was uncomfortable. I could tell."

"He's a good actor then," added MaryAnn. "He gave up a night with you just to give you the impression that he's a good guy."

"No, he really is a good guy. I don't think he would try to trick me into thinking he's someone else."

Lisa touched Renee's arm. "Listen. You suspected he was a player, and I think you're right. He might have left your apartment and went to meet another woman."

"What?" exclaimed Retta. "He may be a player, but how could he leave an awesome woman like Renee for another one in the same night? It just doesn't make sense."

"Well, it's happened to me," Lisa argued.

"Will isn't like that," defended Renee. "I just gave him the wrong impression and it didn't go over well. To him, I had been his ideal woman for months, and when I behaved like that last night, it changed his whole perception of me."

"You're too close to the situation now," replied MaryAnn. "Nobody can be as good as you think this guy is. You've put him on a pedestal and aren't seeing him as a real man. You see him as some kind of ideal hero who can take you out of your mundane job and give you happily ever after." She paused. "Maybe he's not all that he's cracked up to be."

"He just seems so perfect. We were even almost in a car accident, where every car around us, front and back, was hit. Will's car didn't get a scratch. He missed the car in front, and the car behind us somehow stopped in time. When the smoke cleared, dozens of cars and trucks were involved with steam coming out of many. Yet the police let Will drive on out of there like some kind of royalty."

"That's amazing, but don't let something like that determine if he's a chosen one," said Lisa. "He was just very lucky, right?"

Renee stared at her for a moment, then nodded. "I just don't know. You could be right. But if someone up there is watching out for him, maybe he really is as good as he appears."

They continued working with the sounds of tape being stretched across boxes, people talking in the background, and music playing in the distance. Numbness set in as Renee contemplated that Will may not have been the hero she once thought he was.

# Chapter Thirty-Six

**A**LIGHT RAIN IN THE EARLY MORNing hours was usually a welcome treat for Will, but he hadn't been able to sleep all night. His mind raced with all kinds of scenarios and just wouldn't relax to get rested up before his long trip. His eyes kept opening to stare into the darkness, trying to convince his brain he was almost asleep. The evening dragged so slowly that it seemed to torment him to make things even worse. When the hints of sunlight crept around the blinds in his windows and slowly reached its fingers across the room, it was actually some kind of relief that the terrible night was almost over.

Giving up on sleep, he sat up in bed and went over the events of the previous night at Renee's apartment. Was there any chance this could have just been a bad dream and Renee wasn't really the woman that came on to him a few hours ago? No, he hadn't slept enough to even have a nightmare, and it was all because of those events he was prevented from finding a restful slumber. This was real.

Faced with a dilemma, he hoped he could meet with his friends before getting on the plane this evening. It was too early to call anyone at this time, although they were such good friends they would even get up now to meet him if he asked them to. Will set his suitcase on the bed and slowly selected the clothes needed for the trip. Fortunately, the hotel had a laundry service so he only needed to pack about four out-fits. His mind wouldn't focus though, so it made this usually simple task more difficult than ever. How could this woman affect him like this? This woman? She was the girl of his dreams, or so he thought.

Will kept returning to the worst case scenario. Renee wasn't really the one for him. He had made a mistake. He had always searched for a wholesome woman with a pure heart, but this one was willing to cross the line in a way he didn't like. Yet, in every other way, she was perfect for him. How could she ruin it all in just one evening? He needed some good advice now, since his heart had one opinion and his mind had another. Patrick was the godliest man he knew, and his other friends were just about as wise as Patrick. If he could just talk to one or more of these guys, he could deter-mine what to do.

As the sun came up and the downtown area started wak-ing up, Will took advantage of this quiet time and read. He al-ways enjoyed these times in the morning, but today he craved it more than ever. He sought wisdom, hoping for some kind of divine revelation, eventually coming to terms with the pre-vious night's events. They were over now and he had to move on with the new day.

His phone rang and was glad to hear Patrick's voice. "Hi, Will. I knew you'd be up early. You're going out of town tonight, so do you want to meet for lunch like we usually do before you go?"

"I'm so glad you called. I'm going to try to see Renee at lunch, but would you be able to meet me for breakfast in-stead? It would be great if any of the guys can join us."

"And so it begins. The woman has taken the place of your friends at lunchtime the day you have to travel. So sad. Oh well. Where do you want to eat?"

"I'm almost at that little place on Forsyth Avenue, so how about there at 8:30?"

"Good deal. Wait a minute. Did you sleep at the office again?"

Will hesitated. "Yes. We can talk over breakfast."

"Alright. Oh, I just remembered Daniel and Frank have to work today, but Gregory

may be off. I'll check and bring him along if he is. See you there."

Will set down the phone and continued packing. At least he would get to spend time with one or two of his friends. What would he do without them? He went to his closet and selected a comfortable shirt and casual dress pants to wear on the plane overnight. Hanging them temporarily by the bed, he picked out something to wear today. Blue jeans and a long sleeve turtleneck would be good on a cool morning like today, especially if they ate outside.

Will needed to call Renee to talk with her before having to catch his flight, but he was hesitant. Maybe he should discuss his situation with Patrick first. He put a pair of dress shoes in the suitcase and sat down to slip on some casual shoes. When he finished tying them, he stood up and ran downstairs. It was odd not seeing Sue at her desk, and the place seemed deathly silent.

Stepping out into the mist-like rain, he walked briskly to the café. They would certainly eat inside this morning. He greeted the waitress with a smile and she returned it.

"Hey, Will. Your usual?"

"Yes, please." He should know her name but he was terrible at remembering things like that. He went straight toward a table in back and sat facing the door. The waitress soon brought him a cup of coffee and returned to the kitchen. He opened several packages of sugar into it and stirred it slowly. Patrick rushed in and reminded him of a dog shaking after a bath.

"Don't mind the rain. We really need it," Will said as Patrick joined him at the table.

"Oh, I don't mind the rain, as long as I can sit on my porch and watch it without having to go out into it," replied his friend. "Actually, I'd meet you in a hurricane if you needed me, so don't worry about it."

"I guess Gregory had to work too, eh?"

Patrick nodded as the waitress returned. "Good morning. Would you like some coffee?"

"Yes, I could use something warm right now. Then I'll have two eggs, hash browns, and toast."

"I'll be right back with the coffee."

"Nice choice. That's my usual here," added Will. "I really wanted to talk to you about Renee."

"Renee. What's up?"

"You know I've been telling you I think she's the one I've been searching for all these years?"

"Yes, your so-called soul mate."

"Well, my soul mate came on to me a little too strong last night and I walked out on her. What do you make of that?"

"Are you sure her intentions were what you're suggesting to me now?"

"She set up the evening with one thing in mind. I'm certain of it. I just never thought she would be like that. It was as though she was under the impression it's what I wanted, but it's not. I could get that from almost any woman."

"Maybe you've been wrong and she's not the right girl for you after all."

"But what if she was only behaving like that because she felt it was the only way I'd keep going out with her?"

"Did you do anything to make her think that?"

"No, of course not. I've just been trying to think of other possibilities."

The waitress brought out Will's plate. "Yours will be out in just a minute. Is there anything else you need?"

"How about two large glasses of orange juice?" Patrick asked.

"Coming right up," she replied.

Patrick stared at Will's vacant expression. "What if you're reading too much into this and she's still the same woman you've been enamored with all these months?"

"She is the same woman, but her behavior last night was out of character."

"Have you talked to her about this yet?"

"No, I rushed out of her apartment and went straight home. I wanted to talk with you first before calling her today."

"I'm flattered, but you know more about these kinds of situations than I do."

"Yeah, but when something like this happens, I end it then and there and it's not a happy situation. I'm concerned this could turn out to be the same, and that's what bothers me."

"I hate to put it to you like this, Will, but if a woman has those intentions with you, it's very likely she's had them with other men before you, and would probably have them again with other men after you. She was married once and has a child, so what if she's used to that kind of behavior?"

"Not what I wanted to hear."

"I know. However, maybe this is the first time she's ever tried this with someone, and she only did it with you because she thought she had to, for whatever reason."

"It doesn't make sense, though. I've never led her to believe I'm that kind of guy. I've always been the perfect gentleman with her."

"Then talk to her and find out why she behaved like that."

"I just feel like my whole world is crashing in around me. What if she's really that kind of woman? One who would jump in bed with her boyfriend after only a few months?"

"You know the answer to that. If she feels that's what needs to happen, then she's not the one for you."

The waitress returned and put Patrick's plate down on the table. She also put down two glasses of orange juice. "Anything else, gentleman?"

Patrick looked up at her, "No, this is perfect. Thanks." She disappeared behind the kitchen door again, and they each sampled their breakfast for a few minutes.

It was as though this was the end of an ideal relationship. Renee had brought so much fun into his existence, yet it seemed that she could have been the wrong person after all this time. Meeting with her in a few hours might prove to be one of the most painful meetings of his life.

# Chapter Thirty-Seven

**W**ILL DROVE TO THE BUILDING where Renee worked and stopped at the front desk to ask for her. They called her name over the loudspeaker, which probably embarrassed her. Not the best way to get her into a positive mood to start out this discussion. He waited impatiently, dreading every second before she finally walked through the door. She looked at him but didn't smile like she usually did.

"Hi, Renee. I have to go out of town tonight and I'll be gone for a couple of weeks. Would you meet with me for your lunch break so we can talk?"

Her frown remained and she actually appeared to be angry. "I only have thirty minutes, so if you can get me back her in time, then we can go."

"Great. My car's right outside." He glanced at the receptionist, who immediately turned away.

He held the office door for her and walked beside her toward his car, covering her with his umbrella in the drizzling rain. Opening her car door, she sat down while he ran around to his side and climbed in. Without asking where she wanted to eat, he took her to the same place she had initially walked out on him. It gave him an ominous feeling, which he couldn't shake, but he parked and they both got out, selecting a table inside because the morning rain still covered the outdoor table and chairs.

Will said something to the waitress, who left them alone for a few minutes, then sat down with Renee.

"So what happened last night? Don't you really find me attractive or has that been a lie?"

The immediate attack was a surprise. "Renee, you're perfect and I like everything about you. You are the most attractive girl I've ever met, physically as well as your mind."

"Then why didn't you want to have a romantic time with me? I planned the whole evening, only to have you throw it all away. What game are you trying to play?"

"Everything we've done has been incredibly romantic to me. The dance lessons, the dinners together…"

"You know what I'm talking about. I had something special planned for us. We had the whole apartment to ourselves with no interruptions."

He paused while the waitress brought drinks to the table and walked away quietly,

obviously sensing some hostility there. For a moment, he watched a loving couple walk into the restaurant, stepping out of the rain, but smiling to each other. That's what he had hoped for today.

"I didn't think you were that kind of girl. I'm disappointed you would even…"

"Give me a break. You've been with hundreds of women, and you expect me to believe you wouldn't …"

"Yes, I do. You and I have only known each other for a few months. What you had planned is something so special …" Will paused. "I had hoped you wouldn't throw yourself at me, or any other man, like that."

"Throw myself at you? I thought I was your girlfriend. What am I? Chopped liver?"

"You are the most special person in the world to me right now, but I'm also not ready to take that step. I'd like it to be with you someday, but …"

She laughed and glanced around the room. "That's just not realistic so I truly can't believe you. Men especially could never wait. I've seen the way you stare at me sometimes. I can only imagine how you look at other women when you're not with me."

What had happened to his dream girl? Had he truly made a mistake with this one? "It is realistic. It's not easy in today's world, but if something is that important, it can be done. Yes, you physically drive me wild every time I see you, but I still have to control my thoughts. I'm sorry you don't trust me enough to believe it when I give you the truth."

"How can I trust you when you've admitted to being with so many different women?" she exclaimed a little louder than he had hoped.

"Please calm down and talk in a civilized manner. We're in public and you need to control your emotions."

"Will, I am in control. Don't tell me to control my emotions. I'm just tired of you not being completely honest with me."

He paused, glancing away for a moment, his insides in knots. He was falling back into his past, destined to be alone for the rest of his life. His happy ending was only an illusion that teased him and reminded him just how painful it was to search yet never find that special someone. As though waking up from a nightmare, he needed to get away from this scene as quickly as possible. Time to retreat to a safe corner.

"You know, I can't take this anymore. As difficult as this is for me, I can't deal with your crazy behavior. It seems as though men and women are just incompatible. I thought we were the perfect couple, but now you're acting just as psycho as..."

"What's that supposed to mean? Now I'm a psycho?"

"No, but listen to how you sound. My dream girl would

have never come on to me the way you did last night. It's just not the way I am. And when I try to be a man of integrity, a true gentleman, it's still not good enough for you."

"You are a gentleman, but why don't you just admit you're more of a ladies' man than you let on to be?"

"I'm sorry to disappoint you, but I'm not the man you think I am. I'm better than that. Maybe someday, you'll look back and realize I'm not as bad as you make me out to be."

"Nobody could be as good as you want me to think you are. You're living in a dream world. Wake up and get back to reality, Will. I need a man who is open with me, who won't continue to hide behind this image of perfection. Just step down from your pedestal once and for all."

Will exhaled and stalled his response, shaking his head. He didn't want reality at this point in time. He didn't want to wake up from the joy he'd experienced with Renee this year. Was this really the woman he had fallen in love with over the past few months? He didn't even know this one in front of him.

"I'm not sure what you need, but from what I've learned last night and today, it seems as though it's not me." Will paused again, still staring into her eyes. "For the past few months, I really thought it was me. I hoped it was me. I'm sorry to disappoint you. I'll do you a favor and stay out of your life from here on out."

Will stood up and walked toward the waitress, handing her a twenty dollar bill and speaking to her quietly. He continued out the front door and into the light rain without turning to look back at her. Dark clouds reflected from the puddle next to his car as he paused before getting inside. As usual, a song from the past came into his mind and broke his heart even more as he considered the sad lyrics. This was his destiny, to always be reminded of his eternal sadness. His past was back to haunt him again. The restaurant door slammed behind him, ringing a small bell, and his tears blended on his cheeks with the water coming down from the sky.

# Chapter Thirty-Eight

RENEE ARRIVED AT REBECCA'S school and went inside to wait for her little girl to be released. Hopefully nobody would recognize that she had been crying all afternoon. She washed up in the ladies' room, wiping off smeared mascara and splashing cold water on her face in an attempt to take away the redness in her eyes. She gazed at the mirror one last time and shook her head, not caring anymore what people thought when they saw her. It really didn't matter and she wasn't in the mood to discuss her personal life with Will's sister.

She walked out and Rebecca ran up to her with a big grin. "Hi, Mommy."

"Hi, Sweetheart. I missed you today."

Fortunately, Kim was busy with other mothers and just waved to Renee in mid-conversation, so that was her opportunity to slip outside without having to talk to anyone. Kim must have realized something had happened, since she stopped and looked concerned. Renee quickly led her daughter to the car and drove off. Rebecca gave her mother all of the details from her day, mentioning some of the crafts she worked on, games they played during recess, and a project she needed to start. This was good, since it gave her the chance to just nod and listen to her daughter all the way home. They parked and walked hand-in-hand into their apartment. The little one skipped while Renee walked quickly to keep up.

"Are we going to see Will today before he leaves for India?" Rebecca asked excitedly.

Rats. Renee had hoped to avoid talking about Will, but she needed to make sure her daughter knew the facts. They stepped into the kitchen and Rebecca stared up at Renee as she waited for an answer.

"Honey, Will won't be coming over anymore."

"What do you mean? He won't be able to make it today, but we'll see him when he gets back from India. Right?"

"No, we're not dating anymore. He's going to start going out with other women, so he won't be picking us up again."

Tears filled Rebecca's eyes, which uncontrollably brought them out of Renee's as well. "But Mommy, why?"

"Well, I can be hard to get along with sometimes and I made a mess of things between Will and me. He really needs to find someone better to spend his life with so he can be happy. I make his life miserable sometimes."

"That's not true and you know it," shouted her daughter indignantly, which surprised Renee. Rebecca sobbed and continued, "He said you were beautiful when your hair was a mess." She sobbed again. "I saw him kiss you at the front door and he looked very happy."

"Yes, I think he was happy a few times but I eventually messed things up and it's not easy to fix."

The little girl's tears kept coming and Renee tried unsuccessfully to console her by sitting next to her and wrapping her arms around her little girl. "You do mess things up, Mommy, but if he's important to you, then it's worth fixing, isn't it? Why wouldn't you try to make it better?"

She was a smart six-year old. "He needs someone who won't always get angry and be jealous all the time."

"He wants to be with you! I know he does. Why don't you see that, Mommy? He's right in front of your eyes and he's Mr. Right."

Her daughter's outburst only made things worse for Renee. How could she respond? "Rebecca, you don't understand…"

"I understand that you don't even see a good thing when it's right in front of you. You've even said it yourself." She paused as she caught her breath, then exclaimed, "If you don't marry him, then I will," and Rebecca ran to her room leaving her mother speechless. Renee sat alone and sobbed.

***** 

Parking at his usual spot at the curb, Will quickly stepped out of his car and walked into his office building. Sue talked on the phone, so she just waved to him as he nodded and kept going to his desk, shutting the door behind him. He hung up his jacket and stood there, contemplating whether or not to sit. He had a few final things to wrap up before his trip, but was afraid of the images that would be presented to him on his computer if he sat down and woke up the screen saver slideshow. His heart couldn't take seeing photos of Renee at this moment.

He held in the power button on his computer, forcing it to crash and ensuring that a slideshow couldn't possibly startup. He then sat down, leaned back, and picked up a stack of papers from his desk. Sue had finished making his travel arrangements and left them there for him to review. He checked his watch and looked back at the itinerary. Flying out in the evening, spending the day and night in Frankfurt, fly out in the morning, spending the night in Mumbai, early morning flight to Bangalore. Same as usual. The sooner he could get out of here tonight, the sooner he could put things behind him, move on, and focus on his job. He had been in this situation before and he would get through it again. The key would be to pour everything into his next assignment.

A photo of Renee on his desk caught his attention and he stared at it emotionless for a few seconds. Leaning up and reaching for the distraction with his left hand, he put it face down so he couldn't see the front. His eyes didn't move from the frame for quite a while, but he eventually stood up and walked through the door to his upstairs bedroom with the itinerary. He had to make sure there wasn't anything else he needed for the trip.

His cell phone rang and he answered it without looking.

"Mr. Sayre. This is your old pal, Patrick. Could you do me a favor?"

"No, this is a busy time for me. I'm about to leave for the airport. Sorry."

"Oh, alright. Where are you stopping before you get to India?"

"Germany. Then I need to finalize a few things with my customers in Bangalore later in the week and part of the following week."

"You don't sound any better, Will. Are you sure you're okay?"

"I'm fine. Well, not so fine. I ended it with Renee today. I know she's difficult to be around sometimes, but it just didn't seem right to leave her like this. She came on strong to me last night and is angry I didn't go along with it. It didn't appear she was sorry she acted like that, so it's probably the kind of woman she really is. Yet why do I feel like I've made the biggest mistake in my life? Anyway, I'll get through it and we'll have a good game of basketball with the other guys soon."

"I hope so. If you want to talk more in the next few days, call me anytime. I'll make myself available for you. Even in the middle of the night, okay?"

"I appreciate the offer. I may just take you up on it."

"Well, have a good trip and we'll see you when you're

back in town."

"Thanks, man. Talk to you later."

Will tossed the phone on his bed as he looked at his open suitcase. He examined the clothes there for a moment, then stood up and walked around the bed. Still expressionless, he stopped and stared in his closet for a few minutes. He hadn't felt this despondent in years. It wouldn't be an easy trip because he couldn't get Renee out of his mind, even though she was already out of his life.

If all women were like this, he would never be able to spend his life married to the same one. A love for a lifetime must just be a myth. He was certain Renee would be the one, but he couldn't even get six months of happiness with her before she showed what she was really like. He was a decent guy. Several women in this world would be glad to spend years with him. He must have more problems than he ever recognized. No, it was obvious that once a man got to know a woman, she would eventually reveal all of the crazy things about her that make her unsuitable as a partner. Was it even possible for marriages to last fifty years anymore? His parents had reached their twenty-fifth anniversary before they were killed a few years ago, and they seemed happier than ever at the time. Was a happy marriage only a thing of the past though?

His heart ached as he realized he would probably forever remain a bachelor, never to understand why women behaved the way they did. The sooner he accepted that, the sooner he could go forward with his life. What a depressing thought. He had to drive to settle his mind. He went out to his car and passed through familiar sights in town, deciding he wanted to spend the rest of his day listening to music. He knew where he needed to go.

Alone in his dimly lit studio, Will played a dual-necked guitar along to his most depressing collection of breakup songs from the 1970's. The music was loud. He played the melodic parts of the songs on one guitar and lead guitar solos on the other guitar. The envy of the local music scene with this guitar, Will was proud of his prize. He would bring it along the next time he played onstage with some of his friends. Facing his speakers, he closed his eyes and lost himself within the music as he played his parts. Forming interesting faces with his mouth as he played some of the notes, it was as though he was there with the band, recording with them in the studio all those years ago. He could relate to the songwriter's mood as he played along without singing. Sometimes he mouthed specific lines that applied to his own feelings, his own current situation. He blocked out everything else.

Will was back in time, dealing with another loss, and his heart poured out into the songs. No, he was in the present time, dealing with his current loss. It was almost too much to handle, so he played on. 'A Man I'll Never Be' by the band Boston came on, and he paused momentarily. Keyboards were setup in front of him, and he made sure the volume was set properly to match the song from the speakers. Restarting the song from the beginning, he began playing on the keyboards, with the big guitar still hanging on his neck. A melodic introduction to a powerful song. He then stepped back and played along on his melodic guitar, listening intently as the words appeared to be written for him and this very moment. As the intensity of the song increased, Will switched to the lead guitar and played them note-for-note along with the song. He was there with the band, as the singer expressed Will's own feelings of not being the man that Renee expected him to be. Closing his eyes again, he played on as the music surrounded him like never before.

After the guitar solo, Will went back to the keyboards and played along there, then moved to his melodic guitar again. The words to the song were his own thoughts, his own feelings, his own situation. It was too sad to compre-hend now. He played along to the lead guitar as the music guided his movements, his expressions, his past, his future. No, this couldn't be his future. The song built up again and Will switched the sound of the keyboards and held the chords down like a church choir for a few seconds, then set it back to the piano sound to finish the song. He stood there in silence, contemplating what had just happened.

Was he really that different from the man Renee wanted him to be? Was she confused? Did she really want him to desire a woman like that? Could he have misunderstood her actions and handled the whole situation all wrong?

# Chapter Thirty-Nine

**C**OOL BREEZES AND BLUE SKIES with cloud brushstrokes usually improved a person's mood, especially when combined with the sounds of birds whistling all around. Yet Renee was more disheartened than ever. She had messed up Will's life by meddling with his past and making more of it than she should have. She tried to be someone she wasn't, and now Will didn't want anything to do with her. She was probably not fun to be around at her workplace anymore either. Even worse, her daughter wouldn't talk to her or spend time with her unless Renee made her sit in the same room. Will seemed to have the Midas touch, but she had just the opposite.

She looked out the back window from her couch, eating a tub of Mackinaw Fudge ice cream, Will's favorite. Everything outside was spectacular. The sights, the sounds, the aromas, the temperature. Yet her life had taken a turn for the worse again. It never failed to disappoint her, so she was determined to just accept bad things as they came her way and move on to the next disaster. It was usually because of a bad decision she had made, and this time was no different. If she kept eating junk food like this, she would inevitably gain a few pounds but it didn't matter now. She had just thrown away the best thing that had ever happened to her, not counting her daughter. What could a few extra pounds hurt?

Her phone rang, but she didn't want to talk to anyone. She would just sit here until the ice cream tub was empty and not move for anyone. It rang again. That bite had a nice piece of chocolate in it. Yum. Another pound added to her waist. A third ring. Maybe it was her daughter. She stood up and answered her phone after another ring, "Hello?"

"Hi, Renee. This is Patrick Wilson, one of Will's friends. Do you have a few minutes?"

How could she move forward if things from her past kept coming back? "I don't know. Will and I aren't dating anymore and …"

"I know and that's why I'm calling. When you two were an item, he was happier than anytime I'd ever seen him, but now he's miserable. He's out of town now, but he hasn't answered my calls yesterday or today. It's unusual for Will. I hate to see him like that and I think it would help if you and I talked a little."

"I'm sure you mean well, but you know Will. He's set in his ways and doesn't have any room in his life for someone who behaves like me. I bring on a lot of extra baggage that would ruin things. It's better to let him get on with his life."

"I disagree. You've changed him so much for the better and I'm concerned about him now that you two aren't together. Would you like to meet my wife and me for lunch to talk in person?"

Renee covered her eyes with her free hand and dropped her head. "Why would you want to meet with me?"

"You may not realize it but you are the most important person he has ever met in his life. He's convinced you're the one he's destined to spend the rest of his life with."

"He may have thought that at one time but not anymore."

"No, he does think that even now. He believes it's a mistake you two aren't together, but he doesn't know how to fix it. Please join us for lunch. It's our treat. You'll enjoy meet-ing someone who knows Will better than anyone else. Except for his sister. And maybe his personal assistant. Possibly you. But anyway, I know a lot about Will that you don't know. What do you say?"

"Okay, where do you want to meet and what time?"

"Excellent. You won't regret this. Let's meet at Keller's Café on Highland at 11:30. Would that work for you?"

"Yes, I'll see you there."

She hung up. Why did she agree to meet with one of his friends? Will was on his way to India and would probably spend the next week with one of his girlfriends in Europe or Bangalore. It was just his nature and there was nothing she could do about it. Rebecca was at a neighbor's house, so she would be fine while Renee went to lunch. She would just get this over with and then she could move on. Getting dressed was a drag for her and she had no motivation to even go out-side. She forced herself to drive there, thinking about Will the entire way. He was probably out to a late dinner with some pretty European girl or Indian girl right now on the other side of the world.

She parked and walked on the warm sidewalk toward the restaurant. Of course, it just happened to be a little outdoor café that Will would enjoy. He had probably brought a doz-en women to this same place over the past few years. Very fitting. Now which one of these guys was his friend? She should have asked what he looked like.

A young, muscular man in a short-sleeved shirt and a black goatee stood up from a table full of people and walked toward her with a welcoming smile.

"Hi, I'm Patrick. I recognize you from Will's photos that he stares longingly at every day."

"Hi," replied Renee without feeling as she shook his hand.

"I took the liberty of inviting a few of Will's close friends to join us, so you can have access to years of Will's friendship. You can ask us anything you want, but let me tell you a little about Will before you ask anything. Oh, and this is my wife, Carol, Daniel and Barbara, Gregory and Jasmine. Everyone, this is the one and only Renee that has affected our friend so deeply."

They all stood up and came to her. Renee weakly returned their greetings, not remembering any of their names. She joined them at their outdoor table and asked the waitress for a glass of water with lemon.

"So why did you all bring me here?" Renee asked dryly.

"Remember, I said that you can ask questions later," Patrick replied. "Let me start first, if you don't mind."

Renee nodded and stayed quiet.

"For a long time, Will has traveled and dated all around the world. There's no question about it. I have no doubt that he's never taken even one of those relationships to the next level, if you know what I mean. He's not that kind of person. He is so focused on waiting for Mrs. Right and has spent years searching for that girl."

Patrick paused, as Renee just raised her eyebrows and shrugged her shoulders. "So I've heard," she replied.

"He basically dated as much of the world's female population as he could in order to find the one girl he could settle down with," said Gregory.

Carol made a face and said, "That's not really the best way to explain it but the concept is the same. Will has been so desperate to find the one girl who could make him feel the way you've made him feel. None of his many dates matched his high standards until he met you."

"Exactly," Daniel said. "Each time we met him for a game of basketball or for lunch during the past few years, Will was focused on his work, with a search for his dream girl a constant quest. Once you came into his life, he was a changed man. He stopped dating anyone else and was happier than we had ever seen him."

"You are his dream girl," Patrick added.

"Can I say something here?" Renee asked, as they all nodded. "I appreciate all of your kind words and I know you must like Will a lot to want to help him out. There's more to it than what you mentioned. It's not easy being with Will at a park or a restaurant and wondering what other girls he's taken here or there. I know it's probably childish but it's always in the back of my mind. I also made a mistake and behaved in a way that I shouldn't' have last week. I took some bad advice and I've paid for it. Plus, in case he hasn't told you, he's tired of my crazy attitudes and he's done with me. It's not up to me. He's right too. I'm irrational sometimes, I have difficult moods that I can't control very well, and he doesn't know how to handle them. It's too much to ask someone to deal with."

They all laughed. What was so funny about that? She was serious.

Barbara spoke first. "Moodiness is a reality for most women, and men in the world have a difficult time dealing with it. It's hard enough for women to deal with it, but it drives men crazy trying to understand the behavior of a woman whose hormones have taken over."

All of the men at the table nodded emphatically and Jasmine added, "Once a couple realizes that, and they work together to minimize the mood swings as much as possible, it will bring them closer together as a couple."

"It's not easy," said Patrick, "but it's worth it. Will has never had experience with a woman in PMS, so he just needs to learn how to cope with it. It's a reality and he's a smart guy. He cares for you so much that he would do anything to make your life better. Also, he has taken a lot of girls out to different places, so chances are good that anyplace you go with him has been a place he's taken someone else in the past.

But that's all there was. You're the one he wants to make a memory with and you're the one he'll remember the most at every place he takes you."

"His life is basically starting over right now with you," said Gregory. "What happened in the past doesn't matter. What matters now is what you and Will do from this moment on."

Silence filled the air for a few moments as Renee took in these words. Will really had some good friends.

Patrick continued, "Whatever happened a few nights ago, Will knew it wasn't you. He told me just before he left that he couldn't be with someone like that. He was afraid it was the real Renee, that you were probably like that with a lot of guys, but deep down he doesn't believe it. He needs you to tell him it wasn't. He craves that confirmation more than you can realize right now."

What was going on in her heart now? She actually wanted to run to Will now and never let him go. These friends of his were right and he was a perfect match for her. They really were meant to be together. Tears streamed down Renee's cheeks as she made the decision at that moment to win back Will's heart and work with him to make their relationship a success.

"I want to thank each one of you for taking the time to convince me. I'll call Will in the morning and let him know that I want to make things work between us. You all are the best friends a person could have, and I hope to be a part of your friendship for a long time."

Patrick added, "We always enjoy a friendly argument with Will since he's so passionate about things, even something as simple as the quality of a certain type of mustard, his favorite cheeses…"

"The perfect burger," interrupted Daniel.

"Mountain Dew," added Gregory.

"An impressionist painting," continued Patrick.

"A song from the sixties," said Renee.

"The list could go on," said Patrick. Everyone laughed, even Renee, and somehow she relaxed. Life wasn't so bad after all.

"One time, he returned from The Netherlands," said Daniel, "with a dozen different types of cheeses and just as many types of mustard. He insisted that we try them all so we could experience the unique flavors of each, even though some of us don't like mustard and I can't eat cheese." Laughter erupted around the table as the men appeared to remember that day. "The flavors were so amazing to him that he had to share them with us. He's really a considerate guy. A little eccentric sometimes, but incredible."

Jasmine said, "Yes, he does seem so perfect and confident all the time."

"Oh no. I can hear it now. You're going to ask why I can't be more like Will," replied Gregory to his wife.

"Does he have any flaws?" Renee asked the group, looking around at the various faces at the table.

"He has an obsession with Mountain Dew and drinks it by the gallon," said Gregory.

"Don't you mean by the liter?" asked Jasmine.

"No, I never converted to metric," responded Gregory. "Will probably drinks a gallon a day."

Renee laughed. "Well I don't like the taste of it, so I would put a stop to that."

They all stared at each other in silence at those words.

"No, I mean I'll make sure he cuts back to a healthy level," replied Renee as they nodded with obvious relief.

"You may want to work on how much sugar he puts into his coffee too," added Daniel.

"He really doesn't eat very healthy either," said Barbara.

"Every time I've eaten with him, he has a healthy meal,"

replied Renee.

"That's what he wants women to think," said Patrick emphatically. "He puts up a healthy front, but he snacks like a lunatic, devours bacon, cheese, salad dressing, and it drives me crazy watching him eat it."

"It drives you crazy because you're jealous that you can't do it too," said Carol.

"Yeah, none of our wives will let us get away with it," added Daniel.

"He's not very good at basketball," said Patrick as the men at the table gave each other fist bumps. "Also, he thought he understood women until he met you, Renee. He told me he should write a book and call it 'Men Are Practical, Women Are Insane.'"

An awkward silence engulfed the conversation until Carol said, "That's really not very funny. I'll pretend you didn't say that." Patrick raised his eyebrows and shrugged his shoulders, but remained silent, probably hoping to avoid any further scolding.

"Here's something you didn't know about Will," said Daniel. "He has such a huge appetite that he eats a full dinner before he goes out to eat with you."

"What? How can he stay so thin?" asked Renee.

"He must have a very high metabolism," said Gregory. "If I eat the stuff he eats, I'd gain five pounds every week. And he still looks better in a tight shirt than I do."

"Plus he does work out in his personal gym upstairs at his office," Patrick added.

"Well, he has more spare time than we do because he has his personal assistant take care of everything for him," said Gregory as the rest of the group busted out with laughter.

"I'll work on getting him to do more things for himself," said Renee.

The group talked among themselves about Will's interesting quirks, all laughing because their friend was quite a character. Renee took it all it in, savoring the close friendships that these wonderful people had with the man she cared so much about. As the men discussed Will, the ladies talked more with Renee as they ate lunch together and she revealed more about herself than she expected. Surprisingly, they had already heard about some of her details from Will. Should she be concerned or flattered that he would have shared so much about her with his friends? The fact that he talked about her so positively was indeed a good thing. She couldn't wait to hear from Will and see him again. Could it be that life was about to get better for her again?

# Chapter Forty

**R**ENEE POURED HERSELF A CUP OF coffee and sat down on the couch to watch the news before taking her daughter to school and going to work. She looked forward to calling Will and trying to straighten things out between them. She really wasn't listening but had the TV on as a habit while she ate breakfast or relaxed. She glanced around the room as the headlines blurted out. These bookshelves probably needed to be dusted. The TV showed a map of a country around the world and the announcer got her attention immediately when he mentioned India.

"There was a plane crash early this morning on a flight from Mumbai to Bangalore."

"Hmm. Will said he always takes the same flight from Mumbai to Bangalore. The 6AM flight." She sat her coffee down and turned up the volume to hear it better.

The man kept talking and he mentioned the name of the airlines, the flight number, and no survivors. There was at least a nine hour difference between India and North Carolina so she calculated out the hours. Could this have been a different flight from Will's? How many flights went to Bangalore from this airline? She stood up and gasped. This was indeed his flight. He was scheduled to arrive in Bangalore, India this morning, on this plane.

Her breathing increased as her eyes stared blankly at the screen. "He must have missed the flight today though," she said to herself as her eyes watered and her hand moved up to her mouth. She couldn't catch her breath as the tears streamed down her cheeks.

"There was one American on board but the details can't be revealed until his next of kin has been notified," the announcer continued and Renee's mind blurred out everything else.

"This can't be happening. I didn't have a chance to apologize to Will before he left. I need to call him right now and make sure he's alright. Maybe I should call Kim and see if she's talked to him."

A little figure stepped into the doorway and asked, "Mommy, why is the TV so loud?"

Renee wiped her eyes and looked at Rebecca while walking toward her.

"Good morning, Sweetheart. There was a plane crash early this morning and I wanted to hear the details about it. I'm sorry I had it so loud." She picked up her daughter and pointed the remote toward the TV until the volume was back to normal. Rebecca's expression told Renee that she was acting a bit abnormal. She tried to calm down so she wouldn't worry the little girl.

"Are you hungry for breakfast yet?" asked Renee as she gazed into her daughter's eyes and walked her toward the table.

"Mommy, what's wrong? Why are you crying? Was it Will's plane that crashed?"

"No, don't even say that, Honey. He's probably safe at his hotel," but she burst into tears again and buried her face in Rebecca's long blonde hair with a wave of irrepressible sobs. Her daughter was also crying so she tried once more to gain her composure.

"It's OK, Rebecca. Will always manages to stay out of trouble, so he'll be fine. We'll call him on the phone in a little bit and see when he's coming home."

"You said that you and Will weren't talking anymore."

Renee smiled at her and replied, "No, I talked with some of his friends yesterday and they said Will really wants to be with me still. We're going to start dating again as soon as he gets back from his trip." Gloom filled her thoughts as she made that statement. He just had to come back.

She sat her little one at the table and brought a box of cereal and a bowl to her. Renee went to get a spoon, but the phone rang and her eyes met Rebecca's with a terror she had only experienced once before when she found out her husband had been killed. The phone rang again but she couldn't move toward it to pick it up.

"Please answer it, Mommy," said her daughter as she released a flood of new tears.

Renee stared at the phone and it rang a third time. She took a few steps and lifted it from the receiver. A wave of dizziness hit her. The sounds around her were muffled as though she was in a dream. That's where she wanted to be now, in a bad dream that she could wake up from and forget about.

A voice came from the phone. She put it to her ear as she leaned her back against the wall. The voice cried and spoke at the same time.

"Renee, is that you?"

"Yes. Kim, is it true?"

"I've tried to call Will, but it goes straight to voice mail. I think he was on that flight. Sue said she booked the reservation herself and couldn't stop crying when I called her."

Renee closed her eyes, let go of the phone, and slid to the ground, covering her face with her hands. Her daughter hugged her now. She wouldn't be able to hide her grief

264

any longer. Renee let it all out while she sat on the floor, Rebecca's sobs blending with her own. She stayed there for a few minutes, not wanting to move or do anything else, but realized she had hung up on Kim. She would have to call her back in a few minutes. Maybe she could find out more about this morning's events.

"Rebecca, I need to call one of Will's friends. Would you go and get dressed?"

The little girl stood up without a word and ran to her room. Renee stood up and glanced around. Everything still appeared to be the same as it had before she turned on the TV. Yet nothing was the same now. She walked to her purse and pulled out her cell phone to find Patrick's number. Renee paused and looked up, wondering if by some chance Will would answer if she called him now. She closed her eyes and prayed like she'd never prayed before, then looked at her phone again. She tried but fumbled while she dialed Will's number. Her heart skipped a beat when she finally got it right, but it sank when the call went straight to voice mail. It was too much to ask for.

She wiped her eyes more than once as she paged through her directory, but soon found it and called Will's friend. It also went straight to voicemail. This still didn't mean anything. Maybe they were both busy or both already on a call. Or what if Will was on the phone with Patrick? Perhaps at that moment someone from the airlines had called Kim to notify her that her brother was killed in this morning's crash. She had tuned out the news but it was still on, so she walked in her living room to see if there truly was a crash. It was possible she had heard it all wrong. She watched the usual weather reports. Why didn't they get to the point and announce the name of the American killed on this morning's flight? Didn't they realize how important this was? Then of all things, it went to a commercial and Renee couldn't take it anymore.

She turned it off. Rebecca stood quietly in the doorway again.

"Hi, Beautiful. You look terrific in that outfit."

"Mommy, can we go see Nicole and Ms. Kim?"

Renee stared at her daughter. She was a bright kid. Will's sister must be hurting even more, and probably needed someone to take Nicole for her now. "You're absolutely right. Let's go see if she needs anything." She picked up her purse, reached for Rebecca's hand, and led her outside to the car. The skies were as blue as ever and the breeze felt wonderful. Will would have mentioned something about how perfect this day was. Rebecca stayed unusually quiet. Renee didn't know what to say to her, so they drove in silence. Her daughter had grown quite close to Will over these past few months. She wasn't the only one.

They arrived at Kim's house, only to find a lot of people already there. Bad news spread quickly. She and Rebecca walked up to the front door. It was like a dream. Someone opened the door without saying anything and let them inside. Renee looked at faces but there were still no words spoken as she seemed to glide past them all.

Doug was on the phone, probably trying to verify the name of the American on this morning's flight to Bangalore, but he appeared to be frustrated. Kim sat near him, expressionless, until she saw Renee. She then stood up and quickly moved toward Renee, hugging her and then Rebecca, giving them a gentle smile.

"Where's Nicole, Ms. Kim?"

She picked up Rebecca and gazed into her eyes. "She's in her room. I know she would want you to visit her."

Rebecca gave her a wonderful hug that went on for several seconds and Kim put her down. The little girl walked quickly to find Nicole and soon disappeared in the crowd.

"I tried to call Will's friend, Patrick, but didn't get an answer."

Kim nodded, then looked at her and said, "We're not going to school today, so if you want to leave Rebecca with us while you go to work, it would really help Nicole."

Renee turned to Kim but couldn't even think about working today. She wanted to be with Rebecca but figured it might actually be best to let her stay with Nicole. "I really appreciate the offer. Although I had come to see if you and Doug wanted me to take Nicole with us."

Kim shook her head. "No, I'll stay with her and Rebecca. You go ahead."

"Alright. If you find out anything, please let me know."

"Of course," said Kim as she hugged Renee. "Will always knew that an airline crash was a possibility, so he told us several times not to worry about him. He said he made an effort to be right with God at any given moment because we never knew what could happen."

Renee nodded and looked around once more. She smiled at Kim, then made her way to the front door. She wanted to ride over to Will's place. Even though nobody would be there, she drove to it anyway and stepped out of her car. She just stood still on the sidewalk in front for several minutes. She glanced up at the decorative windows on the second floor where Will's bedroom was. This was a perfect building for Will.

Renee even checked the door to be certain nobody was there. She was reminded how jealous she was about a pretty girl like Sue being his 'Personal Assistant' and laughed at how foolish that was. She glanced at the front window, noticing her own reflection, wishing she would see Will's reflection walk up beside her. She turned, only to see an empty sidewalk. Of course he wouldn't be there.

Renee walked to some of the nearby places Will had taken her and reminisced about her times with this special man. She regretted saying some of the things she had said to him. He was the best friend she ever had. He made her feel special in whatever he did and he seemed to honestly enjoy putting her on a pedestal. She would never be able to replace him. At that moment, she realized what Will had gone through all this time after his flawless woman walked out of his life forever. She could finally relate to that emptiness and understood his loss.

She walked by the little restaurant he liked, while his kind words from that day came to mind when they sat outside enjoying a sunny day like today. There were so many things she would never forget about this man who only came into her life for a few months and yet changed her forever for the better.

Her phone rang. It was Will's sister again. She wasn't ready for this news yet.

# Chapter Forty-One

**R**ENEE STARED AT HER PHONE FOR a moment, noticing the name of the caller, then slowly put the phone up to her ear and answered it. "Hi, Kim."

"Hi, Renee."

"Have you heard anything more about Will?"

"Are you at work?"

"No, I couldn't concentrate at all so I took the day off. What's going on now?"

"Good. We're going to take Rebecca to Will's house in a few minutes. Can you meet us there?"

Renee paused for a moment. Kim must have to start arranging for the funeral or getting Will's body back from India. "Wait a minute. Will's place? I'm there now, but nobody's here."

"No, you're probably at Will's office but his house is at 333 Brentwood Lane, just past the new post office. Sometimes he just slept at his office rather than going home in the evenings."

Will's office? Why didn't Will ever take her to his house? Didn't he say that he lived upstairs at his office? He even said he stayed at his office most of the time when he was in town. Why would he have another house? "Yes, I think I know where it is. It'll only take me about ten minutes to get there."

"Alright, see you then."

That was that. Quick and straight to the point. It would be best to spend the day with Rebecca anyway, so it should work out fine. There's nothing more she could do here and reminiscing was too sad at this point in time. Maybe it would be better in a week or so to visit the places he used to bring her. It was difficult not to break down into tears every few minutes and she didn't need people staring at her or bothering her now.

Renee took her time driving to Will's house, even though Kim and Doug had things to do. Maybe she should offer again to keep Nicole with her and Rebecca so they could make arrangements without having to involve their little girl. Nicole was so cute and it was difficult to imagine what she was going through, knowing her favorite uncle wouldn't be around anymore. She walked to her car, picturing Will's little convertible sitting there by the sidewalk in the shade where he liked to park sometimes.

It seemed odd that Will never mentioned living somewhere else. Perhaps she didn't know Will as well as she assumed. Was there some reason he never took her to his house? Maybe he really was married and didn't want her to find out. Was he ashamed of her? No, there she went again jumping to conclusions and thinking the worst about him. She had promised to never do that again, so she pushed those thoughts out of her mind. Kim would have said something anyway.

She drove past the post office. What would Will's house be like? He was a bachelor so maybe he would have been embarrassed to have people see where he lived. Yet he said he spent most of his time at the office. He must not have gone to this house much. Very strange.

She turned onto Brentwood and drove down a stunning tree-lined street that she had never been on before. This was an impressive area. Had she made a wrong turn? She drove up to the open gate and saw a giant 'S' on it as she followed the driveway toward an elegant house, noticing the mailbox said '333' on it. There was a lake on the right side with a spectacular two-story house overlooking it on the left. It was like an old Victorian home out of the 1800's. Who lived there? Glancing around for Will's home, she couldn't see any other houses. The driveway turned left, then curved to the right and followed the lake where that large brick house stood over. It couldn't be Will's house but if not, then where was she going?

Why would Will have not mentioned he lived somewhere else? That 'S' on the gate might be for "Sayre," but it couldn't be, could it? Never taking her eyes off of the house that appeared to be at the end of this long driveway, she pulled up to the front door and parked next to Kim's car. Several other cars lined the circular driveway. Who else would be here at a time like this? Family and friends must have been given the news about Will's crash and decided to meet at his house to mourn together. That made sense.

Renee slowly stepped out of her car and glanced at the finely manicured bushes under a blue, cloudless sky. She suddenly broke down into tears and did her best to restrain herself as her heels clacked on the sidewalk. She paused at the front door and tried to regain her composure before going in to face his family and friends. She knocked and practiced giving a smile, realizing her eyes were still moist. The door opened and she quickly wiped her right eye, presenting a fake face to the person who opened the door. She didn't recognize him, but he gave her a friendly grin back.

"Come on in. You must be Renee. I'm Frank."

"Thank you," was all she could manage, and she carefully stepped up and past him, making sure she didn't trip and embarrass herself. The dark wood floors shined, leading to painted walls that ended with a decorative chair rail and changed colors up to the ceiling, which was lined with exquisite crown molding. Colorful renaissance paintings were placed strategically along the entryway and hall, and she figured they were replicas of the classic Renoir, Degas, Monet masterpieces that Will enjoyed. He taught her so much about the different styles that she actually recognized two of them before a voice interrupted her train of thought.

"Hi Renee. I'm so glad you could come out here." Kim appeared from one of the doorways and almost ran to her, hugging her tight. Kim lost all control and broke down into sobs, burying her face into Renee's long hair. The news must have been confirmed and Renee also started crying again. She didn't try to stop this time and let the tears flow freely. Kim stepped back, extending her arms, and put her hands on Renee's arms, gazing into her tear-stained eyes with a weak smile.

"I have something to show you," and she led Renee without a word toward the doorway from where she had just entered.

What would Kim want to show her now? Why was she walking so fast? Renee glanced at the décor and was impressed, although she knew Will had a style all his own. She wanted to slow down and explore the other rooms they passed, but it was as though she was in a museum on a rushed tour. Maybe she would ask Kim to take her around the house once they finished meeting today. There was still so much more she could learn about Will from exploring his house.

They walked into a spacious room with a grand piano and sunlight streaked through the sheer curtains, filling the room with warmth and life. The colors were bold, but different from the previous rooms she had just walked through. Several people stood around and turned their heads toward her as she walked into the light. Who were these people? Oh, that's Will's friend Patrick, and there's Will's personal assistant. She certainly was attractive. Renee did recognize most of them as she took in some of the unknown faces. The

272

door on the other side of the piano opened and she noticed her daughter and Kim's daughter, holding hands with Will as they strolled into the room, grinning from ear to ear. He was wearing pajama pants and a sweatshirt.

Wait a minute. What did this mean? It couldn't really be Will, since he was in a plane crash just a few hours ago, halfway around the world.

"Mommy, Will's alright. He didn't go to India this time and missed his flight."

Renee's hand went to her mouth and tears instantly welled up and touched her cheeks again, as Will silently walked over to her and wrapped his arms around her to a hushed room. Kim stepped back, taking the girls by the hand and squatting down to talk to them as her brother just held Renee. Through her tears, she saw people smiling at her. Was this just a dream? Dizziness set in as her ears became muffled. Should she even look at Will? If it was a dream, this was where the nightmare would begin as the handsome Will turned into a hideous monster and laughed at her before fading away. Will spoke to her but she couldn't hear his voice. It vibrated through her body as he hugged her tightly and spoke again.

"Renee, I'm so sorry for not being understanding and for thinking the worst about you. I'll never be like that again."

She didn't move or respond since she still didn't know what to think. How could he be here in front of her when he had left for India two days ago? He tried to pull back but she held him tighter and wouldn't let him go, knowing that if she released him know, he would be gone forever when she woke up.

"I canceled my trip at the last minute and my colleague, Chuck, went out there in my place. He was killed on the crash in India this morning. I just confirmed it with the airlines after Kim and everyone came over and woke me up. I've been in bed for the past few days, not even wanting to do anything or talk to anyone."

Renee slowly pulled her face out of Will's shoulder and looked up into his eyes through her tears. He was blurred but was the most welcome sight she had ever seen, even with his hair a mess. She reached up and touched his face with both of her hands while he kept his hands on her waist, and she smiled for the first time.

"I'm so sorry to hear about Chuck but I'm glad you stayed home. I thought I'd lost you forever."

"I thought I'd lost you and I just couldn't function at all this weekend. I know you're not really that kind of woman and I'm sorry for thinking that way. I need you more than you'll ever understand."

At those words, Renee buried her face again and sobbed uncontrollably. She couldn't speak, so he just squeezed her and leaned his head against hers. Will was back from the dead and her life would never be the same.

# Epilogue

**A** YEAR WENT BY, WHILE **W**ILL RO-
manced Renee around town every chance he
could. He made commitments to both Renee
and Rebecca and sold his consulting business. He let Renee
use his office for her new interior decorating business, as his
personal assistant stayed on there and became her personal
assistant. They enjoyed a brief engagement and his fiancée
made all the wedding plans with the help of his sister. Will
stayed out of them as much as he could, figuring that he
would be fine with whatever made her happy.

On the wedding day, the early morning weather was
picture-perfect. Will spent it kayaking with his friends at his
favorite spot to watch the sunrise, then they all ate breakfast
at his favorite outdoor café. People teased him about losing
his bachelorhood once and for all, but he welcomed the end
of that part of his life. Will looked forward to his married life
with Renee and being a father to little Rebecca more than anyone realized. More than anyone except Kim, who understood
him better than he knew himself.

While Will relaxed on this special day, his friends filled
him in on what Renee's morning was probably like. Rushing
to get this and that done, spending time on her hair, spending
time on her dress, spending time on her nails, etc, etc. He
was glad to be a guy. However, throughout the day, thoughts

about his parents came up and he missed having them here to be with him and his new wife. They would have liked her a lot. Both were in Heaven already and would meet her there someday for sure.

Patrick interrupted Will's silence. "So are you really sure that Renee is 'The One'?"

Will paused and looked up at his friend. "I've talked with her about that, and she said the only reason she's 'The One' is because I chose to make her 'The One'. She thought she had found her one and only in her first husband, but he was killed. I was certain I found mine before too, but that didn't turn out. The 'one and only,' 'Mrs. Right,' or whatever you call it, is only a myth. 'The One' is actually the person you enjoy being with the most, the one who builds you up, the one who makes you feel special, and the person you want to spend the rest of your life with."

"She's a wise one, young grasshopper."

"Yes. I told her if I had known that years ago, I could have saved a lot of time. Instead of wasting the past few years searching, I could have just chosen that blonde stewardess in Sweden in 2008 and been happy ever since."

Patrick laughed and asked, "Oh, and she didn't dump you then?"

"She slapped me and said I must have waited for the one woman I just couldn't live without."

"You made the right choice, my friend."

"And I choose to grow old with her and love her every day."

The men were a little late arriving at the church to get dressed, but Patrick, who was the pastor for the ceremony, was also late since he had spent the morning with the groom and groomsmen. They came in through the groom's special entrance so Will wouldn't see the bride, and Patrick disappeared somewhere into the church building. The rest of them rushed to get cleaned up and dressed in their grey tuxedos, laughing the whole time about something or another. It didn't take them long to get ready, of course, and Patrick came in to join them for a few minutes before they all went out to wait for the bridal party to start walking down the aisle.

After a brief huddle, the men wandered out to their appointed positions and stood. Will led the way, periodically glancing out at the people in attendance. The music was classical Mozart, Bach, Beethoven, and Debussy, which was about the only input Will had for the wedding. As the music changed and people stood to look at the back of the church, Will's heart rate picked up as he anticipated Renee's entrance.

Rebecca and Nicole were first down the aisle as flower girls, and Will's friends escorted Renee's friends from work next, with his sister as the matron of honor. A brief pause in the procession built up the suspense and when Renee finally stepped into view, Will stood in awe. The light behind gave her the appearance of an angel. With each step closer to becoming Will's wife, he allowed her to capture his heart more and more. With her help, he had finally escaped from his past and would forge a new beginning with his special partner in life.

Will couldn't stay focused on the service, even though Patrick was the pastor, and his eyes kept roaming toward Renee. His mind wandered like it always did. It was funny how surprised Renee was when she learned that Patrick was a pastor. She must not have realized pastors were people too, especially one who could be as smart, fun, and full of integrity as him. He glanced up at the ceiling. She had also been surprised this church doubled as their basketball court and had basketball goals that folded up into the ceiling. Maybe she would want to come and watch Will and his friends play basketball here someday. She was so athletic she might actually be better than him at basketball, and that brought a smile to his face. His specialties had always been baseball, football, and soccer, with basketball never being a favorite. His friends recognized that and would only play sports which were his weaknesses. That was okay. He made them look good.

He missed his cue as Patrick had to repeat something to him. Renee gave him an interesting expression and scolded him with her eyes. He couldn't help but laugh. They said their vows and exchanged rings, then Patrick said he could kiss the bride. Will instead turned to Rebecca, leaving Renee with a cute, confused expression, since she wasn't aware of his plans at this point. He asked the little girl to come up to the top step, and she shyly joined him and Renee. He knelt and recited a vow of commitment to always be there for Rebecca, which caused his bride to break down into tears. He then offered a small ring to the little girl, who gave him the same cute expression as her mother, and placed it on her finger before standing to join hands with Renee again. Will secretly handed Renee a mint, and when she felt it in her hand, she laughed but shook her head. He had wanted her to do that cute little sneeze, but she didn't fall for it.

"You may now kiss the bride," repeated Patrick and the church erupted with applause as their lips met. A fast paced Beethoven song filled the air to give a celebratory atmosphere, as Will and Renee led the rest of the bridal party back down the aisle and disappeared into the happily ever after.

Rick Gangraw is the award winning author of "Secrets in the Ice" and "Deathly Silent." He and his family live on the east coast of Florida and he wishes he could spend more time at their cabin in Upper Michigan. When he's not dabbling in fiction, Rick enjoys sports, kayaking, camping, and working on his family history.